THE ALIEN FACTOR

THE ALIEN FACTOR

STAN LEE

with STAN TIMMONS

ibooks

new york

www.ibooksinc.com

DISTRIBUTED BY SIMON & SCHUSTER, INC

An Original Publication of ibooks, Inc.

Copyright © 2001 by ibooks, inc., Stan Lee, and Larry Schultz

Special thanks to J. Madison Davis and Larry Schultz,
for service above and beyond the call of duty.

An ibooks, inc. Book

ibooks, inc.
24 West 25th Street
New York, NY 10010

The ibooks World Wide Web Site Address is:
http://www.ibooksinc.com

ISBN 0-7434-3475-7
First ibooks, inc. printing October 2001
10 9 8 7 6 5 4 3 2 1

Edited by Steven A. Roman

Jacket art copyright © 2001 by John Ennis
Jacket design by Mike Rivilis
Interior design by Westchester Book Composition

Printed in the U.S.A.

12 OCTOBER 1942
NEAR MESQUER, FRANCE

THE SHRIEK rose up in the middle of Marcel's dream like a furious dragon breathing vengeance and fire. The earth trembled, and a blinding light slashed between the seams of the farmhouse shutters. He blinked, thinking at first that it was the light from a Bosch truck, but the shriek was nothing like an engine. It grew louder, painfully louder, until it deafened him. He slapped his hands over his ears and screamed, but he had no voice against the sound.

The shafts of light swept across his room like white-hot swords, momentarily lighting the picture of his mother and father on the bureau, his threadbare work gloves, and his plaster figure of Joan of Arc. The gilt on her upraised sword flashed and her serene face seemed to move, to look at him before the light passed to the wall, the door, the chair on which he removed his sabots, and he just had time to think:

It is God, Marcel thought. *It is the angel. I am to be anointed, like St. Joan. I will save France. I will save my father.*

But the shriek exploded into an earthquake, the blast tearing the shutters off their hinges and tossing him from his bed. He landed hard on the stone floor. The light ebbed and the shriek was replaced by a groan, weakening, weakening. He raised himself and made out that his parents' picture had been knocked flat. His gloves and bedclothes had been blown to the floor, but the statue of Joan still held its place, her smile serene, her sword raised, her armored steed gnashing its teeth as it reared.

I am to be anointed, Marcel thought again. The light faded. He thought at first he was fainting, but he felt the cold floor, the jab of one of his sabots in his side. Had he heard the voice of God? Had the angels told him what he was to do? Did it come like this for St. Joan: a flash of unnatural light, an unholy sound, and then silence? His arm tingled. He couldn't raise his hand. He felt a strange lump in his forearm and then a grating pain as he moved it. He had broken his arm when he was thrown from the bed. Was this God's will? He lay back, ears ringing, and saw the gentle light of a paraffin lamp outside his door.

His grandmother pushed back the door, her face distorted by the fear of what she might find. She sagged at the sight of the smashed shutters, but Marcel's grandfather gripped her upper arm as he pointed down at Marcel.

"There!" he said, his voice just making it through the ringing in Marcel's ear. Marcel raised himself on his good arm as his grandmother shoved the lamp into her husband's wiry hands and dropped to her knees, clutching the boy's head against her breasts.

"My boy . . . My boy . . ." she sobbed, and Marcel wasn't certain whether she was thinking of him or his father, who had gone to market one Saturday and never come home.

Marcel pulled away enough to see the tears streaming down his grandfather's hatchet face and into his mustache. He had never seen the old man cry. His throat felt full. He choked on it and felt himself sobbing as his grandmother took his head in both hands and frantically kissed his nose, his eyes, his salty cheeks. He moaned what he had called her when he was just beginning to talk. "Papeau . . ." he said. "My Papeau . . ."

"Your Papeau is here," she whispered. "Papeau is here. Grandpere is here."

He sniffed loudly, feeling ashamed for having blubbered. For a year, after the disapperance of his father, he had been being a man—

a twelve-year-old man who had sworn to St. Joan that he would work the farm and keep it right until the day his father returned. This was the cottage in which Marcel had been born, and his father before him, and his grandfather. This was the cottage in which his mother had died, giving birth to a girl who outlived her mother only by hours. By worldly standards, it wasn't much, and he had worked until his hands grew thick and hard. With the bloody blisters of his feet he had polished the inside of his sabots smooth. But God smiles on the humble, his Papeau often said, and blesses the sorrows of life on this earth with bliss in the next.

Grandpere went to the window, cupping the lamp with his hand. "It must have been a shell," he said. "A new kind."

"Or a bomb," said Papeau. "The English don't care how many French they kill."

Marcel's grandfather looked at her in anger. "If they kill Bosch, they can bomb me all they like." He craned his head out the window. "Maybe it was an entire plane. Maybe Americans."

"There might be survivors," said Marcel. "The pilot."

"They might need help," said Grandpere.

"We don't dare," said Papeau, squeezing Marcel closer. "The Germans will swarm like flies."

"If they turn up, I will help them."

"Think of the boy," said Papeau. Grandpere lowered his eyes. Clearly, the humiliation of being old and powerless as his country was being violated weighed him down.

"If you ever see flyers, get away from them," Papeau said to Marcel.

The boy nodded, then winced. "My arm," he said. "I think it's broken."

Papeau hugged him again. "Come to the kitchen. Grandpere will look." She glanced up. "If he isn't too busy looking for *trouble,* that is."

"I'll splint it up good," the old man said, ignoring her jibe. "I've broken my own arm seven times. If you splint it right, it grows perfect, even stronger."

There was a distant rattle. Grandpere squinted into the darkness.

"Get away from the window, you old fool!" said Papeau.

"Machine gun," said the old man.

"Get away from the window!"

Grandpere glanced at the paraffin lamp in his hand and backed away, stumbling on the pieces of the shutter. "They will shoot at the light," he said.

"Help the boy."

When they got Marcel to his feet, he paused and took a deep breath. "I thought . . . I thought it was an angel. The one that came to St. Joan."

"You were dreaming, perhaps," Papeau said gently.

The old man hmmphed and shrugged. "The Bosch must have brought down a bomber. They were finishing off the flyers with the machine gun. That must explain it."

"Help the boy to the kitchen, you old fool," Papeau said sharply. "That's all that concerns us."

"Get the brandy, woman," said Grandpere.

As they lurched out of the room, the boy turned back to see the plaster St. Joan fade into the darkness.

Marcel's forearm was swollen and blue, but after much painful squeezing, Grandpere concluded that only one of the bones had been injured, probably cracked but not broken through. He tightly bound it with strips of burlap between staves from a five-liter barrel, then sagged to a chair and tossed back the brandy Marcel had only sipped. They heard the barking of dogs, shouts, and the cracks of three rifle shots in the near woods. If there had been flyers, they were surely dead now. No one spoke. It was nearly dawn.

Grandpere's head lolled forward and he began to snore. Papeau went about her morning as if nothing had happened, setting a fire in the stove, reheating the broth they had eaten for dinner and breaking up the hardened bread to soak in the bowl.

Marcel rose from his chair. "Clemence will need milking."

"Let your grandfather do it." She reached to shake him awake, but Marcel grabbed her arm.

"I can do it. Let him sleep."

She looked at her husband, then back at Marcel.

"I can do it," he repeated, wiggling the fingers of his splinted arm. She nodded. He picked up the milking pail.

"You tell her she'd better start paying her way, or she'll be stew."

Marcel smiled and went out into the cold gray morning. Clemence had once been the pride of his father's farm, giving strong calves and gushing enough milk to feed all of them. Now, she was getting old. The milk had decreased and lost a lot of its richness. If they could have replaced her, they would have, but they were lucky to have any cow at all.

He paused in the middle of the farmyard. The barking dogs were in the forest on the next hill, but there was no excitement in their voices. They weren't on a fresh trail.

Abruptly, he knew he was being watched. The hairs on the back of Marcel's neck crept up and he spun, expecting to see one of the Germans behind him.

Nothing. Just his grandmother's garden patch; and beyond that, the grave of their old dog, Danton. And yet . . .

And yet Marcel knew that something was wrong. But what was it?

Then he realized what it was: the birds weren't singing to the sunrise. There was an eerie silence as the wind stirred the trees.

"Who's there?" said Marcel.

Nothing. He stood quietly for a few moments, part of him afraid there would be an answer—but none came. He shivered from the cold mist and walked on to the stable.

Clemence turned her great head toward Marcel as he opened the door.

"Hello, Madame," the boy said. "How are you this morning? I trust your rest was not too—"

He suddenly lost his voice. The feeling had come over him again, this time more powerfully. The sensation of fingers caressing the back of his neck and scalp.

He spun and looked into the farmyard.

Nothing.

He looked back into the stable. Two rows of three stalls on each side. The workshop in the back, with the warped door half open as usual. A maul hanging on a nail. A scythe Grandpere had been sharpening yesterday. There was light in there, too. Grandpere had either forgotten to close the window or it had been blown open by the explosion. Heart pounding, he crept back and looked in. The window was open, but it was still on its hinges. He smelled the oil on the scythe.

He went back to Clemence. She seemed particularly perky this morning and when he touched her neck, she suddenly turned her head and licked him on the ear.

"Hey! Hey!" he said, wiping with his tattered sleeve. "You almost knocked me over, Madame." He patted her forehead and kissed her on the nose.

He slid the bucket under her, drew up the milking stool with his foot, and blew into his hands to warm them. He felt good, he thought. His forearm hurt very little, and when he reached for Clemence's udder, it felt full. "My, you do require my attentions, Madame!" He caught two teats and had barely touched them when they began to gush. Each gentle squeeze brought loud rushes of milk, again and again. The pail was about to overflow when the flood finally ceased.

"My God, Madame!" he laughed. "You have escaped the—ah—the fate you seemed destined for." He carefully moved the pail away from her, watching for any sudden movement of her legs. Even in the blue light of the dawn the milk seemed yellow and rich. He set it on the floor and dipped his finger in it. It tasted rich, as if it were half cream. It was so rich, in fact, that he wondered if Clemence had contracted some odd disease, but it was good, so good, that he dipped two fingers in it and licked every droplet off.

And then there was a noise, a strange shift in the straw.

Again, he had the sensation of fingers in his hair.

The flyers, he thought. One of them is hiding here. In the back stall.

But that made no sense. He had passed the back stall when he had peered into the workshop.

Maybe the flyer had crept in while Marcel was milking. He thought of what his grandmother had said about helping the flyers. He thought about what his grandfather had said.

"I will help you," he called out. "Don't be afraid." English or American pilots might not understand French, he thought, but he had no idea what to do about it. He took a deep breath and edged forward, raising his hands. "I will help. Don't be afraid."

He reached the side of the stall and tried to peer over it. He saw nothing unusual, then bent at the waist to look around the edge. At first he thought he saw nothing, then a dizziness came over him. His vision blurred. There was an area in the middle of the stall that had distorted, as if it were a photograph being bowed and unbowed, as if Marcel were looking at the stall through an irregular piece of glass. He gripped the stall wall thinking he was going to faint, that he was dying, that the milk had been poisoned. He crumpled to his knees, panting, and saw fragments of a walnut shell among the straw.

He felt the fingers in his hair again and, just as suddenly as he had been dizzied by the strange deforming of his eyesight, he was filled with a great sense of comfort and wellbeing. He felt like he was six again, falling asleep in his father's lap while Papeau sang an old hymn.

And so, he raised his eyes.

He blinked.

It couldn't be.

On one knee before him was a being whose entire body radiated a chalky, greenish light. It seemed to be wearing a jumpsuit or factory worker's overalls, which shimmered like liquid mercury. The being was no taller than Marcel, well under two meters tall. Its limbs were long and spindly, like spider's legs, and its fingers had round joints and bulbous fingertips. One arm hung straight at the being's side and when it raised itself to stand, the arm continued to hang limp and useless with an iridescent liquid dripping from the fingertips.

Marcel closed his eyes, counted slowly to ten. When he opened them, the being was still there. He raised his eyes upward to look straight into the being's face and clasped his hands in prayer.

"My God!" he whispered. "You are my God."

Its head was out of proportion to its body, so that overall it looked like a marionette. Its eyes were large and dark, two sharp ovals forming a V, and covering nearly a fourth of the face. Its tiny, lipless mouth was a bloodless surgical incision. There was no nose. Yet the face was ageless, free as the face of St. Joan of lines of worry or anger or guilt or loss. It was a face that seemed to be waiting to be born.

It was, Marcel felt, the most perfect and pure and beautiful face he had ever seen.

I am chosen, he thought, and tears of joy rolled down his cheeks. As he stared at the being's chest, the colors shifted again. Dark spots appeared on the strange vestments, scattered like ants, then reassembled into a shape—a character, perhaps.

No, a cross. The symbol of St. Joan of Arc.

The cross of Lorraine.

Marcel began to tremble uncontrollably, clutching his hands together. The cross became larger and larger until his vision blurred, and he dropped insensible to the stable floor.

12 OCTOBER 1942
OCCUPIED FRANCE,
NEAR THE BOIS DE NOE

OBERFÜHRER WERNER Borck had taken a lot of convincing to come out to the crash site. A new set of laborers had arrived two days ago. The sorting of them was always tiresome, but General Furst needed all available officers to participate in it. This one might have been a watchmaker. Was he good for calibrating and monitoring the air flow valves? That one had been a miner and perfect for extending the tunnel network. Yet another one was only a peasant and dimwitted, strictly a manual laborer, but often men like him made good guards. And then this one, with his thick specs and tiny arms, was probably only fit for record keeping. And so on, through three hundred men, French "volunteers" for the war effort. These men had been snatched off streets or arrested for petty crimes, such as carrying irregular papers or loitering. If the building of the huge underground rocket factory went well, they might be allowed to write home. They might even be released in a year, to be replaced by Soviet prisoners or Jews. But, if the work went badly, they might as well be Jews, General Furst had made clear, and his entire staff would be answering to the Führer himself.

Borck was primarily the security officer for the entire project, and no sooner were the last ten volunteers led to their new jobs that afternoon, than a guard spotted a flash of light on a nearby hill.

With the help of the dogs, a man was caught carrying a pistol and a brass telescope, probably the source of the flash. Obviously, he was spying on the project and there was a possibility he could give information about the resistance organization in the area—if he could be made to talk. That was Borck's specialty, making people talk, breaking them to his will. He had risen rapidly through the SS because of this ability, honed by an abbreviated term in the medical school at Heidelberg. He had been happy to see that one of the first Jews arrested had been the professor who had gotten him expelled.

But the man with the telescope was a tough one. He was not impervious to pain—his screaming revealed that—but somehow through three sessions of "treatment" he revealed nothing. This was a personal insult to Borck, a problem that resisted solution. He searched the man's clothes for any clue of who he was and what would make him give in. At one point, the man screamed in Spanish and babbled in another language, which might have been Basque. Burning him, sawing off a toe, a finger: these things made him shriek and pass out, but just when Borck thought he was about to break, he broke into song: "Malbrough sa vat en guerre." By sunrise, Borck decided to try truth serum. Incredibly, the man had a seizure and died, straining against his handcuffs and spewing blood from his mouth and ears. Borck did not recall reading of this in the medical literature. It was strange, he mused, and intended to find out more about it, but, first, they needed to find out anything they could about this man by questioning in the neighboring towns. There was always someone willing to talk, even without torture, someone who'd want to curry favor with the new masters. Borck would sleep for two hours, wash up, and find out whatever there was to find out. He never allowed himself to fail. Never. Only the inferior races fail.

He received the first message from a skinny young radioman who had scribbled it out on a scrap of brown paper. It came from the regiment manning the coastal gun emplacements forty kilometers away.

"Flying craft shot down. Send intelligence officer immediately."

Why "flying craft"? Why not "airplane" or "bomber"? He assumed that they wanted him because they had caught the pilot or the crew.

"Tell them to bring the prisoners to me," said Borck with irritation.

Borck seemed barely to have closed his eyes when the radioman rapped on his door again. There were no prisoners. The crew had escaped. They were searching for them and needed further assistance. The colonel there insisted that Borck come immediately.

Borck stormed to the communications room and had the radioman contact the colonel, whose name was Kunster.

"Colonel, what is all this? Over."

"You must come, sir. Over."

"You shot down a plane, so what? Was the crew killed? Find the crew and bring them to me! They'll hide nearby for several hours. Over."

"Oberführer, sir, I cannot explain over the radio. Over."

"Colonel, unless I hear anything different, I intend to sleep."

"All right, but the radio is not secure, so you must take full responsa—"

Borck snapped down the microphone button. "Colonel! I am losing patience with this! Bring me the crew or the papers from the plane! That is your order! Is that clear? Over."

"It isn't an airplane, Oberführer!" shouted the colonel.

"Then what is it? A dirigible?"

"There is nothing like it. The Americans must have invented it! You must come! Immediately!"

"Are you mad?" demanded Borck.

"Come! See! If I am wrong, courtmartial me!"

The colonel's impudence startled Borck. And, yes, if this turned out to be a fool's errand there would definitely be a courtmartial.

"This is a very suspicious request," said Borck.

"Wurzberg has the finest cobblestones," said the colonel, and Borck leaned forward. "This is not a joke. You must come. Now!"

"I'm on my way," said Borck.

It didn't really make sense in this context, but Borck now knew that Colonel Kunster was putting his face to the fire. The colonel had used this week's code words, known only to the highest officers of the regiment. They meant, "Invasion Imminent."

12 OCTOBER 1942
NEAR MESQUER, FRANCE

Marcel blinked. Above him, he saw an owl's nest high in the rafters under the tile roof. He must tell his father. No, his father was gone. The chickens were all gone. There was no reason to bother the owl any longer. He closed his eyes for a moment and floated in his calmness. The weariness of all of his days working as a man had left him. He was as refreshed like he had slept for a year.

Suddenly, then, Marcel remembered everything that had happened before.

There was a movement. He slowly rolled his head to the side, and sucked back a strangled cry.

The angel was kneeling over something oblong that lay parallel to Marcel on the other side of the stall. It was about two meters in length, wet and shiny like a huge grub turned out of the earth by a spade.

At the sound, the angel turned his bulbous head to look back at Marcel. Its black eyes studied him for several seconds, and Marcel thought how he had seen many pictures of angels, but none of them had looked like this.

The angel slowly rose and crossed to him, its left arm limp at its side. Marcel moved to sit up, and winced at the pain in his arm. The angel paused, then stretched out his right hand. The fingers unrolled like yarn off a spool, and his bulbous fingertips touched Marcel's blue thumb.

Their eyes locked, and Marcel was awash in a warm, inner peace and knew again that the angel, strange as he was, was God's angel, was good.

The bulbous fingers picked at the burlap that bound the splint in place, but could not pick apart Grandpere's knots. Marcel moved to help and the angel started.

"It is broken," said Marcel. "The light knocked me out of bed."

The angel stared. Marcel slowly began to pick at the knots again. The splint painfully fell off. The angel leaned closer to the bruised and swollen arm. A greenish light rose from his shimmering tunic, and he touched the lump where the forearm bone had cracked. Marcel winced at the pain. The angel looked at him, then at the lump again. Marcel saw that the angel had four joints in his spidery fingers. His arm throbbed, as if removing the splints had freed the pain to race up his arm. The angel looked at him again and Marcel had the sensation of fingers caressing his scalp. Black dots formed on the angel's breast and whirled into the cross of Lorraine.

All at once, the angel limped to the bucket of milk Marcel had left on the floor. He paused a moment, then dropped to his knees. He leaned over the milk and his tiny mouth pursed once, twice, then began to extend outward, forming a cylinder slightly fluted at the end. It elongated to about the length of a hammer handle, then the angel lowered it into the bucket, in one quick motion drawing liquid in.

Marcel's eyes widened in astonishment. The village priest had often said that the miracles of the Lord were beyond human comprehension, and Marcel began to sense the anguish behind the serene face of St. Joan. He now knew how hard it was to accept one's own anointment as God's messenger.

The angel rose, twisted his head, as if working out a crick in his neck, then returned to Marcel. The tube that had been his tiny mouth remained extended and looked like the proboscis of a fly. Marcel drew back against the stall wall.

All at once, the angel's right arm shot out and gripped just above the elbow of Marcel's injured arm. Marcel felt pain, but was in a trance-like state, unable to move. His mouth opened and closed like a fish's.

With a noise like a sigh, the angel pointed his proboscis at Marcel's arm. A liquid as thick, but as liquid, as warm whipping cream gushed over the arm.

Marcel squirmed to pull away, but the angel held him fast until the arm from elbow to the heel of the hand was covered in the liquid. It began to harden, looking first like candlewax, then growing harder and more translucent until it was white and shiny, like milk glass. Like the strange huge grub on the other side of the stall.

The angel gushed out the last of his liquid, then held Marcel gently until all of it had hardened. The pain subsided in Marcel's arm. The glasslike case felt warm and comfortable, like settling back into a bath.

The angel straightened itself and Marcel thought he saw a slight change in the coloration of his face. It stepped back and staggered, retracting the tube. Soon its mouth was as before, a tiny surgical incision. It turned, took two steps toward the giant grub, then one spindly leg crumpled to its knee.

The angel was exhausted, thought Marcel. It needed to sleep.

He stood and walked toward it. The angel looked at him.

"Rest," said Marcel. "I will protect you. Sleep."

The angel did not move for several seconds, then dropped to both knees. He made a sound like a strong wind blowing across a wine bottle, then fell onto his back, straightening out beside the grub-like blob. He spread his spidery fingers over his chest, then ceased to move. His stiff position reminded Marcel of the tombs of the knights at the Chateau Miravin. The lids of their sarcophagi had been carved in a similar repose.

When the angel had not moved for several seconds, Marcel listened for breathing. He heard nothing but the grinding of Clemence's teeth as she chewed her cud.

Marcel backed toward the grub-like shape. When he stopped to look down, he recognized that the material of which it was made was the same as that which now encased his arm. With a glance toward the sleeping angel he gently extended his fingers to touch it. Warm, smooth—it was like glass in a summer sun. He peered down into its murkiness and saw a dark area and then another, and jumped back.

There was an angel inside. It was sealed in it as if it were in a coffin. The sleeping angel had intended to seal Marcel in such a case as well, he momentarily thought, but it had run out of milk and then collapsed.

No, he thought. How could an angel mean harm? The second angel was in a cocoon, or a chrysalis. Perhaps angels went through a phase like a butterfly in order to grow their wings.

What would this do to his arm?

He was suddenly aware of his grandmother calling him. "Marcel! Marcel! Are you there?"

The angel stirred, barely moving his head. Marcel ran to the stable door, knowing that he did not want Papeau to see the angels yet.

He stepped into the open door, keeping his encased arm behind the frame.

She was only a few steps away, hands on her ample hips. "What happened? Did you pass out? You gave me a fright, boy! You must have been in there twenty minutes!"

"I dozed off on the straw. I'm sorry, Papeau."

"Is there milk? If Clemence doesn't pay her way, it's into the stew."

Marcel didn't know what to say. The pail had been full to the brim, but the angel. . . . "I will be in the kitchen in a moment," he said.

"Are you sure you can milk?"

"Yes, Papeau. It doesn't hurt."

A flash of sadness and then pride in her brave grandson crossed her face. She turned to hide it and go inside.

Marcel looked at the glass encasing his arm, then back at the stall where the angels hid. What would he do? This was going to take some explaining.

When he returned to look in the pail, which was totally drained, he thought Clemence's udder looked full.

That couldn't be.

He reached for it.

It was as hard as a soccer ball, full to the point of bursting.

12 OCTOBER 1942
THE ATLANTIC COAST, FRANCE

The half-track ground its gears, straining to make its way over the sharp hills that ringed the small bay. Wanting to doze but unable to do so, Oberführer Borck and the patrol of twelve men in the back clung to their seats to keep from tumbling out. Several times Borck considered the possibility that he was being drawn into a trap, set by the Resistance or Allied commandos, perhaps because of his capture of the man with the brass telescope. If so, he thought, it was a good trap. Colonel Kunster used the code words, and they are changed every week, sometimes more often. If this isn't a trap, it better be serious, thought Borck, grinding his teeth.

The truck finally lurched over the top of the last hill and plummeted down the road toward the coastal gun emplacements. The seaweed smell of the Atlantic fog rushed over them, flapping the soldiers' rifle straps. The moonlight briefly played on the water below. It took only minutes before the truck creaked to a halt at a sentry post. To Borck's surprise, Colonel Kunster waited with the sentries.

"Thank God you're here," said Kunster, leaping into the half-track.

Borck snapped to his feet. "You had better explain yourself, Colonel. You gave warning of a landing. What landing? Where?"

"Oberführer, you will not believe it until you see it. I had no choice."

"Why not your commanding officer? You brought down a plane?"

"Not a plane—or nothing like any plane I've ever seen. This is a matter of the highest priority, strictly an intelligence matter."

Borck pinched the bridge of his nose.

"Oberführer, if this isn't a matter for Berlin, you may execute me on the spot."

Borck sneered. "I may take you up on that." He expected Kunster to react. He did not. "Very well, then, take me to this—this wonderment."

Kunster once again promised Borck he wouldn't be disappointed. He gave directions to the driver and the half-track noisily backed up, turning to head up a bumpy dirt road winding up the face of the hill. As they neared the top, Kunster shouted something that Borck couldn't hear, pointing toward the summit. Borck looked and saw a notch in the line formed by the treetops. Something about fifteen meters across had crashed through the canopy and clipped out a semicircle.

The half-track slid sideways a bit cresting the summit. The road moved into a wooded area, a perfect place to ambush them. Borck kicked the boot of his sergeant to warn him to be alert, though the forest, like most which had been scoured for fuel, was fairly open at its floor. Only a few branches from the collision with the plane lay scattered in the ferns. The half-track turned again, and suddenly the craft was visible.

Borck was rising to his feet even before the half-track screeched to a halt. All of his men stood gaping.

Stuck in the earth, against an outcropping of stone, was a silvery disk. It wasn't very large. A tall man standing on another's shoulders should have been able to reach the top, with maybe the height of another man buried in the earth. It had no markings on it. No windows. No openings of any kind. Its surface was smooth, though unpolished. Light refracted on its surface like it does in an oil slick.

"This is your air—? Aircraft?" asked Borck.

"Yes."

"It flew?"

"Yes."

"How?"

Kunster shrugged.

"There are no propellers."

"It glides?"

"Perhaps it was towed behind a plane, then released."

"We saw no plane."

"But if it's shaped correctly, gliders can travel for tremendous distances."

"Gliders aren't this heavy. Gliders aren't made of metal," said Kunster. "If you can call this metal."

"What do you mean?"

"You'll see. What's more, gliders don't have an engine noise."

"You heard its engine?"

"It wasn't like any engine I've heard before—it made a high, shrieking noise. It deafened several of my men for a while. My ears are still ringing. When it hit, its entire—" he gestured helplessly "—fuselage lit up like flash powder."

"Begin at the beginning, Colonel. How did this happen?"

Colonel Kunster explained. He was finishing some reports about 0200 when his men spotted a light, no more than a blink, low on the horizon. They assumed it was a ship and, as was normal, reported its position. Quickly, the order came back that it could not be a known Axis vessel. The men rushed to stations, in seconds loading their antiaircraft guns and the big weapons of the emplacement, a pair of 700-millimeter cannons.

The blink was spotted again in less than a minute and seemed to be moving straight at them. A battleship, possibly, or a low flying bomber. They strained to see through their binoculars. The blink was no longer a blink. It was steady, and even over the sound of men shouting and getting into place, they heard the noise. Kunster described it as the scream of a divebomber at top speed, only more shrill. It closed faster, faster, and he shouted the order to fire at his command. The shriek, however, now filled their ears and then even the space between atoms and one of the artillerymen panicked, or fell, or simply fired one of the big guns, even though it had been raised too high, in preparation for a shot at an offshore warship.

"I did not even hear the shot," said Kunster. "I had covered my ears in pain. The noise of the craft penetrated to the bone."

The craft, a blur of white light, turned night into day. Exactly what happened then, wasn't clear.

"The projectile must have struck the edge of the craft. It began to flip, like a coin. It somehow just cleared the ridge—" he pointed back at the clipped area of the trees "—dropping out of our sight and then came to rest here."

"Do you take me for an idiot?" said Borck. "How could a 700-millimeter gun have hit it? Its not that big. It should have ripped apart!"

"That is what I saw. The muzzle recoiled. The craft began to flip."

"Like a coin."

"Yes. And, in any case, there is a large mark on the other side. Like someone struck it with a huge ballpeen hammer."

Borck drummed his fingers on his belt. "What could withstand such a hit?"

"You tell me, Oberführer. We came over the hill and there it was. Glowing."

"Glowing?" Borck shook his head and was about to ask about the liquor supply at this post, but, yes, the disk was there, stuck in the earth.

"In the glow, we saw men moving slowly up into the rocks."

"There were men?"

"Yes, they moved awkwardly. One of them collapsed, and the other dragged him. That is what Corporal Weiss saw. He got the clearest shots."

"British? Americans?"

"The glow was diminishing. He saw only shadows."

"And have you caught these men?"

"I have every available man searching. The dogs picked up a scent, then lost it."

"And there are bodies in the craft?"

"We cannot get into the craft."

"There is no hatchway? No door? How did the others escape?"

Kunster was angry at Borck's condescending tone. SS men often spoke this way to regular army, and Kunster's army rank, higher than Borck's SS rank, seemed to make no difference. But Kunster was too astonished at the events of the last day to say more than. "I don't know, *Oberführer*."

"This bears seeing," said Borck, and they set off for a closer look.

Seamless, iridescent, the disk looked like it was made of a solid piece of aluminum. When Borck and Kunster approached it, the other soldiers hung back. From edge to edge it was a little less than ten meters in diameter, but standing before it, Borck was filled with awe. He thought of the sun disk that the ancient Pharaoh Akhenaton had worshiped. His fingertips tingled, and the hair on his neck bristled. He felt some kind of pulse, a throbbing too low to be heard. "It is still on," he said. "What is it trying to tell me?"

Kunster shot him a glance. "You see. No rivets. No doors. Nothing."

"Perhaps it is radioactive."

Kunster's eyes widened.

"Have any of your men been in close contact with it?"

"Several touched it. None have complained about being sick."

"Is it possibly a bomb?"

Kunster shrugged. "If it is, it is a dud. I don't know many bombs that can take a hit, even glancing, from a shell."

As Borck strode around the rounded edge of the disk, he could see that it thickened steadily from the edge to its center, where it bulged to about five meters deep. He climbed over a rock until he could see the gouge where the shell had struck. The indentation in the smooth surface looked exactly as Kunster had described, as if a giant ballpeen hammer, the arm spread of a man, had struck it.

"So," said Borck, "whatever it is, it isn't indestructible." He turned and looked up into the rocks. "And they fled this way?"

"Yes," said Kunster. "We went two kilometers in that direction, but the dogs lost the scent."

"Then that way," said Borck, pointing in the opposite direction. "My men will find them."

Kunster began climbing up after him, but abruptly stopped. "What in God's name?!" he said.

"They doubled back," said Borck. "Haven't you seen an American western? They always double back. My guess is that this is some experimental American glider that—" He realized that Kunster was hearing nothing of what he said. "What is it?"

Kunster stared up at the huge dent in the disk.

"Colonel!"

Kunster raised a shaking hand. "The gouge!"

"What about it?"

"It was larger last night."

"What? Don't be stupid."

"It was more ragged, I tell you. It was worse."

Borck rolled his eyes. "It's a trick of the light."

"No," insisted Kunster. "It has changed. It has *changed!*"

12 OCTOBER 1942
NEAR MESQUER, FRANCE

Marcel opened the thick door to their kitchen and hefted the full pail onto the table.

His grandmother poked at the fire in the tiny stove and stuck in another piece of firewood. "What took so long, boy?" she said. "Your soup has gotten cold—" She turned and saw the pail.

"My God! Clemence gave you this? It is a miracle!" She scurried to the stairs. "Come look at this! The milk!" She turned, beaming. "The explosion must have scared her and opened her up. And it looks so rich!"

In pure delight, she threw her arms around the boy and buried his face in her shoulder. When she stepped back, however, she felt the strange, glassy covering on his arm. She slowly lifted his hand. "What is this? You've stuck your arm in a glass tube. Where did this come from?"

"Papeau," he said, not certain how to begin, "it is a miracle. An angel. France will be freed."

Her eyes darted back and forth, between his encased arm and his curious expression.

"What's going on, woman?" said his grandfather, descending the stairs. He carried a walking stick and the small rifle with which he had often shot them dinner. "Clemence? Is she ill?"

She raised Marcel's arm. "Look at this."

"What happened to your splint?"

"The angel did it. He cured Clemence."

His grandparents looked at each other.

"You must tell him to go away," said the old woman.

"We will give him what help we can," insisted the old man.

"He must go, though. The Germans are all around."

Marcel grabbed his grandmother's arm. "What are you saying? Go? Why?"

"Marcel, if the Germans catch us helping an English flyer, they—"

"English flyer? There is no flyer. It is an angel. Just like the one who came to St. Joan. The cross of Lorraine appears on his chest—"

"On his chest? Whatever are you talking about?"

"It is an angel! The milk! What about the milk!"

His grandfather was confused by Marcel's words and shook them off. "Why did you take off my splint?" He reached for the glassy cast. "Take that thing off."

"The angel put it on me. I feel no pain." He wiggled his hand. "See?" He was about to explain how the angel had spun the cast from his own mouth, but hesitated.

"It must be something aviators use," said his grandmother.

"It feels warm," said the old man.

"What will we do?" she asked.

He rubbed his gray whiskers. "We will feed him, at the very least."

"And then we will send him on his way."

"Perhaps I can speak to Levrier."

"But you don't know for sure. He could be working for the Germans."

"He has always been a Communist. I have heard things that make me believe he is in the Resistance."

"You 'have heard' things! You don't believe the Germans wouldn't corrupt such a man, then spread it about that he is in the Resistance? If you heard it, others have heard it."

"Woman, I will not chase off an ally of France as if he were a rabid fox!"

"If there were only me," she said firmly, "and you, old fool, it wouldn't matter."

"Papeau," interrupted Marcel. "Grandpere. It is an angel. I swear to you."

His grandmother suddenly turned. "Hush," she said.

"What is it?"

"The noise." She moved to the open door. As soon as she opened it, Marcel heard the grinding of an engine approaching.

"The Bosch!" said the old man.

Papeau hurried into the farmyard and peered to the north. The half-track was moving along the edge of the vineyards at the next farm. The soldiers in it stood, searching the vines, while an officer pointed. "My God! My God!" she shouted. "Send the flyer away! Quick! Quick!"

"No!" shouted Marcel, breaking for the stable.

"Get him!" shouted Papeau.

The old man gripped her arm and glared. "Calm down! We will say that we saw someone running up that hill. We don't know who. Up there. That hill."

The woman stared at the closing half-track, bit her lip and nodded. "What about Marcel?"

"He is doing his chores."

She nodded and wiped her nose on her sleeve.

Marcel closed the stable door behind him and crept toward the back stall. The chrysalis-like blob was radiating a weak internal light, as if the angel had bottled an aurora borealis. The angel within the chrysalis was clearer now as the light danced around him, his black eyes staring upward. Marcel noticed an orangish, swollen area on the side of the encased angel's head. His thin arms were crossed over his chest like those of an ancient pharaoh, the angel's fingers spread like the ends of the flail. Next to the chrysalis, the other angel lay unmoving in the same position, except that his left arm lay limp by his side.

Marcel opened his mouth to wake him, but nothing came out.

How do you address God's angel? "Sir"? Gently, he reached down to prod him and, just before he touched him, he saw the shimmering tunic begin to flow and swirl, black dots swarming like beetles on a dead goat. He touched the angel and its mouth parted, sucking air.

"Sir? The Germans are coming. The enemy. They will be here any second." The angel raised itself to a sitting position, breathed in several times, and crawled wearily toward the chrysalis.

Marcel watched him. Did an angel need to hide? Surely not, but there was something wrong. Perhaps angels weakened when they appeared in the earthly realm. Why was the other angel in what amounted to a sarcophagus? What should he do? He looked around the familiar stable for a place to hide them. Stalls. Perhaps in the one stuffed with hay? They would poke it with their bayonets.

He heard the half-track drawing closer. He turned to pull the angel into his grandfather's workshop and out the back window, but his foot slipped out from under him. He thudded to the floor unhurt, but saw that his sabot had stepped into a slimy gelatin. It had a pinkish tint.

The angel was looking at him. Suddenly, Marcel understood why it was that the angel's arm hung limp. He was wounded. This slime was his blood. Could an angel be wounded? God had ordained that his own son should die on the cross. Certainly, he could ordain an immortal to suffer.

The half-track was creaking into the farmyard. Marcel grabbed the end of the chrysalis and began to drag it toward the workroom. The angel, on his skinny knees, pushed to help but had little energy for it. Marcel made certain the window was open, then dragged the chrysalis under the workbench. The angel climbed under with it, and Marcel backed under, as well, piling a barrel, tools, whatever he could find to block the view. He concentrated on one thought, hoping he could plant it in the German's minds. "We escaped out the window. We escaped out the window." He heard the half-track stop, and then, oh God!, the bark of a dog.

* * *

Four soldiers leaped out of the half-track and took up positions in a wide circle around it. The one closest to the old man pointed his rifle directly at the center of his forehead.

"*Guten Tag,*" said Borck, stepping down.

"You have nothing to fear from us," said Marcel's grandfather, putting his arm around Papeau's broad shoulders.

Indeed not, thought Borck. *Your only weapon is your smell.*

"We saw him," said Papeau, "but we did not help him."

" 'Him'? And who would that be?"

"The pilot, he ran over that hill there!"

Grandpere tried to shush her.

"A pilot? How did you know he was a pilot?"

"Wasn't that a plane crash last night?" said Grandpere. He tried a weak grin. "It knocked me out of bed."

"British? American?"

Grandpere tried to think of an answer. "An Englishman," said Papeau.

"Very good," said Borck. "And how did you know he was an Englishman if you hadn't spoken to him?"

Papeau looked at Grandpere. "Well, we're not really sure. His uniform looked like an English uniform. That's what I thought. Of course, he was far off in the distance. He ran up that hill there."

"So you say." Borck thought he could smell them. He moved several paces to his right to get upwind of them. "Did you see anyone helping him?" They shook their heads. "Because if you did, those persons would have to be assumed to be part of the Resistance. We want no trouble with the Maquis in this area, eh?"

"No, sir," said Grandpere. "I stay out of politics. I am too old."

"He falls asleep when others discuss politics," Papeau said.

"You do understand," sniffed Borck, "that if we find an airman concealed on this farm, we would be forced to conclude that you are with the Resistance. It would mean immediate death." He cocked his head. "I will give you another chance."

Papeau looked up at her husband. He straightened up as if it were 1915 and Marshal Foch was passing. "You may look as you wish, but he went over that hill."

Borck stared at the old man for several seconds.

"Corporal," he said, "the house. You two, the stable. Sergeant, the dog."

As the men scattered to his orders, Borck removed a cigarette from a case. It was Turkish and scented with clove. He had taken the pack from a Jewish scientist that had initially worked on the Project. There was code word for the Project, but that's all they called it, "The Project." He smoked one of these cigarettes when the smell of death was in the air. He was certain the old farmer and his wife were lying. He would kill them, soon, but this would be not nearly as interesting as others, who inspired him to kill slowly. These people were just animals that needed to be put out of their misery. A waste of bullets, really. He could order his men to do it when the time came, but they respected you more as an officer if you did some of the dirty work yourself. He smiled at the old couple. The old man weakly smiled back.

The sergeant was having trouble untying the dog and had to put down his rifle to do so. The corporal emerged from the cottage carrying the old man's rifle. "There is no one inside, Oberführer," he saluted. "There is this."

"I hunt with that," said Grandpere. "It belonged to my father."

Borck bent and looked closer. "Hmm. Civilians were to turn in all weapons."

"Why, that's no weapon, sir," said the old man. "It's as old as I am! I use it for rabbits, sometimes pigeons."

Borck lifted it with one hand. "No weapon? I doubt the rabbits would agree with you."

He glanced over the hood of the half-track at his men fumbling with the stable door. The sergeant led the dog around to the rear.

Marcel looked at the blank eyes of the angel, who seemed to be listening attentively to the sounds of his hunters. Marcel sat with his heart in his throat, nearly fainting when he heard the rattle of the stable door.

The angel reached into his tunic as Marcel gaped. He reached not *under* the tunic, but *into* it, like he was reaching into a tub of water, like he was scratching the inside of his own ribs.

Marcel heard boots on the dirt floor. The sound of a pitchfork stabbing into the hay.

The angel pulled out his hand as if plucking out his own heart. He held a metal sphere, smaller than a boule, and Marcel thought it was some kind of weapon. The angel peered down at it for several seconds, shifting his fingers and rolling the ball in his hand.

The soldiers were moving closer, and now there was another sound, that of a dog panting and sniffing along the outer wall.

Seams suddenly appeared on the angel's globe, and it slowly began to open like some otherworldly flower. The petals began to spin, whirling like fan blades with a barely audible whine. A foggy dome of light, shifting colors like the aurora in the chrysalis, formed just above the petals.

"Look at that," said one of the soldiers.

"The poor thing is nearly dead."

"I hate people who abuse their animals."

The whine of the metal ball grew silent, but the search dog began to whimper and cry out at the pain of a noise beyond human hearing. Marcel thought the ball was some kind of siren, but what kind?

The angel twisted his torso, flinging his limp arm against Marcel, who didn't understand. The angel did it again and Marcel grabbed its cold forearm. The angel shifted in the cramped space and awkwardly dropped his leg over the chrysalis, just as the soldiers kicked back the workshop door.

One quickly stuck his head in, then pulled it out. The second did it as well, then entered, sweeping his rifle side to side.

Marcel gripped the angel's arm and remembered a prayer. "The Lord my God is an army no fortress can withstand/The Lord my God is a bulwark no force can overwhelm." He glanced at the angel and was suddenly aware that it was ringed in an aura of yellowish haze.

The angel stared into the whirling petals of the ball without moving. The whole space they occupied was filled with the haze; Marcel saw it clinging to his own body and suddenly knew the soldiers would see this light. He looked out.

One soldier poked under the opposite table, while the second examined various tools and cans of nails on the shelf. He found a can of tobacco. It must have been the one Marcel's father had searched for many months ago and accused Marcel of stealing. The soldier pointed to the barrel and tools concealing the space in which Marcel and the angel hid. He aimed his rifle as the second soldier moved cautiously to get a better look.

They were caught, Marcel thought and he cringed closer to the angel, bumping his head on the table above.

"Who is there?" said the soldier, throwing the bolt of his rifle.

"Come out, come out," said the other one. "Now!"

Marcel stared at the angel, who did not move, but continued to stare into the whirling ball.

The soldier kicked the barrel and his view was clear. His face was only a meter away. He was looking directly into Marcel's white face. If Marcel had breathed, the man could have felt it.

All at once there was a great roar, and the soldiers spun toward the window. The search dog had leaped into it, barking and snarling, his teeth white and dripping, straining on his leash to get inside.

"God in Heaven!" shouted the soldier, staggering backwards.

The sergeant looked in the window behind it.

"I almost shot it!" said the other.

"Halt," shouted the sergeant, barely able to restrain the beast. "She smells something!"

"There is no one here," said the annoyed soldier. "Get that damned dog back!"

"Don't talk to me like that, Private, or I'll set her on you!"

"She smells the cow or maybe the airman was here, but there's no one now."

The dog looked directly at Marcel and barked, the force of it seeming to shatter Marcel's bones. The angel turned his head slightly toward the dog, hovering the metal sphere in his hand in front of him.

Suddenly, the dog blinked, grew silent, and rested its head on the bottom of the window frame. It whimpered and dropped out of sight to the ground.

"That dog is worthless!" said the private.

"You watch your mouth," said the sergeant. "And check the floor for trap doors! Schatzi smelled something!"

"The floor is dirt," stomped the private, only a hand's length from Marcel's sabot. "It hasn't been disturbed in five hundred years."

Again they looked directly at Marcel and the angel, as if they could almost see something, but it wasn't there.

"Schatzi smelled something!" insisted the sergeant.

"Your underwear," mumbled the private. "Come on."

The soldiers left. A few seconds later, Marcel heard the sergeant and the dog moving around to the front of the stable. He waited for them to come inside, but they didn't.

The yellowish aura which had enclosed them faded. The petals of the miraculous sphere slowed and closed. The angel's head wobbled as if he were exhausted, then dropped back. From the pursing of his tiny mouth, he seemed to be breathing hard. He dropped the sphere into Marcel's lap. When Marcel picked it up, it was as smooth and seamless as a billiard ball. He squeezed it with both hands to stop his fearful shivering.

"Where is the boy?" Borck demanded.

"The boy?" asked Grandpere.

Borck quickly slapped the old man, knocking him to the ground.

The old woman knelt beside her husband and shouted, "You beast!"

"I'll give you 'beast'!" said Borck. He spun and kicked out, catching her in the shoulder and knocking her back. The old man struggled to rise, but swooned and fell back.

Borck prodded him with his toe, then stomped down on his fingers. Grandpere cried out. "Where is the boy? The boy has a room.

The boy has clothes. There are three soup bowls. Where is he? Hiding the airmen?"

The old man tried to say something. His wife was clawing at his arm, blubbering.

Borck spun and picked the old man's tiny rifle up from where he had propped it against the bumper. "Is this a weapon? Is this a weapon, old man?"

Grandpere shook his head.

"It's just a pop-gun. It's just a toy, eh?" He pointed it straight at Papeau. "Good, we shall play then!"

The old man jerked up, blocking a clear shot.

"Where is the boy?"

"Kill me! I don't care!" shouted Papeau. "Filthy pig!"

The crack of the rifle seemed to freeze time. No one moved. The elderly peasants sat thinking they were dead, that it didn't hurt as they had expected and then waited for the pain to come.

It didn't.

Borck smiled and noted with distaste the spittle at the corner of the old man's mouth. A rabid dog, needing to be put down. "You see how easy it is? Tut-tut, and I missed. Well, that was so amusing that unless I am distracted by information about the location of the boy, about where he is concealing the airmen, or perhaps something of interest about the Resistance–" he narrowed his eyes "–I will certainly do it again."

"I told you: over the hill. That way."

"The boy?"

"He went after morels. He likes to hunt morels. We make soup. Soup is all we can afford."

"They starved their cow," said the corporal.

"Liar," said the old woman.

"You should see it, Oberführer, a bag of bones."

Borck shot a glance at the corporal for speaking. "You know, *Monsieur*, I have heard that some of the Jews sent their children to the country to be hidden among the peasants. You seem quite old to have a child . . ."

* * *

Only a moment before, Marcel crept out of the hiding place. He checked out of the window, saw nothing but the pasture and the wooded hill beyond. He then stepped carefully out of his sabots and made his way carefully across the floor toward the opposite wall. There was an open knothole in the wall through which he might see, as well as hear what the Bosch were up to.

He paused, however, by the workshop door. Clemence had collapsed to the ground. Her ribs rose and fell as she labored to breathe. The change was astonishing. Only a few hours before she had never looked healthier. Now her eyes were glassy and her skin seemed drawn tight to her skeleton. He had been right, he thought. The sudden profusion of milk was the result of a vicious disease. He remembered then the grotesqueness of the angel's strange proboscis. He looked back at the angel, still resting with its leg across the strange chrysalis. He touched the glassy cast on his arm and felt almost sick.

He heard the crack of his grandfather's rifle and hurried to look out the knothole. He saw Borck fiddling with the catch to break the gun at its hinge and insert another bullet. He couldn't hear as well as he had hoped. The half-track partially blocked his view. The sergeant rubbed at his dog's ears, but the dog seemed drugged. Borck paced, then suddenly kicked Grandpere in the side. The old man writhed in pain and Papeau threw herself on him to protect him, raising her hands, begging with clenched fingers.

Marcel shot to his feet. A scythe. A pitchfork. Anything he could attack them with.

But as he jumped up, he nearly collided with the angel.

The angel pointed to the open window and the trees beyond. Marcel instantly understand.

"No," he said. "Please. My Papeau, my Grandpere."

The angel insistently pointed.

Tears poured down Marcel's cheeks. "I know you are from God," he begged, "but don't ask me—"

The sensation of fingers in his hair returned, and once again the cross of Lorraine assembled itself on the angel's breast.

Marcel gradually felt at ease. His grandparents were in God's hand. They would be safe. He knew this the same as he knew that the sky was blue. When the angel pointed again, he knew he must go. Where? That he didn't know, but he had faith that the answer would soon be revealed to him. As he went to the window, Marcel saw the steel ball lying on the ground beside the chrysalis. He hesitated, looked back at the angel, whose head seemed to drop in assent. Still watching the angel, he made the sign of the cross and picked up the steel ball, sticking it in his jacket pocket. Leaving his sabots behind, he ran barefoot across the pasture, carefully keeping the stable in the Germans' line of view.

He was halfway to the tree line when he heard another shot. He didn't dare think what they were doing. He ran even faster, as if he could outrun the next shot.

The old woman squirmed on the ground in agony. The bullet, no larger than a pea, had shattered her arthritic knee.

The old man wept and pleaded and begged. "Not her! Not her! Please! Me instead!"

"Then tell me," barked Borck. "Distract me!"

"Please! I don't know anything! I'm just a farmer. The boy went for morels. Please! In the name of God—"

The old man froze, looking toward his stable.

"What?" demanded Borck.

"Oberführer!" said the sergeant as the other men gawked, slowly raising their rifles.

A strange creature with a bulbous head and great black eyes staggered into the sunlight.

"The angel!" whimpered the old woman.

What uniform is that? Borck thought. Some kind of liquid shimmered across the chestpiece, undulating like water in a breeze.

"Take off your helmet," ordered Borck. He fumbled for his sidearm, then aimed the Luger directly at the airman's head. The creature stood silently looking at him, his left arm hanging at his side, his strange, long fingers curling slowly in front of his chest.

"My God," said the sergeant. "What is that?"

"American?" asked Borck. "Englander?"

The creature stared.

"I demand answers!"

He straightened his arm and stiffened his back, walking fearlessly toward him, the sites lined up precisely between the eye holes of the helmet. He could shoot him, but he knew he couldn't. He suddenly knew there was more to this strange creature than anything to do with the Allies. It was obvious. Who on earth could invent such an aircraft? Was it possible that this was a pilot from Mars? From the stars? If he was, that aircraft could win the war. Not only that, what this creature could tell them! What the revitalized Germany could do with the technology of a race from another planet! Perhaps they already knew about the war. Perhaps they were here to help place the superior race in command of the planet. The Thousand-Year Reich was to have allies from space.

Black dots suddenly appeared on the creature's chest. They swirled and massed like bees at a hive door, then shaped themselves into a sharp-edged swastika.

Borck lowered his Luger and gaped, but the creature's head rolled to one side. He tottered and crumpled.

"He is dead!" mumbled Borck's sergeant.

"Damn!" said Borck, imagining all his possibilities evaporating.

The swastika on the creature's chest guttered out like a candle.

16 OCTOBER 1942
SUPREME HQ,
ALLIED EXPEDITIONARY FORCES
LONDON, ENGLAND

Contemplating the relevant documents on his desk, General Thomas D. Anthony tried to make them unify into a coherent picture, what his adjutant called "connecting the dots." The intelligence that he had been collecting for Operation Torch was not really a challenge. Locating the French forces in North Africa wasn't all that difficult with so many French willing to betray their German and Vichy masters. The main problem was cutting a deal with the contentious French leaders. Who would be the best man for the Allies to exploit: Giraud, DeGaulle, or the collaborationist Darlan? If these battling egomaniacs could be soothed somehow, there might be no resistance to the landings, and the Americans could roll across Algeria and attack Rommel's Afrika Korps from the rear. Thank God all that politicking with French generals was for Eisenhower and the others.

Anthony had worked on the project to convince the Germans through false intelligence that the Americans intended to land in Dakar far to the south in Senegal, rather than in Morocco. It had gone extremely well, and Anthony also monitored that situation. But for weeks nothing had indicated that the Germans suspected anything. They were too interested in Rommel's push to drive the Brits out of Egypt. They couldn't defend Dakar, anyway, and were counting on Darlan to do what he could. If Rommel crushed Montgomery, he could just turn around and crush the troops they imagined coming up from Dakar. It was astounding that the Allies had broken Enigma, the unbreakable coding machine; Anthony, his staff, and the Brits were reading secret German dispatches every day. The problem was always, what do they mean? If a message said Rommel was being treated for a stomach problem, that was clear, but suppose it only gave a list of materials, or contained a set of numbers. Would the answer "55" in a message be the number of tanks? Metric tons of sugar? New uniforms? Bombers? Figuring out what the Germans meant when they said a certain thing was the Harvard-educated Anthony's specialty.

Lately, it was this strange collection of activities midway between Vannes and Nantes that had intrigued him. The area was fairly rocky with a number of caves, many of which had been used by wineries and for storage. Nothing really unusual had happened when the Germans came in, until they began moving slave laborers to one particularly large cave. A young intelligence officer had picked up the movement of mining equipment, but there had never been any indication that mining had ever gone on there. No, it was much more likely they were building some sort of bunker. Perhaps a kind of underground fortress that could not be destroyed from the air. Later, however, other information came. At least three scientists with expertise in metallurgy had been ordered to the place. In addition, an eminent Russian emigré whose specialty was atomic research, had been forced to leave the University of Paris for Saint-Lyphard. This, along with several other indications—orders for lab materials and equipment—led the Allies to believe it was some kind of research facility, probably for armoring, though RAF Brigadier General Hume made a good argument they were working on ball bearings, essential to so many machines. The rail line they had been laying to the mountain seemed to prove they wanted to get large quantities of something or other in or out of there.

But then there had been all of this sudden weird activity, which Anthony had connected with the shooting down of an experimental

Allied aircraft fifteen miles away from the cave. Coded messages had been going back and forth between Berlin and Saint-Lyphard. No less than an SS general had quickly slipped in and out of Saint-Lyphard. The coded messages had suddenly gotten more cautious, even though Anthony did not believe the Germans knew that Enigma had been broken. Hitler himself, and Goering, seemed to have gotten interested in the downed Allied plane.

Why?

There was no experimental plane, certainly not operating in that area. You don't test an experimental plane by sending it into a war zone. The building of the rail line had gotten even more frantic. They had sent one hundred Jewish slaves to assist. And then the message that the laboratory in Berlin was almost ready for the "gift of Saint-Lyphard."

Planes had been lost, of course, but none near Saint-Lyphard, nothing "experimental." One of the branches might be concealing something from Anthony, that was always a possibility, but why? All this had to be about something the Germans had misunderstood. They only thought they had an experimental aircraft. But how could they be deceived so long? They had something there. They had moved a number of things outside the cave and into huts. They had declared an area of two kilometers around the cave a *Zutritt Verboten*—a "Forbidden Zone," meaning any unauthorized personnel could be shot on sight.

What puzzled Anthony most was a cryptic message from the general who had visited Saint-Lyphard to the Reichstag:

WHEN HE TALKS, THE WAR WILL BE OURS.

Anthony had read weirder messages than this one. The Big Nazis were in love with the occult, so he even checked if there had been an oracle in that cave in ancient times, but that was so implausible that even as he checked it, he knew he was wasting time. They had found a Roman god? Yeah, right.

He mused over the various strands of this puzzling tapestry for an hour and still could not see what they pictured. There had to be some action, though. The general's message had sounded like the usual Nazi boast, but he had the feeling that it was more than that. Had the Germans found a way to build an atomic bomb? What did a downed aircraft have to do with it?

He had to find out.

He drummed his fingers on his desk for several minutes, then asked his secretary to get General Eisenhower's office.

17 OCTOBER 1942
THE SATED SWINE PUB
EAST END OF LONDON, ENGLAND

The French singer—a dark-haired woman named Nicole DuPrix—was working the crowd of soldiers, sailors, and airmen as only a French woman could. Her skirt was just high enough, her voice just smoky enough, her eyes just inviting enough to guarantee that every heterosexual male in the room would feel a pressing need beneath his fly buttons. And when she began to sing "We'll Meet Again," she mingled her sexiness with the sadness of all those friends you'd never meet again in this lifetime, and you fell in love with her, at least for the length of the song.

As she repeated the last verse, the Brits began to sing with her, some of them weeping. Most of the Americans joined in, but without the rueful thoughts. They hadn't seen action yet. They were well-scrubbed, clean-shaven, and, like prep school football players pulling on their leather helmets, ready to win this thing.

Captain Joe Logan, however, felt nothing. He had been working hard for weeks to feel nothing. Sometimes he almost came close to succeeding. He belted back another scotch and surveyed the room through the cigarette smoke. He felt as if he were watching a dull movie. All those chipper Americans—his own people—were just Hollywood phonies, pretending to be real. The Brits—oh, they were real, they'd been through hell and more, but he couldn't feel any connection with them, either. Logan knew that he shouldn't be alive, and maybe he wasn't, fully. Sometimes when he remembered the raid several weeks before, he wished he wasn't.

The singer drew a huge round of applause, slid off her stool, and shouted, *"Je suis Nicole, messieurs! Vive la France!"*

"Viva la Fra-yunce!" shouted a big American. Soldiers crowded around Nicole, offering her drinks. She looked like a sparrow caught in a cattle stampede.

"Cap'n," said a gravelly voice. "Cap'n."

Logan looked up at Sergeant Pawlowski. "MPs in the street."

Logan shrugged. Captains and NCOs weren't supposed to fraternize with enlisted men. Perhaps it made ordering a guy to his death a mite tougher. "If it worries you, get out of here."

"I'm with you," Pawlowski said, sitting. "Anyways, what they gonna do? Bust me? Send me home?" He set another scotch down for Logan, then sniffed the mug in front of him. He saw Logan eyeing him.

"Hard cider," he said. "It's like an English thing."

"They have hard cider in America, Punchy."

"Not in my neighborhood." He sipped. "It don't taste too bad. Good for a thirst." He gulped half the mug.

"Watch the kick."

Punchy shrugged. "It's like water."

"It's got a sneaky overhand right," Logan said without smiling.

"Very funny," said Punchy.

"Punchy" Pawlowski had been a boxer, moving up in the rankings as he steadily mowed down twenty opponents, fifteen by knockout. Seven by the third round. His fists were compared to cannonballs. For the sake of a big purse, he was hyped out of his league and knocked back into the footnotes of boxing history by an overhand right by Primo Carnera. Tap, and he went down like the *Titanic*.

Nobody lost to Primo Carnera, not even your grandmother.

"Fists like cannonballs, a jaw like a Faberge egg," said one newspaper.

All that teasing and the memory of the arena fading to black kept

Punchy watching for ghost overhand rights when he should have been watching the left jabs. Max Baer beat him up good, then a comer named Hersh, and suddenly Punchy was being offered club fights. He sometimes fought under two different names on the same night just for the money. And then, of course, he was offered a swan dive. The mobster said he could do it or die, and held out the fifty dollars. Punchy leveled him, then broke the jaw of the guy's body-guard. At that moment, any quick way to get out of town was a good way. He joined the Army. Hell, it was July 1940 and there was fighting in Europe, but it wasn't like America was in it.

Nicole had climbed up on top of her stool and thrust a glass toward the ceiling. "We will toast now! *Vive la France! Vive la France libre!*"

"Hear! Hear!" shouted a Brit, and then the whole room shouted *"Vive la France!"*

"To Franklin Delano Roosevelt," an American slowly and rever-ently said from the top of a table, "who saved America and is soon to save the world."

"Franklin Delano Roosevelt!" said the crowd, as the American tumbled drunkenly from his perch.

A sergeant-major wearing a kilt rose onto the seat of a chair. "To his Britannic majesty, King George VI, king of England, Wales, Ire-land, and most importantly, Scotland. May he long reign with Her Majesty, the Queen, at his side!"

"Screw the Queen!" said somebody.

The room was instantly silent. The sergeant-major lowered his craggy face—a frightening face. "Pardon me?"

The tide of Americans parted, leaving one soldier trying to pull a fuzzy drunk to his feet and out of there.

"Was that you?" said the sergeant-major.

"Screw the queen," said the American again.

"He don't mean nothin'," said his friend. "He's just . . ."

The sergeant-major stepped down from his chair.

"Please, boys . . ." begged Nicole. Her piano player closed his keyboard, grabbed his hat, and tiptoed out the back.

There was no other sound than the sergeant-major's shoes crossing the wooden floor.

"Here we go," said Punchy.

The sergeant-major stopped in front of the drunk, and clasped his hands behind his back. "Would you mind repeating that?"

"Screw the Queen! You deaf? Screw the Queen!"

The sergeant-major smiled broadly. "Ah, laddie, you can't do that. You can't even approach her!"

Nicole's eyes widened. She began to titter, and the room erupted in a roar of laughter. Two Americans clapped the sergeant-major on the shoulders. He tilted his head jauntily, spun on his heels, and began to walk back to his drink.

And then the drunk threw a bottle. Whoever he hit it wasn't the sergeant-major, who glanced back over his shoulder at the shoving and shouting and, soon, the flying fists, flying chairs, and noses gushing blood. An American in glasses came at the sergeant-major with a chair. As it came down, the sergeant-major stepped to one side, caught the man by his belt buckle and lifted him off the ground, flipping him back as the chair dropped down on his face. Another man came at the sergeant-major from his other side with a bottle, but the sergeant-major seemed to sense it, turned, and swept a backward kick that mowed him down. The sergeant-major smoothed his twisted kilt.

Joe Logan tapped Punchy on the forearm to watch the sergeant-major, a coracle of tranquility in the eye of a hurricane. The guy dusted off his attackers like flies, and could have been thinking about picking up his laundry as he did so.

A mug shot by, barely missing Logan as he tilted his head to the side. It smashed on the wall behind him. Punchy brushed glass fragments off his lap, then watched the battle royal with a grin. He cocked his head as if asking Logan to dance.

"Go ahead, have fun," Logan shouted, barely audible in the din.

Punchy waded into the crowd and took down a Royal Marine with a simple jab. He backhanded an American flyer a full head higher than he was, and the guy's eyes rolled like cherries in a slot machine.

Logan heard a piece of a scream and turned to see Nicole, pulling at the back of a fat man's suit. The fat man was the only man in civvies in the whole brawl, but he was wringing a Canadian soldier's neck, flopping the man around as the boy flailed helplessly. Nicole was trying to stop him, clawing his back and hurling an unbroken string of obscene French.

The fat man was distracted a little by her and turned his head. Somehow, the Canadian caught the fat man on the ear, which infuriated him. He choked the boy in earnest now, never mind the gnat who worried his back.

"Oh, hell," said Logan. Somebody was going to get hurt over there, he thought, and it isn't going to be one of ours. He drained his drink, picked up Punchy's cider mug, and started for them.

The Canadian was nearly blue when Logan pushed several sweaty bodies out of the way to get to them. Nicole was riding the fat man's back, trying to grab his greasy hair.

Logan swung the mug into the fat man's face and his eyes went glassy, even though he didn't fall. Logan brought back his fist to finish him, when a tangled blob of spitting and fighting humanity tumbled into them. They all went down like dominoes. The Canadian landed on his face. The fat man spun around the end of the bar, and somehow Logan and Nicole ended up tangled under the front edge of a dripping table.

"*Merde!*" she shouted when she caught her breath.

From down there, the fat man's belly looked like a rolling hill in Ohio. The Canadian wasn't moving, and Nicole crawled out to him. Before she reached him, however, he rolled over, coughing and holding his neck.

Brawlers were still stumbling, falling, and hitting each other with anything handy. Logan crawled out, hooked Nicole around the waist, and pulled her back under the table.

"Stay here!" he shouted.

She struggled against his arm, and he felt a wiry strength you wouldn't expect from such a small woman.

"You'll get hurt," he protested. "Stay here! *Restez!*"

She turned her head and momentarily froze, looking back at him. "This is horrible!" she said, no longer trying to pull away.

"I don't know," said Logan into her ear. "The whole world is nuts and we have a nice quiet corner to ourselves. What more can you ask for?"

Some spilled liquor dripped over the table edge and patted on her nose. She jerked back, saying *"Merde!"* He wiped it off with his fingertips, then licked it off.

"English beer," he said. "Warm."

She took his hand and licked it, as well. "I like it warm," she said.

"I'll bet you do," he said.

The noise of a flung chair landing on top of the table made them duck, and they looked out at the chaos. Punchy, who had evidently decided to show the sergeant-major that he wasn't the toughest son-of-a-bitch in the place, had now mowed his way to him, leaving three unconscious men behind him.

The sergeant-major had just picked up a man and thrown him over the bar. Punchy came up to his side, planted his feet, and must have shouted something. The sergeant-major turned. Punchy smiled and drove an overhand right at his jaw.

It almost connected. With reflexes like a cat, the sergeant-major flicked back his head and brought up his fist under Punchy's jaw.

Punchy dropped like a sack of grain. The sergeant-major gave the crumpled ex-boxer a glance, then reached behind the bar for a bottle of whiskey. He reached into his sporran, dropped a silver coin on the bar, and casually walked out the back door.

Logan whistled. "Primo Carnera all over again. What's French for 'glass jaw'?"

"That is the Great McGonigle," she said. "He is very strange."

"Why is he the 'Great' McGonigle?"

"Cher," she grinned, "you do not want to know."

MPs were blowing their whistles and flailing their batons to get into the door. It was a new phase of the battle, in which the combatants allied themselves against a common foe.

Logan glanced at the back door. "Nicole, my lovely, I think discretion is the better part of valor at this moment. We've got to stop meeting like this, *n'est-ce pas*?"

She smiled. "Sixty-two Musgrave Square, *Capitain*," she said. "It's not far."

"Call me 'Joe,' " he said.

"Perfect," she said. "Stockings are nice."

"Yeah," he said, "on the right legs."

19 OCTOBER 1942
OCCUPIED FRANCE, NEAR NANTES

If he allowed himself to think about it, he would simply stop. Stop moving, stop trying, stop caring.

Stop living.

He was already a ghost. Always hungry. Always taking the next step and the one after that by repeating the name of Levrier, the Resistance fighter his grandfather had mentioned. He had asked for Levrier in Mesquer and was told he was in Guérand. In Guérand, no one had heard of Levrier until Germans rolled up in a car and began asking the local constable about a boy from a farm near Mesquer. He had murdered his grandparents, they said, and burned their house. The tavern owner was hiding Marcel in his cellar when the constable came around, asking the patrons if they'd seen him. Under the owner's harsh stare, those who had seen the boy suddenly lost their memories, but it was likely that at least one of them would recover it if he thought there was a possibility of a reward. The tavern owner told the boy he was on his own, but gave him the name of a charcutier in Nantes.

Traveling at night, Marcel hid himself during the day, having fitful dreams in which he relived the day of his flight. The angel pointing out the window. The crack of a shot. The gasping, gasping. His heart nearly exploding as he drew closer to the trees. His tumbling in the ferns as his legs gave way. Then looking back at the high, snaky column of black smoke. The cottage roof exploding in flames. The stable crackling as the orange fire shot up its side.

All of what had been his life was gone. His grandparents were dead, he was sure. And why deceive himself? His father was dead, too. If Papa were alive, he would have returned. One way or another he would have returned. His grandfather had said he was sure that his son had slipped away to join the Free French army in Equatorial Africa. But how could his father get there? No, it was far more likely that the Germans had simply shot him. Several weeks before he disappeared, someone had killed a German in Vannes and they had chosen ten men at random for the firing squad. Maybe they plucked Papa from the street and shot him for calling them the Bosch, or simply because they didn't like his look. No, Marcel's former life was dead. He was alone, except for God, and God was demanding much more than Marcel could have imagined.

The only thing that held him together was the idea that it had been the same for the peasant girl from Arc. In the end, God had asked her to accept being burned alive. Yet, in her death, she had lived on and France had been freed. God demanded a high price, but he repaid tenfold. The angel had come. Marcel had been protected. Somehow he was part of God's plan to save France. When he found Levrier, perhaps he would find out what that plan was.

Sometimes Marcel felt the presence of the angel. He awoke from his nightmares sometimes thinking that the odd face and the black eyes would be directly in front of him. The strange metal ball the angel had given him. He caressed it, cupped it in his hands when he was cold, and though he sometimes thought he felt warmth in it, it remained only a metal ball. It did not open or flower or give any sign of the miracle that had occurred in the stable.

The glass cast in which the angel had wrapped his arm had become part of him. It seemed weightless. He felt no pain or irritation from its being there. It didn't even itch. He kept it hidden under a big coat he had stolen from a barn near Guérand. Neither the tavern owner nor the old woman who caught him sleeping in her vineyard had noticed it. She had given him bread and cheese and knew the Germans were looking for him, but she asked him for no further explanations and shooed him off as soon as she could. His big coat, however, was heavy and hot during the day, and he had to get rid of the cast sometime. His arm felt fine. He whacked it with a thick stick, and studied it for cracks. Nothing. He whacked it harder. Nothing. On the third try, the stick shattered. He picked up a jagged rock and tried to scratch the cast. The sharp edge slid over the surface like new shoes on ice.

He braced himself, placing the cast on top of a boulder. With a grunt, he brought down a fist-sized stone. It bounced off, putting a sting in his striking arm. The cast was unmarked, but the stone had crushed flat on one side. The boy was now frustrated, determined to break his arm free, even if he hurt himself. This time the stone ball cracked into two neat hemispheres. In doing so, it had cut the palm of his hand. He looked at the blood and thought of Christ's stigmata. The cast, however, was as smooth as the day it had hardened.

Marcel suddenly felt impious. Maybe the cast was intended to be a sign to convince the skeptical. He mentally prayed for forgiveness for his impatience at trying to undo what God had wrought. "Levrier," he whispered to himself as he rose to his feet.

He looked up at the darkening sky. "Lead me to Levrier, St. Joan. Lead me to Levrier."

19 OCTOBER 1942
KREIGSFABRIK 347
(THE FORBIDDEN ZONE)
OCCUPIED FRANCE

D r. Vassily Orlov pushed open the creaking steel door and emerged from the cell. He locked it behind him with the thick key. Borck had been watching from the other side of a wall of bars. Before Orlov reached it, Borck had snatched the key from the guard and opened it.

"Well?" demanded Borck. "Well?"

Orlov adjusted his glasses and tugged his ear. "You are correct, Oberführer. The creature is alive, but it may be perilously close to death."

"You must keep it alive!"

"Oberführer, the biology is so different."

"Your own life depends on keeping it alive. Is that not clear?"

Orlov took a sample tube from his pocket. "This is a liquid which I found on the floor near the creature's shoulder. It may be blood. I cannot know if it is blood at this point."

Borck, his hand shaking, reached out for the tube and raised it toward the light hanging from the ceiling. The "liquid" was no longer fluid. It had solidified into a hazy suspension of sparkling particles. "This looks nothing like blood. What else could it be?"

"I don't know," said Orlov. "We are in the realm not just of the unlikely, but of the impossible."

"It is not impossible," said Borck. "It is there. In that cage."

"And it lives," said Orlov. "But I do not know how. It may be in some sort of dormant state. Or it may simply be dying. I believe that it may have been shot when it was being chased."

"Then treat it for a gunshot wound!" He thrust the tube back at Orlov.

"I cannot get under that material that covers its torso. I cannot know what is under it—the wound, bone, whatever."

"You must save it, Orlov. I order you to save it!" Borck's voice came off the stone ceiling like a rain of spikes.

"Oberführer," Orlov said like a father to an irrational child, "believe me, I want to speak to this creature, make contact with this creature as much as you do, but I cannot operate on something of which I have no concept of its biology. What if its heart is in its shoulder? Its brain?"

"How ridiculous!"

"No," said Orlov. "Some dinosaurs had ganglia, clusters of nerves, in parts of their bodies, other than the brain, and these clusters had a brain-like function. Invertebrates often have nervous systems that are not as centralized as the higher animals."

"This creature is no insect," said Borck.

"No," said Orlov. "But it does not mean that it did not evolve in a totally different way from the mammalia."

Borck threw the key at the started guard and paced. "Scientific theories! This is too important. It must not die."

"That is why we cannot take chances. The scientific knowledge to be gained from this is mindboggling!"

"Scientific knowledge!" snapped Borck, his voice echoing down the stone corridors. "In that cell there, and in the hangar chamber, are the keys to dominion over the Earth forever."

"What are you doing with the spacecraft?" asked Orlov.

"I have men going over its surface inch by inch, listening with stethoscopes, looking for any sign of a seam, a rivet."

"Could the craft be cast from one solid piece? Hollowed out?"

"We will find out. We must find out." Borck smacked his fist into his palm.

"And the tunic? What kind of cloth is that?"

"*Is* it cloth, Doctor?"

"Oberführer, I cannot tell you whether it is cloth or a fluid. There is nothing like it on Earth. I must have equipment. And help."

"The greatest scientists of the Reich will be here. Count on it."

"I fled Russia for this," said Orlov intensely. "And the Wehrmacht captured Paris just so I could be here. It is destiny, Oberführer. I shall not fail you."

Borck blinked. Orlov's grandiosity surprised even him. But these were not the times for shrinking. The Superman does not shrink. There was a way to unlock these mysteries and for the thousandth time, Borck went over the details in his head. . . .

When the creature had collapsed in front of him in the farmyard, he had rushed forward with his pistol raised against a trick, but when he bent forward, he saw a slight movement in its lips. That strange head wasn't a helmet. It took him a moment to collect his thoughts, then he waved his men to check the stable and behind it.

He knelt beside the supine creature and gingerly reached out with his gloved hand. The thin neck felt hard and cold and a bit sticky. Borck felt nothing like a pulse. He lifted the spindly arm and looked at the strange hand. More like the branches of a tree than those of a hand, the fingers had four joints. There were two thumbs on opposite sides, also four-jointed, and three middle fingers. All of the digits were of equal length, though the thumbs were set a little lower on the hand. Each fingertip had a round, bulbous end, like the pads on a cat's foot. There was no sign of a pulse or anything like it in the wrist or in the elbow joint.

Borck then turned his attention to the fluid-looking tunic. He pulled his SS dagger from his belt and attempted to lift the cloth. But it didn't behave like cloth. The point broke the shimmery surface, but when Borck tried to lift it, it slid off, like silk might slide off a smooth rod. He tried to pinch the material between his fingers, but it would not be caught, and the surface rippled. The black dots which had formed into a swastika were no longer visible.

He prodded the creature's chest with the knife. The tunic rippled, but felt solid. He poked the creature's hard thigh. It was hard, too. The creature did not respond, so he pushed harder. Its resistance reminded Borck of wood. He could feel it give way a bit, but it was nonetheless solid as oak.

If the creature felt pain, it would have felt the knife; however, it had not reacted. Borck considered pushing harder, but did not. He sat and tried to understand what lay before him. The only thing he knew clearly was that the ship this creature had come in, could contain undreamed-of secrets. He glanced back at the old couple crumpled together, weeping against each other. How much did they understand of what they had concealed? Had there been any communication between the old couple and the—what?—spaceman?

"Oberführer!" shouted the sergeant from inside the stable.

"Watch them," Borck had said to the corporal, who could not take his eyes off the strange, unmoving creature.

In the back room of the stable, the sergeant pointed at the boy's abandoned sabots. Borck looked out toward the wide field and saw nothing. Borck knelt for a closer view of the cow. It was barely alive, desiccated into a horrible parody of a cow.

What was this, then? The creature sucked the life out of this cow? How?

He knew the magnitude of this discovery, but he hadn't the faintest idea what to do about it. The creature outside was dead or nearly dead. If he'd only been able to communicate with it, to let it know the importance of this war in restoring the Aryan culture to its supreme position in history!

"Put it in the half-track along with the dead, ah, pilot, and cover them with a tarp."

"What about the peasants?"

"Shoot them," he had said, then raised his arm. "No, don't! We will take them back to the facility. There may be something they can tell us. When you've searched all the buildings again, burn them."

With the smoke rising behind them, they then began their strange ride back to the cave. The old couple was placed in a prominent position in the back, so that anyone could see them: it was a message that no one who defied the Reich will escape, and also protected against sniper attacks. The men, however, had clung to the edge as far away as they could from the lump under the tarp. Even the dog had cowered. Only Borck had sat flat in his seat, looking down at the creature, smoking a Turkish cigarette.

Borck grabbed Orlov's lapel. "The creature is alive? You are sure?"

"The surface temperature of his skin has risen to twenty-one degrees Centigrade, about sixteen degrees below normal human body temperature, and then has stabilized for the last three hours. He does not seem to have been harmed by being placed in the refrigerator, but who can tell? Perhaps it even stimulated the response."

Borck felt as if he were being accused. "I put it in the empty food locker to prevent deterioration. At least then it could be dissected."

The guard who had been posted by the heavy door went inside (probably to pilfer some cheese), and saw steam rising from the tarp in the narrow alcove where the body had been placed. Gingerly, he lifted the tarp with his fingers and felt warmth. Not a lot, but noticeable in the cooler.

"It is no worse for it," said Orlov. "Perhaps."

"We will get the best minds here," said Borck. "We must not only restore this creature's health, but find out who he is and what he knows."

"I need equipment from the laboratory in Paris."

"Make a list. We will send for it."

"It will be easier if I get it myself. Some of it has to be carefully packed. Several items are of my own design."

"Surely you have an assistant."

"She is—was a Jewess."

"Oh, yes," remembered Borck. "That should never have happened." Borck had ordered her relocated just before bringing Orlov
to the Project.

"She was a student. She was clever. They are very clever." Orlov
watched Borck's eyes. "In a limited way."

"We make use of what we must," said Borck, "and then discard
it." He was thinking of the old couple. Was there anything useful
they could tell him?

19 OCTOBER 1942
EAST END OF LONDON, ENGLAND

Logan woke to Nicole holding his face in her hands, whispering *"Calme! Calme!* You are with me, Joe Logan. With Nicole, eh?" She kissed his eyebrows dripping with sweat and tried to pull his face into her bosom, but he pulled away, swinging his legs out of the narrow bed.

"Bad dream," he said. "Too much to drink."

The light of mid-morning had infiltrated the tiny room. She touched his shoulder blade. He flinched and stood, fumbling with his pants. "Where are my cigarettes? Did you steal my cigarettes?"

Nicole's face turned hard. "Your cigarettes are on the chair. By your shirt. Go. I need to sleep."

Logan's hands shook as he tried to light up. After the first drag he was suddenly aware of his nakedness. He curled his body and sat on the edge of the chair. He saw that Nicole had turned her back to him and lay on her side. She was a bony girl, each of her vertebrae accentuated by the indirect light.

"I'm sorry," he said. "Bad dream."

"So you said. *Au revoir.*"

"I can't help having a nightmare, lady."

"So my neighbors have to hear you scream?"

"I imagine they hear a lot of noise from this room."

She sat up, looking him in the face. "Not enough to get used to, Joe Logan! My business is my business—not yours! Now, get out of here." She spun back to face the wall and lay down.

He took a deep breath and rubbed his eyes with both hands. "I'm sorry," he sighed. "The nightmares, they shake me up."

"You think you are the only one with bad dreams? There is a world and more of bad dreams out there. Bad dreams no one can wake from!"

"I said I'm sorry," he snapped, reaching for his undershorts. "And I'm sorry I couldn't find you the stockings."

She sniffed, and he thought she was weeping. He touched her shoulder. "Maybe I can find you a pair later . . ."

She slapped away his touch. "The coffee and the chocolate are enough. Just leave me alone."

He expelled another long stream of smoke. "I don't want to end this way, okay? That's all. I might never see you again. That's the way it is, now."

She laughed, sitting up. "*Sacre bleu*, Joe Logan. Do you know how many times I've heard that line? Why do you try it with me? You've already had what you wanted. Or do you want more? Why don't you tell me how you might die freeing my beloved homeland?"

"Go to hell," he said. "I've had a bellyful of you and your country. If I never go back there, it'll be too soon."

He snatched at a sock on the floor and snapped it on.

"France! What do you know about France? Do you know how they came into the cabaret and arrested everyone? Do you know they stuck a pistol into my husband's mouth and blew his head off? Don't tell me about nightmares!"

Nicole threw back the covers and went to the window. She opened the curtain, indifferent to whether anyone could see her. In the bluish light from the hazy sky, she looked much older, at least a decade older than she had when she was singing.

He stood silently for several seconds, then slumped to the chair with his forearms on his thighs. "I was in Dieppe," he said.

"Dieppe?"

"The raid on Dieppe."

"Please!" She gestured with her hand. "There were no Americans in that."

"Fifty Rangers. Most of the troops were Canadian, but there were fifty Americans."

She studied him for a moment. "And you survived?"

"If you can call it that."

"Not many did," she said.

"No," he said, "not many. It was a total screw-up. We didn't stand a chance. It was worse than they let out."

"It is always worse than they tell us," she said softly.

Logan broke with his memories and began to look for his other sock. She watched him, then said quietly, "Why don't you sleep more? We could both use more sleep."

He saw the weariness in her face. He knew it as if it were his own. He could be five thousand years old, he thought, and not feel as weary as he did.

"We'll go out to eat later," he said. "After last night, that club of yours will be locked up."

"So it goes," she said, pulling the curtain closed.

19 OCTOBER 1942
SUPREME HQ,
ALLIED EXPEDITIONARY FORCE
LONDON, ENGLAND

The messages to Berlin had gotten more explicit, and far stranger. At first, General Anthony suspected there was yet another kind of code involved, the kind of thing in which you said, "We've been hunting buffalo," when you meant "We've been seeking the Panzer group." That sort of thing arose spontaneously in radio exchanges. But in top priority messages to the Big Nazis? He'd never seen it. And these messages hardly seemed spontaneous. There was no playfulness that his German language experts could find in the wording and, what was more, the three messages from Berlin did not seem to be anything other than extremely serious.

It appeared that one Oberführer (the SS equivalent of a German army Major General) named Werner Borck was having difficulty convincing his superiors of something, even though his facility had been visited by a general. It seemed that Fieldmarshal Goering did not believe the general, or, at the least, was looking for greater confirmation of what the general said before actually bringing this to the attention of Hitler himself. The information had also been stopped from rising up the chain of command in the SS, so that Himmler had not been contacted, either.

Now, it was hardly unusual for upper ranks in any military organization to disregard various bits of intelligence, but Berlin *had* sent a general. Why didn't they believe whatever he had brought back? Why were the messages from this Borck so urgent and insistent? And what the hell was he talking about?

At first, they seemed to have mistaken some aircraft for an experimental Allied craft. Anthony had discounted this and decided it must be code for something else. What then? They knew that the underground facility had a scientific purpose. The Germans were always experimenting, and this facility Anthony and the boys in MI-5 had concluded from the materials going in and the scientists who had been moved there, was more research in either rockets or ram-jets. The V-1 and V-2 rockets were troublesome on occasion, but a working jet engine might give the Axis superiority in the air. It might be possible to fly very far at very high speeds—or that's what the engineers said.

But what did Borck mean when he had sent this message:

I MUST INSIST/STOP
WE HAVE CONTACT WITH BEINGS FROM SPACE/STOP
THE FÜHRER MUST BE NOTIFIED IMMEDIATELY

The response had not been intercepted, but Borck then sent a message indicating that photographs and further documentation would be sent immediately, but that time must not be wasted. It wasn't normal for an Oberführer to be this insistent. He would be endangering his career at the very least. Borck couldn't have gone mad or he would simply have been removed, wouldn't he? Hell, the whole Reich was ruled by loonies.

The conclusion Anthony and his staff had come to was that there was a breakthrough of some kind; the British agreed. Dr. Vassily Orlov's sudden relocation to the facility particularly worried him. It was as if he had dropped off the planet. Orlov was one of the best germ scientists at the University of Paris. He had managed to flee Russia by way of Switzerland in the mid-1930s after he'd published a paper that wasn't in line with the official "science" of the Soviet Union. He had moved easily into the emigré population in Paris and made himself known as an extremist anti-Bolshevik. He was the kind of man who would easily support Hitler's crusade against Communism. Orlov was attacked by a French biologist when he said in a café he was waiting anxiously for the conclusion of the fighting around Stalingrad so that he could go home and sow anthrax on the steppes. The biologist was later found floating in the Seine, beaten almost beyond recognition.

What if the breakthrough involved biological warfare? Nothing slowed an army better than illness. What if they had found some way to deliver disease by rocket? They would fire a rocket over London, say, and disperse a deadly influenza for which they had developed a serum? There was a lot of science fiction to this idea, but there was a lot of science fiction in the buzz bombs before they began dropping out of the sky. The Germans had shown no hesitation to punish civilian populations and in the last World War had used poison gas. Even Hitler had gotten a dose of it in the Great War. So far, though, the Nazis hadn't deployed it. But that didn't mean they wouldn't use disease. The Nazis were certain that they were justified in anything. There was no one more dangerous than anyone who was certain.

The British, however, thought less about Orlov being summoned there than a young physicist from Heidelberg. Orlov had been summoned. It did not mean he hadn't been clubbed at night by a patriotic Frenchman or some other Communist. To the Brits, the summoning of the physicist indicated that the breakthrough was about the atomic bomb. According to the scientists, the bomb would be an unrivalled source of destruction. It would make all conventional explosions seem like firecrackers. The Germans were pushing a program in developing the atomic bomb, and, if what Anthony had heard was true about such a bomb, he certainly hoped the Allies were secretly engaged in seeking it as well.

Anthony needed to find out what was going on in the Forbidden Zone, Kriegsfabrik 347, near Herbignac. He was running out of options and feared he was running out of time.

He had been given the authority by Supreme Allied Command to do whatever was necessary to disrupt the activities in the Forbidden Zone. He decided to use it.

He buzzed his secretary. "Sergeant Emerson, tell Colonel Marston I want to see him."

The intercom crackled "Yes, sir," and Marston soon came in.

"Close the door," said the general. "Have you got that mission worked out?

"It seems simple," said the colonel, "but . . ."

"But what?"

"But more than a little risky."

"This is important, Marston."

"Yes, sir."

Anthony sat back in his chair and laced his fingers. "I'm thinking Captain Logan."

Marston started. *"Joe* Logan? Isn't it kind of soon?"

"Yes. It is."

"He survived Dieppe," said Marston. "If he survives this, too, I'll want to know what horses he bets on."

Anthony took a deep breath. "Believe me, Colonel, I also pray he leads a charmed life. If this isn't a suicide mission, I don't know what is."

20 OCTOBER 1942
NANTES, OCCUPIED FRANCE

Marcel hid in the alcove of a doorway opposite the Charcuterie Flanne, just after midnight. A policeman walked by about three humming "Valentina," but he didn't look in. A stray cat awoke the boy by licking at his hand, then curled up to sleep beside him. Marcel nearly wept at the creature's gentleness. He had felt totally isolated for days.

Just before dawn, a man appeared in the window of the second floor of the butcher shop. He had no shirt on and straightened his suspenders over his thick shoulders. Chewing on a toothpick, he looked in both directions along the little street for some time, then went back inside.

Marcel took a deep breath and hurried across. He saw no one in the street, though another window opened further up.

He twisted the door bell. He saw many hooks for hams in the rear of the shop, but only two swung on them.

"We're closed," said a voice above the door.

Marcel backed up. The man in the suspenders looked down at him. "We're closed," he repeated.

"I was told to come here," said Marcel.

The man looked up the street, then down. Then disappeared. Reappearing from a tiny staircase at the rear of the shop, he unlocked the door, checked the street again, and pulled the boy inside.

"And who are you?" demanded the charcutier.

"My name is Marcel. I was told I could find Levrier here."

"Levrier? I know nothing about any Levrier. I have two hams, not very good, and two varieties of sausage. It's not like meat grows on trees, you know. I used to have much more."

"Please, sir. I must find Levrier. My grandfather said he was a Resistance leader. I was told I could find him here."

The man shrugged. "Unless one of the pigs I ground up yesterday was named Levrier, I can't help you."

Marcel's throat clamped tight like a great, hard fist. What would he do now? What? He closed his eyes tight to fight back the tears, then spun in his shame to go.

"Wait," said the butcher, no longer as flippant as he had been. "You'll be needing some breakfast. You don't look like you've eaten for days." His strong hand clamped down on Marcel's shoulder, as his eyes once again checked the street. "Come in the back," he said, pushing Marcel behind the counter.

In the back, the pork butcher's knives and saws hung on the wall. Worktables stretched the length of the room to a series of sausage grinders at the end. A small rickety table with two worn chairs was in the corner.

"Sit here," said the butcher. "I have some eggs hidden in the back. We'll have a fine meal, I promise you."

Marcel felt so sick, so worthless, he wasn't even certain he could eat. He had failed God and he had failed France. What could he do now?

He lowered his face into his hands and then heard the creak of a floorboard.

A man in a black coat and a beret stood by the grinders. He calmly took a revolver from his pocket and aimed it at Marcel.

"Who are you after?" asked the man.

"Levrier," said Marcel. "My grandfather told me about him."

"What did he tell you?"

Marcel realized he had fallen into some kind of trap. "Just that he would give me work," he said. "Our cow died and—"

"You're a liar. What do you want with Levrier?"

Marcel hesitated. "To free France," he finally said.

The man looked at him curiously. "That's a worthy objective, son. And how do you propose to accomplish what all the army could not?"

"With God."

The man cocked an eyebrow.

The charcutier returned. "All is clear," he said.

"This must be him, then," said the man. He put the pistol in his pocket and pulled the other chair up close to Marcel. The charcutier stood over them, arms crossed.

"You are Levrier," said Marcel.

"It's possible," said the man. "Actually, it isn't possible because there is no Levrier. My real name doesn't matter."

Marcel was a little confused by this. "I thought you were the Bosch."

"We could have been. There are enough people in the world willing to sell out their country. I am not one of them, however. Neither is Flanne, here."

"Thank God," said Marcel.

"Or someone," said Levrier. "Why are the Germans after you? They are tearing up the countryside looking for you."

"They killed my grandparents."

Levrier and Flanne exchanged a glance. "They've killed lots of people. I don't think it matters to them who knows."

Marcel had come so far to deliver his message, and yet he froze. For the first time, he realized how mad it would sound. He was afraid his voice would catch. He must state it with the calmness which St. Joan must have stated it, but he wasn't certain he could.

"Well?"

"The angel. He came to me."

"Angel?" Levrier squinted. "What angel?"

"The angel of the Lord," said Marcel.

Levrier pursed his lips to keep from laughing. "I have been a Communist for many years, son. Angels are not very interesting to me. It's nothing personal, understand. Don't take offense. I just can't see why you would seek out a man who could never believe you."

"Maybe the Germans believe him?" said the butcher.

"They believe something," answered Levrier. "You tell me all about this angel of yours. Who knows? Perhaps I shall be miraculously converted, eh? A feather in your cap for the hereafter—converting old Levrier."

"You're laughing at me," said Marcel.

"No, son, I am all ears. Tell me about your angel and afterwards, Flanne will feed us, eh?"

The oyster-eyed Levrier rested his elbows on the tabletop and nodded as Marcel told him about the brilliant flash, his going out to milk the old cow and finding the angel, the rich pail of milk, and the cross of Lorraine. Flanne threw up his hands and turned to leave.

Levrier shushed him. "Let the boy speak! Go on, son. And the arm was limp? He was wounded? How can an angel be wounded?"

"I don't know."

Flanne snorted, and Marcel plunged into despair. They didn't believe him, they never would believe him.

Levrier smiled gently and said, "It isn't necessary to explain everything." He looked up at Flanne. "If he could explain everything, he would be a liar, wouldn't he?"

"An angel!" said Flanne. "He's feeble-minded."

"Shush!" He tapped the back of Marcel's hand with his fingers. "You go ahead, son. I want to hear everything."

Marcel began again, slowly, awkwardly, checking to see Flanne's reaction. He explained how the Germans came. How he hid in the stable with the angel. How the officer in the black uniform had shot his grandmother in the knee.

"And where were you?"

"In the stable, as I said."

"And the Germans did not search the stable?"

Marcel hesitated, then explained how the angel had made the

metal ball flower and they had become unseeable to the soldiers. Flanne shook his head, and Levrier leaned back in his chair.

"Son . . ." said Levrier.

"Here!" said Marcel. "I can prove it. He gave it to me." He reached into his coat pocket and pulled out the metal sphere, sitting it on the table in front of them.

Levrier and Flanne leaned forward. "It's a ball bearing," said Flanne.

"To what?" said Levrier. "It's the size of an apple."

"A ball bearing for a big gun, like on a battleship."

"It is not a ball bearing!" said Marcel.

"When has he been near a battleship?" Levrier said to Flanne. He picked up the sphere in his thick hand. "It feels strange, warm."

"It was in his pocket," Flanne said.

"Where does it open, son?"

Marcel shrugged. He had searched its surface a hundred times and found only smoothness.

Levrier turned it and pressed it with his fingers. "Perhaps it is like a Chinese box," he said. "But it feels solid." He shook it by his ear, rolled it from palm to palm. "What metal is that?"

"Some kind of steel," said Flanne. "Maybe it's a kind of shot, like for a shotgun, only for artillery."

Levrier nodded.

"It is not from a cannon!" Marcel protested.

"Keep your voice down," said Flanne.

"It doesn't look like anything other than a ball, son," said Levrier, handing it back. "Can you open it?"

Marcel shook his head. Even with God on your side, nothing was easy. This was hopeless. How can you convince an atheist of the presence of God? He wanted to be invisible at that moment, to be nonexistent. He wanted to fade like cheap ink in a downpour, astonishing these two disbelievers. He wanted it more than anything.

Levrier jumped suddenly, dropping the ball on the table. "It moved," he said.

Flanne laughed. "The ghost stories have gotten to you."

"I swear I felt something. It tickled me."

"Your arm is asleep," said Flanne.

"It wasn't quite like that. I only felt it in my palm. Here." He pressed his fingers against the heels of his hand.

Flanne picked up the ball, hefted it, and set it back on the table. "Ball bearing," he said.

"You spooked me," said Levrier.

Marcel snatched the ball off the table and stuck it in his pocket. "Explain this, then!" He pulled back the sleeve of the big coat.

"It's glass," said Levrier.

"You've got your arm in a glass tube," said Flanne.

"It is a cast. I fell on my arm at the explosion of light. The angel put this cast on me." He did not want to explain how the angel had spit it onto him. He quickly stood and dropped his coat. They leaned in to look at the cast.

Flanne grabbed it and gave it a tug. "What if I pull it off?"

"It won't come off," said Marcel, jerking it back.

"Suit yourself," said Flanne.

"Have you ever seen anything like that?" asked Levrier lightly. "A glass cast!"

"It isn't glass," Marcel said.

"No?"

Marcel crossed the room and plucked a heavy meat cleaver from the wall.

"Hey!" said Flanne. "Put that back!"

"You must believe me!"

Levrier extended his hand. "Don't do anything foolish."

"I'll show you! It is not glass!" He raised the heavy cleaver over his head. "It cannot be broken."

"Son," said Levrier, "you'll cut off your arm."

Marcel looked down at his forearm and remembered how the rock had split, but then hesitated. What if the cleaver *was* strong enough?

Flanne was on him before he completed the thought, twisting behind him and ripping the cleaver from his upraised hand.

"No!" struggled Marcel. "No!"

"You lunatic!" said Flanne.

Marcel continued to struggle and swung his cast as a weapon, barely missing the butcher, who grabbed him by the neck and with one hand almost lifted him off the floor.

"Stop!" said Levrier, pressing his hand over the boy's mouth. "The door! Flanne! The door!"

They froze. The shrill ring of the charcutier's doorbell was followed by an insistent rapping. *"Herr Flanne! Rauschen Sie, bitte!"*

Levrier pulled his revolver and pulled Marcel toward the rear door. Flanne peeked into the front of the shop.

"Hide," he said. "It is only Munschen."

Flanne went to open the door. "So early, my friend!" he said loudly, and then only bits and pieces of the conversation came through to the back.

Munschen had brought a basket of fresh meat he wanted made into bratwurst. He had very specific instructions about the recipe and he wanted them by noon. He said a number of his men had been chasing Jews up north and he needed to reassign them in the afternoon. Flanne casually asked if there was something going on up north. "What have you heard?" asked Munschen. Flanne said he used to get truffles from a farmer near Herbignac, but that a Forbidden Zone had been created. Munschen muttered something vague about searching for a downed flyer. Flanne changed the subject by saying he was about out of casing; supplies were hard to come by. Munschen promised to speak to his commander. A good word, and the Charcuterie Flanne might be contracted to supply the local garrison.

"I will make these sausages unforgettable," Flanne promised.

The German left. Flanne came into the back with the basket. He lifted the brown paper covering the meat. "My good friend Lieutenant Munschen," he said. He spat on the meat, then sat it on the counter. "They come to Flanne the pork butcher because they are cannibals. They eat their own kind."

"If you get to supply the garrison, I'll supply the arsenic," said

Levrier, releasing his grip on Marcel. "You sit down over there, son. We must decide what to do."

"God has sent me to free France," said Marcel.

"I hope you are right," said Levrier. He pulled Flanne just into the corridor leading to the back door.

"He's a lunatic," whispered Flanne.

"But why do the Germans want him so badly?"

"And what is really in the Forbidden Zone?" asked Flanne. "Munschen said something about a deportation center, but not that many 'undesirables' have been taken in there."

Levrier thought for a moment. "Maybe it's just a ball bearing factory."

"With angels."

"Look," said Levrier, "assuming the boy is mad, we can interpret what he says as this: a plane crashed and one of the crew hid in his stable. The SS wants him badly. Why? They think he has something— that ball, the glass—or he knows something. Maybe something he doesn't know he knows. Whatever it is, I don't want the Bosch to have it.

"It's the principle of the thing," he added with a smirk.

21 OCTOBER 1942
SUPREME HQ,
ALLIED EXPEDITIONARY FORCES
LONDON, ENGLAND

T he drop," said Marston, pointing at the map.

"Why there?" said Logan, holding down the end as it tried to roll itself back up.

"We want to make you as hard to find in France as you were in London."

The map room was strangely silent. The general had ordered all personnel to leave so that the three of them could talk alone.

"I was supposed to have another five days off," Logan grumbled.

"So you've reminded us several times," General Anthony said. "But that doesn't answer the question."

"If the drop is seen," said Marston, "or security doesn't hold, they will think the purpose of it is to go after their fuel dump here at St. Nicolas, about twenty miles away. Their effort will go toward protecting it, while you and your men will be moving rapidly in the opposite direction."

Logan measured it with his thumb. "And how rapidly can we be expected to go—what is it?—about fifty miles?"

"It is likely," said Anthony, "that their spotters will pick up the plane as it comes in over the coast. They are on high alert after our raids on St. Nazaire and Dieppe."

"They seemed quite alert at Dieppe," said Logan.

Anthony met his eyes briefly, then looked at the map again.

"Well?" asked Logan.

Marston cleared his throat. "The Forbidden Zone has the highest form of security. In fact, this particular one has got the best we know of. It clamped down tight about a week ago, and remains so. I guarantee you can't afford them to be looking for you."

"So, we're supposed to walk fifty miles and knock on the door of the Fort Knox of Deutschland and shoot Hitler when he opens the door, right?"

"The Resistance is to meet you and help with transport."

"And then what?"

"You carry out the mission," said Anthony.

"Which is?"

"I haven't decided yet."

Logan raised his hands. "Well, sir, when you think you know, be sure to let me know."

"It may change as more information comes in."

Logan stared at him.

"Joe, this all started out as something weird, something inexplicable—a ghost blip on a radar screen that just doesn't make sense. But then we start putting things together, and it looks like something very important is going on. I won't kid you, we're not sure what, just that suddenly the Krauts think they can win the war with it."

"With what?"

Anthony paused. "I don't know."

Logan dropped his head. "You don't even know what it is, and you're sending out a suicide mission."

"Who said this is a suicide mission, Goddamit? I don't send men on suicide missions, you son-of-a-bitch!"

"What did you call me?" Logan moved to reach over the desk at the general. Marston held him back. "How many men had to die so you could wear scrambled eggs, General?"

Marston and Logan struggled until Logan pushed him back. Marston stumbled against a chair and landed on his rear. When he flailed to get back up, the general said, "Forget it, Colonel."

Logan snarled. "Answer my question, General! How many?"

"Too many," said Anthony after several seconds. "If you stay in, Captain, you'll find out exactly how many that is."

Logan turned his back and vised his head with both hands. Marston climbed to his feet.

Anthony waited, looking through the map at a frozen plain in Siberia, where the U.S. had intervened on the side of the White Russians and where Anthony had learned what it meant to command. "I'll deal you out if you want out," he said, "but I want the best. You've got the instincts for quick judgment. You've got the nose of a rat terrier. It's exactly *because* I want the men to come back that I chose you."

Logan turned, his head still between his hands. He was thinking, he wasn't sure why, of Nicole, forced to sell all she had—including her body—for stockings, for chocolate, for whatever she could get. You paid a price to survive and then you paid compounded interest and then you died anyway.

"If you're not up to it," Anthony continued, "I don't care what the reason is. Just say so."

Logan dropped his hands and, with the weariness of an eighty-year-old man, wandered back to the map. "How many men?"

"I said twelve," said Marston. "The general said fifteen."

"I'll need a regiment," he said.

"This isn't about force," said Anthony. "It's about stealth and quickness."

"I pick them. I'll try to take people you'll never miss."

"Half of them should be Brits."

Logan raised an eyebrow. " 'Should'? Why?"

"We're Allies, remember," Anthony replied. "Ike's orders."

"How about Canadians?"

Anthony shrugged.

"When do we go?"

"This," said Anthony, "you *really* won't like. . . ."

21 OCTOBER 1942
THE FORBIDDEN ZONE

The great metal disk lay under a tarp on a flatbed truck spanning the wide chamber at the front of the facility. It had taken fifty men several days to get it here, but now the best scientists from the Fatherland could examine it in detail. When he had first seen it, Borck had thought it might be impossible to move, but it turned out to be incredibly light for its size. After securing ropes around it and digging it out on one side, it tipped quite easily. The major difficulty was getting any kind of hold on it. Twenty men formed a circle around its edge and worked in unison to heave it onto the flatbed truck. They hardly broke a sweat from the weight, though they stumbled and it shifted and fell on top of a young private from Hanover. His back was broken and he died very quickly. The lieutenant who reported it to Borck clearly took it personally and said, choking on his words, that the medical officer said the boy must have had bad bones. It shouldn't have killed him. They tried again and got it balanced on the bed and wrapped it with all the rope they had. All of those who lifted claimed to have felt a humming from the craft as they did so, and experienced a peculiar numbness in their hands for the next day or so.

Getting it onto the truck wasn't as difficult as keeping it on. The ropes were constantly slipping, even when the men decided to secure the disk under a huge tarp, using it like a bag. The truck moved slowly and men walked on each side, shoving the disk if it slid and making sure it didn't hit anything beside the road. At one point, they thought they'd have to destroy two farm buildings opposite each other which pinched the road, but the lieutenant paced the gap several times and the disk barely cleared.

Thirty men walked with the disk over the countryside in a large circle around it. Their orders were to shoot anyone who got within the circle and saw the caravan, moving at about the pace of a funeral cortege on narrow streets. Most of the French looked the other way when they saw the iron helmets of the Germans, though one peasant approached Corporal Weiss and offered him a sack of tiny potatoes. Weiss merely warned him off. The truck was, luckily for the old man, out of sight behind the trees.

And soon enough, the caravan had reached its objective . . .

"Shall we take it off, Oberführer?" asked the lieutenant.

"Pull off the canvas, but leave it secure," said Borck. "We don't know where the door is. We can't tell which side is up." The scientists were rushing forward to look: Rhinehart, the metallurgist; Rakoczy, the Hungarian-born physicist; Erstewald, the chemist; and Brunnermann, the genius of engineering who had worked at the University of Chicago in the early 1930s.

"They should be cautious," said the lieutenant. "It may slip again."

Borck marched forward as the tarp was pulled away. He felt almost breathless to see it again. This was world domination, he thought. They could circle the planet with these. Strike terror into the hearts of people in New York and San Francisco. Larger ones might be bombers. A craft that could be struck by a XXXX shell and not be shattered, could fly through a torrent of the usual anti-aircraft fire.

Brunnermann's bushy eyelashes bobbed as he strolled around the craft. Rhinehart jabbered excitedly with Erstewald, while Rakoczy bent to look underneath.

"Gentlemen," said Borck, "I cannot emphasize the importance of this enough. You must discover everything there is to know about this."

"It looks solid," said Brunnermann. "It was cast of one piece."

"It is far too light to be solid, and I should warn you that it has already slipped once and fallen on one of my men."

"How can this fly?" said Brunnermann. "If it came from the sky, it was dropped from another craft. Maybe it skipped in off the ocean like a stone. Moving fast enough, that would be no problem. It came in on a straight line, yes?"

"Until it was hit," said Borck.

"There, then, it is not a maneuverable craft. It is solid."

"Herr Doktor Brunnermann," said Borck, "you are forgetting that a creature came from inside this craft and attempted to escape across the countryside."

"From this?" Brunnermann spread his hands. "Where?"

"That is why you are here. Why you are all here. You will solve the mysteries of this craft and of its inhabitants, and you will do it as quickly as possible. You have the possibility of saving humanity from much suffering by making it clear that the Thousand-Year Reich has come."

"You really believe this is from outer space?" asked Erstewald.

"Prove it is not, then," said Borck.

"Now that I actually see it—"

"What about the creature?" Rakoczy asked. "Is there any way to question it?"

"If it lives, we shall." Borck explained that they believed it was wounded, and that Orlov had attempted to bandage the area of the wound. "When Orlov returns from Paris with his equipment, the biology of the creature will be intensively researched, even if it does not live. If it does live, we will find a way to make it communicate with us."

"When will Orlov be back?" asked Erstewald.

"Tomorrow late, we expect," said Borck. "He left two days ago, accompanied by my aide."

"Can we see the creature?" asked Brunnermann. "The nature of the creature would determine the form of its apparati."

"You mean by this . . . ?"

Brunnermann's eyebrows bobbed in annoyance. "A comfortable chair fits a human buttocks, Oberführer. This spacecraft, if it *is* a spacecraft, would be built with its inhabitants in mind. Acceleration, for example—how can a living creature be made to withstand the kinds of acceleration involved in entering the Earth's atmosphere? Not to mention the extremes of heat and cold!"

"What you say has validity, Herr Doktor, but you cannot have access to the creature itself. We will provide photographs," said Borck.

The scientists looked irritated. "Doctor Orlov is concerned about infection," Borck explained. "He wants the creature to have a chance to recover without the possibility of further contact with human bacteria. I promised to leave the creature alone until he comes back."

"We are scientists!" protested Erstewald.

"Concentrate your science on the craft!" said Borck. "The creature may die, regardless." His heart pounded at the words. *It must not die,* he thought. *It must not!*

Rhinehart had drifted to the spacecraft and was touching the rounded edge. "The alloy feels warm," he said. "It has a greasy feel, like silver."

"Silver?" hissed Erstewald. "Silver would weigh too much."

"Perhaps it is in the silver family, then. And alloys can be quite different."

Erstewald rubbed it. "It feels greasy because it is coated with something like oil."

"Oil?" Rakoczy spun on Borck. "Have your men oiled this?"

"And why would they do that?" snapped Borck. "It was hard enough to move."

Rakoczy wiped the edge with a handkerchief and squinted at the cotton cloth. "I think there is something. But I can't be sure."

"Do you feel that?" said Erstewald. "It hums."

The scientists all rushed to lay their hands on the craft. They looked like a group of religious fanatics touching the feet of stone saints in a cathedral.

"Like a transformer," said Rakocsy, hurrying off. "I want my Geiger counter."

Brunnerwald took a nail clipper from his pocket and extended the file. He scrapped at the metal with no effect. "Hard," he said, thinking.

"I felt more," said Erstewald, "when you scratched. Do it again."

Brunnermann viciously drew the file back and forth, while keeping one hand on the hull. "Yes! It follows the motion. Like an echo."

"I feel it," said Rhinehart.

"A second or so of a delay," said Brunnermann. He carefully scrutinized where he had scratched. "There is no mark whatsoever. Nothing. It looks like aluminum. It feels somewhat like silver. But it seems harder than steel."

"We must get a diamond drill," said Rhinehart.

"Yet it can be damaged," said Borck.

"I understand it was struck by a shell," said Erstewald. "But where?"

"Near the edge," Borck leaned to one side and then the other. "Around on the front . . ."

The scientists followed him as he circled the rear of the disk then moved down the side to the truck cab. Nothing there. He rounded the front, looked under, and toward the back. "Of course," he said. "It's upside down. The underside is up."

He stood on the running board on the driver's side, then on the other side. Where the hell—? Finally, he climbed onto the hood of the truck and to the roof of the cab and looked down across the entire spacecraft.

Finally, he saw it.

Not the big indentation he had seen when the disk was stuck in the earth.

A tiny dent, no larger than an orange.

22 OCTOBER 1942
SUSSEX, ENGLAND

G eneral Anthony's Packard barreled through the night south from London, as if his driver didn't care that the headlights had been half blocked for the blackouts and the moon had disappeared behind the fog. Colonel Marston, who had rushed at the news to Anthony's quarters at the Diogenes Club, was pale as a winding sheet. He tried not to look through the windshield or to admit to the acid trying to force its way up his gullet.

"How much further?" demanded Anthony.

Marston listened hopefully. "Twenty miles, General," said the driver, sliding the car through a tight turn.

"Don't kill us," said Anthony.

"No, sir," said the driver. "Is that an order?"

Anthony's driver was a Tech Sergeant named Carlson. In 1927, at the ripe age of thirteen, he had been arrested for driving a pair of stick-up artists to several banks in Ohio. He ran away from a juvenile home and was caught faking his age on the racing circuit in 1932. Given the choice of eighteen months on a chain gang or enlisting, he had chosen the Army. His skill with repairing recalcitrant engines and driving like a bat out of hell had eventually come to the attention of the general (then a colonel) in 1939. Anthony had just been assigned to secretly establish a framework for intelligence cooperation between the States and Britain. He needed a driver capable of evading anyone who might try to capture or kill him. His superiors objected to a man with as dubious a background as Carlson. Anthony knew three things, however. Carlson's driving ability, of course, but also that he had never squealed on his partners and never disobeyed an order, ever.

"It's incredible," said Anthony, deep in thought. "The man should never have left."

"He can't go back now," said Marston.

"Damn!" said Anthony.

About 0300, the Packard screeched turning into the driveway of a secure house in the country. A hundred yards up the driveway, Carlson slammed on the brakes and slid on the gravel, bumping the heavy pole across the driveway. A guard stuck his head in the window.

"General Anthony," said Marston.

" 'Churchill's mother,' " Anthony barked.

" 'Jenny,' " said the guard. He gave a short bleat on a whistle and the pole went up. Anthony and Marston were thrown back against the seat, as Carlson slammed the car into gear. He hardly slowed between the trees leading to the colonnaded Neoclassical veranda.

Anthony was out of the car even before it had completely stopped. He shoved past the guard at the door, saying, " 'Churchill's mother'!" and rushed the lieutenant manning the night desk. "Where is he?"

The lieutenant snapped to attention. "In the dining room, sir. Just step through the drawing room—"

Anthony was already shoving open the heavy white doors.

At the far end of the long dining table, guarded by two MPs, sat a tiny man hunched over a plate of stew.

"You two out of here!" barked Anthony. The man slurped the last of the gravy off his oversized silver spoon and looked up.

The door to the kitchen slammed as the MPs scurried out.

"Good morning, General," said the man. "I was going to eat when I got here, but I fell asleep. I'm not as young as I used to be."

"What in God's name are you doing here, Orlov?"

"It's important. More than important."

"You were made?"

"No, but I had to take the chance. The war hangs in the balance."

"All the message said was 'Your package is on the way.' The usual."

"I told them to send it like that. We cannot know who is listening. When the boat landed—"

Anthony gestured impatiently. "You sent the courier. But why, Orlov? Why did you slip away? What is going on in the new Forbidden Zone? Have they got an atomic bomb?"

"No," said Orlov, "worse. They may have a new ally. If not a new ally, a source of unimaginable technological advantage that may give them the atomic bomb, fuel-less flight, death rays. Unimaginable things!"

"Then why did you leave?" said Anthony. "We need someone on the inside! What did you mean 'ally'?"

"Don't fret, General. I am going back. You cannot stop me. My life is nothing compared to what may be learned."

"Get to the point, Dr. Orlov!"

Orlov took a small glass vial from his chest pocket and laid it on the table. "I brought this. I don't know whether it will prove anything to you, but it is proof."

Anthony picked up the vial and raised it to the chandelier. Something clear with tiny sparkling flecks had solidified in the vial. He thought of isinglass.

"Well? What is this substance? Some new version of heavy water?"

"Blood."

"Blood?" Anthony blinked. Had the Germans invented an artificial blood? A blood disease?

"It is the blood of a creature from outer space," said Orlov.

"Is this another riddle?" said the general angrily.

"No," said Orlov. "I removed this blood from the stone floor in the facility in the Forbidden Zone. It had come from the shoulder of a being who crashed to earth just south of Brittany. He is still alive. They have captured his spacecraft."

"Good God!" said Anthony slowly. Then he shook his head. Surely he was going to wake up from this ridiculous dream. "You've been listening to the Mercury Theatre," he said. Orlov looked puzzled. "Orson Welles. *War of the Worlds.*"

Orlov squinted, then ignored what he didn't understand, lighting a cigarette and holding it backward in the Russian manner. "The facility was originally built for their rocketry research, which is progressing quite dangerously for us I was told there. Peenemunde is at the center of it all, but in case something goes wrong there, they intended to build alternative sites."

"We knew it was something like that. Ramjet engines, atomic fission . . ."

"They have a working jet engine," said Orlov, "and Messerschmidt wants to build fighters with it."

"Why didn't you tell us?" Anthony snapped.

"I heard it in the Forbidden Zone two—no, three days ago."

"We'll get on it. They'll never get enough heavy water to build an atomic bomb, and they'll never put a ramjet in the air."

"Don't be so sure. But it will not matter if they can form an alliance with the creatures. Let me tell you about the craft. It had no propellers, no ramjet, no sign of any engine at all. A direct hit by a huge gun only dented it and the pilot escaped."

"He was injured."

"Probably shot by one of the soldiers pursuing him."

"And he is alive?"

Orlov explained. The creature was either in some dormant state or near death. If it lived, it was impossible to know what it might tell the Germans. It may have come to Earth to help the Germans. It was, after all, flying into occupied France.

"But if it comes from space," asked Anthony, "how can it communicate with them?"

"We can assume, if it is capable of transversing space, it may be capable of anything. It may already speak German."

Anthony nodded. What time is it? he suddenly thought, looking at his watch. Too late, maybe much too late.

"And believe me, even if the creature is not willing to talk, Borck will find a way to make him."

"The security man? He has risen through the SS ranks very rapidly."

"He is capable of anything. When I was called from Paris, a nurse at the Forbidden Zone laughed about what he had done to some of the survivors of Dieppe."

"Dieppe!" said Anthony.

"Borck was the most successful interrogator."

Won't Joe Logan want to know this! thought Anthony, but would he tell him? The way Logan was, he might compromise the mission simply to avenge his comrades and get Borck.

With this information he now needed to rethink the mission, anyway. It might now be necessary to send a larger force to insure the destruction of the place.

"Now," said Orlov, "take me to London."

"We can't do that now."

"You must."

"I know what you want," said Anthony, "but . . ."

"But what? Dispatch me out of Southampton."

Anthony leaned forward. "I am not even certain I am going to allow you to go back. You can't just disappear in Paris and then turn up four days later."

"They think I am packing my equipment."

"What if they have discovered otherwise?"

"I shall still go back, General." Orlov drew on his cigarette. "After a brief visit to London."

Anthony shook his head. Too many long nights this week had turned into another dawn. Maybe he was getting too old for this as well. "We need to think this out. We can't afford to mess this up. It may be foolish to put you back in before you fully brief our best minds."

"General, at this point I am like Columbus standing on the beach at Cadiz. I know almost nothing. If you don't put me back in immediately, you can never put me back in. I can't explain a longer disappearance."

"And you really want to go back in, despite the risk?"

Orlov leaned close enough to Anthony that he could smell the fetid tobacco on his breath. "This is a creature from outer space, General. Nothing I have ever done in a lifetime of science can be compared to this."

The general searched Orlov's eyes.

"Oh, yes," said Orlov, "it *is* worth dying for. Yes."

23 OCTOBER 1942
SUPREME HQ,
ALLIED EXPEDITIONARY FORCES
LONDON, ENGLAND

L ogan had arrived in General Anthony's outer office exactly at dawn, as the general had ordered, and then had been told to wait.

Typical. Hurry up and wait. Anthony's all urgent, immediate, right away, then he's out having croissants and tea with the military attaché at the Savoy.

Logan mentally went over his list again. He had already gone over his list a dozen times. He expected Anthony to reject most of it. Logan would have to insist that these were the men he wanted, and then he might be overruled, and then he could refuse the mission, and what difference would that make? Anthony could simply order him to proceed and he would proceed, with whoever they assigned him. He'd just rather survive the damned thing, and a group like these guys gave him at least a thousand-in-one chance, as opposed to no chance at all.

The way he saw it, to stand any chance of getting in and out of Occupied France alive, he needed one helluva tough group—and yet, he hesitated to choose them. Not even the sharpest crew might be able to get into a Forbidden Zone and out again. He might be sentencing some of the finest Allied soldiers to death just by selecting them. There was the intangible quality of unity that bothered him as well. A group of men was not the sum of their individual abilities. If they could not act crisply as a unit, they would never be all that effective. Their talents would not add up and complement each other. The sum would be lesser than the parts, rather than equal to or greater. Normally, there would be a period of training in which a cohesion could be built. In this case, they would barely say "How do you do?" before climbing into the drop plane to take off on a mission with a purpose to be determined only at the last minute.

All of this was a recipe for disaster.

He'd had quite enough of those, thank you.

At the top of his list was Punchy Pawlowski. He was reliable, tough, and never afraid to walk unblinking at an enemy. As long as Primo Carnera hadn't gone Nazi, Punchy would be a source of confidence and brute force. He could also keep the unruly crew Logan wanted in line.

For a similar reason, he chose Sergeant-Major Robert Bruce McGonigle. He would need some very quick training in jumping, but he had been pretty impressive in a bar fight and had a service record to match. A few more Scots like the "Great" McGonigle and America wouldn't even have had to enter the war. He had fought in Malaya and France, and was rumored to be in consideration for the Victoria Cross. He also knew demolition like an elementary school teacher knows the alphabet.

His second demolition man was nicknamed "Tom Swift." His real name was Murray Sweissenborg and he had taught high school chemistry in Chicago. He wasn't just an ordinary demolition man. He had been an instructor for the Army since 1940, and had been brought to England to train commandos. He was able to find a way to make almost any substance, from shit to Shinola, explode. "Latrines," he had once explained to Logan, "were an unlimited supply of boomety-boom."

He also wanted two radiomen with matching equipment. Bruce Doolin was one of the Canadians who had gotten out of Dieppe. Leo

Stern, Army Air Corps, had played football at the University of Chicago and had been working for NBC on the television thing when he enlisted.

The other skill man he wanted was Tech Sergeant Kit Carlson, General Anthony's driver. He might not get him, but he'd push pretty hard.

That made six. The rest of the group would consist of the toughest, meanest, ugliest hand-to-hand fighters he could find: The kind of maniacs who could pound an elite SS warrior into paste, kill their commander with a toothpick, then use it to clean the blood out of their teeth. The only things that kept these guys out of the nut hatch was the Army, the Marines, the French Foreign Legion, and every other organization which had a regular need to do the unspeakable. In a world without war, these guys were useless.

Jonathan Tyler of the Eighty-second Airborne was in the clink for beating up an Aussie who had made fun of his accent. He'd started out as bodyguard to a moonshiner in Georgia.

Madison James III had come from a good family in Connecticut, but lost all that when a gangster who had murdered his father was found so beaten up it was impossible to determine exactly what had killed him. Lyle had served in the French Foreign Legion, who agreed to transfer him to the Rangers for the duration.

Manny Cosgrove had been in a platoon Joe Logan had trained in California. He was the fastest man in a knife fight that Logan had ever seen.

Two Welshmen, both Royal Marines—it took a while for Logan to remember their names—had impressed him assaulting a pillbox at Dieppe. Both were named Griffiths—one Rhys, the other John.

Logan might come up with others, and might have to substitute for some of these, but these guys could go to hell, kick Satan's ass, and make drinking cups out of his horns. Would they volunteer? Most of them had nothing to lose. A few had a sense of duty. Some would volunteer just to have more ass to kick.

They would be a strange, combustible mixture, more explosive than anything "Tom Swift" could cook up, but they might just be what Logan needed to blow the hell out of whatever it was they were supposed to blow the hell out of.

He heard rapid steps on the stairs, and the general marched into his office, his overcoat billowing out. Marston followed him, looking like an insomniac who'd spent all night with a two-dollar hooker.

"About time," said Logan.

He expected Anthony to bark something about saluting and military discipline and all that, but the general merely continued into his office, saying, "Get in here and close the door."

Logan shrugged and went in. When he did, Marston spun on him and shoved him against the wall, pinning him to it with a forearm across his throat.

"Hey!" said Logan, and he would have brought his fist hard into the colonel's side, except for the barrel of the .45 that crossed his eyes.

Anthony turned and moved closer.

"So," said Logan, his eyes flicking between Marston's face and Anthony's, "what'd I do now?"

"Captain," said Anthony, "you are going to hear something today that affects your mission. It is never to be repeated unless I otherwise give you permission. None of the men on the mission is to know, unless I give you permission."

"Yes, sir." Logan squirmed a bit. Marston pressed the gun harder.

"If you repeat a word of what you hear, you will be shot. There will not be charges. There will not be a courtmartial. I will personally take that .45, or one exactly like it, and blow your brains out."

Logan checked their eyes again. The bastards were serious. He cleared his throat. "What's the deal?"

"Personally," repeated Anthony.

"Okay," said Logan. "Why the ballet?"

Anthony nodded, and Marston backed away. "The point needed to be made. You need to know for sure."

Logan glared at Marston; he still wanted to deck him. He then stepped toward Anthony. "When the hell have I ever been a security risk?"

"Never, that I know." Marston handed Anthony the Army Colt. Logan noticed the handmade walnut grips. Christ! It was the general's own gun. Anthony rounded his desk and began calmly removing his overcoat. "Logan," he said, "I like you. I trust you. You'd rather be right than promoted. And you're a one-in-a-million soldier. We ought to have you at home making babies just in case there's another fight with the Krauts in twenty years. But you wouldn't miss this fight for all the girls in Chicago."

"Speak for yourself."

"Even at that, I can't be sure what you're going to think when I tell you what I'm about to. And it must remain an absolute secret."

Logan wasn't sure he wanted to know any more. "So are we done playing footsie, General?"

"I will be checking with higher authority. Ike himself, probably Churchill after that. It's that big." Anthony took a deep breath. "I decided the goal of the mission," he said, "is this: You are to enter the Forbidden Zone. You are to destroy the facility entirely, if possible."

Logan squinted. "Entirely? A squad of men?"

"Entirely. Utterly."

"Why not get Bomber Harris or the Eighth to do it?"

"We don't think the bombs will penetrate. It is an option, but we have to be sure."

Logan looked at Marston, who had slumped into a chair, then back at the general. "Okay," he said. "I give up. What's going on?"

"Captain Logan," said the general, "have you ever read a novel called *The War of the Worlds* . . . ?"

23 OCTOBER 1942
SAVENAY, OCCUPIED FRANCE

C lose the cellar door," said Levrier, and the five men huddled close around the tiny oil lamp. The air was thick with the smell of mildew, and spiders crawled on the beams above them. During normal times, this cellar had been filled with root vegetables, pickles, and cheeses. The Germans had seized most of that when they had searched the village for arms.

"I'm sorry," said a man in mechanic's overalls. "My cousin. I couldn't get away from him."

"You can't trust him?"

The man shrugged.

"So what is this message?" said Levrier to the man they knew only as "Verte."

"There will be an operation in the north. We are asked if we can assist."

"A raid?" said Bleu. "Where?"

"They won't say."

"And they want help?"

"They don't trust us, they can do it themselves," said Bleu.

"They say it is high priority and want to know how many men can assist them."

"Assist at what?" asked Levrier.

"They don't say, but they asked if we could make a truck available that will hold fifteen commandos."

Levrier turned to the mechanic. "Can we?"

"When?"

"Early next week."

"How long will we need it?"

"At night and the next day."

"I can arrange to have one of the German trucks break down." He chuckled. "Amazing how the parts are hard to get."

"Good!" said Levrier. "What else?"

"They will parachute down at night," said Verte, "and if they get scattered we are to get them together. When they arrive, they will tell us their objective."

"The bridge?" speculated Bleu.

"The new tracks," said the mechanic.

"The tracks to the Forbidden Zone?"

"What else?"

"We could take care of the tracks ourselves," said Bleu. "It's something bigger. What about the fuel dump?"

"Maybe they are backing up a raid on the coast."

"Why this coast?" said Verte. "What about the Forbidden Zone itself?"

Levrier shushed them. "We could imagine all sorts of things. We will find out soon enough."

"Doesn't it bother you," said Jaune, whose rain coat rustled when he moved, "that there will be reprisals?"

"We are at war," snapped Levrier. "Some people don't seem to know that. A few deaths might wake them to the struggle."

"I—I didn't mean we shouldn't do it. If there were some way to warn . . ."

"There isn't, is there?"

"No," said Jaune. "I dislike hurting the people we are trying to save."

"It is the Nazis who hurt them, not us. Every death is a martyr to our freedom," said Levrier, "and the ultimate revolution."

There was a momentary silence.

"You are a hard man," said Bleu.

"These are hard times. We *must* win, or be slaves forever."

"Absolutely," said Verte. *"Vive la France!"*

"Vive la France!" muttered the others.

They began to discuss what weapons they could gather. Bleu knew that five MKb-42s had been stolen from the barracks at Cholet. They could get those from the cell there, but they might need more 7.92-millimeter ammunition.

"I can get some by Tuesday," said Jaune.

"How?" said Levrier.

"They won't even know it's missing."

Other than the stolen Wehrmacht rifles, they had assembled a hodgepodge of weapons left over from World War I, from farmers and hunters, from French soldiers who had hidden or stolen their own weapons in the debacle of 1940.

"Very well," said Levrier after an hour's discussion. "Verte will let them know we are ready. The rest of us will prepare, but we must, up until the last moment, let no one know more than he absolutely needs to know. This is our biggest operation so far and we must acquit ourselves well." He placed his hands on his knees to rise. *"Vive la France! Vive la révolution!"*

"Vive la France!" said the others.

Jaune abruptly grabbed Levrier's arm. "A moment, Levrier. What about the boy?"

"Boy?"

"The boy the Germans are hunting."

Levrier tried to read Jaune's face, but the light was too dim. "What do you mean?"

"The Germans have been searching a huge area for the boy. It was said he was looking for you."

"Really?" said Levrier. "I don't know anything about him. Maybe he's a Jew or something."

Bleu broke in. "It can't be that. I heard the SS took his grand-parents into the Forbidden Zone. A plane crashed near his farm."

Levrier shrugged. "Well?"

"Perhaps he's hiding a flyer or he's got something from the plane. Something the Germans want. They know he was looking for you."

"How do they know that?" said Levrier.

"I don't know," said Jaune. "I just wondered if he'd gotten to you."

"No," said Levrier. "I'll keep an eye out for him, though. If they want him that bad, he may have something important."

"Exactly," said Jaune. "I've got to hurry. My wife doesn't trust me." He moved toward the cellar door.

Levrier grabbed his arm. "No. If I don't make my rendezvous, I'll miss my train. Wait fifteen minutes, then draw straws as usual."

It was their normal practice to leave their councils one by one in some randomly determined order.

"Why don't you draw a straw?" said Jaune.

"I explained," said Levrier sharply. "Good night, comrades."

Levrier pushed up the cellar door, looked both directions in the alley, and listened. A dog barked in the distance. After several seconds, he quickly stepped out and hurried to his right. It was past curfew, and although there was little worry about getting caught by the Bosch in that area of town, he paused at the corner before hurrying up the winding street and through a covered walkway. In a few seconds he could see the end of the alley opposite from where he had exited. Maybe seven minutes had passed. The cellar door rose and a shadowy figure that had the general shape of Jaune emerged. He hurried up the alley in the direction Levrier had originally gone, squinted both ways, then rushed off to the left.

Levrier picked his way from shadow to doorway to shadow until he reached the vineyards just below the old town walls. Out here the moonlight seemed much too bright for safety. The charcutier Flanne waited in the brush on the other side. Flanne opened his mouth to greet him, but Levrier raised his hand, turning back to scrutinize the way he had come. A dog in the distance barked. A moth fluttered at Levrier's ear.

"What is it?" asked Flanne, drawing a pistol.

"Have you ever met Jaune?" Levrier asked, never taking his eyes from the vineyard and the town beyond. "What do you know about him?"

"Not much," said Flanne. "We're not supposed to know much, are we?"

"No. But things fall into place."

"Yes?"

"I tell you this in case something goes wrong very soon. Jaune's real name is Vincent DuCharne. He sold automobiles before the war and had a rich wife who was fifteen years older than he."

"So?"

"There was much gossip about that."

"Your point?"

"I don't know. But I do know that Madame Duprise died last spring. The mason who built her tomb was very glad to get the work."

24 OCTOBER 1942
THE FORBIDDEN ZONE

Borck was pacing his office floor when he received another message from Orlov, saying he was nearly finished getting his equipment together. Perhaps a truck could come to Paris late tomorrow afternoon?

"When did this come in?" demanded Borck. "Why is he using a radio?"

"1311, sir. It wasn't radio," said the radio operator. "He telephoned while you were in the chamber."

"I wasn't in the chamber, then. I was here."

"He said there was no answer, so he rung me."

"I was here." He pointed to the secretary's room. "Corporal Scheimer was here. This is ridiculous."

"Yes, sir."

Borck went to the secretary's message box. There were two more messages from Lieutenant Heisen in the mess. An urgent matter of pilferage, they said. *Who made such idiots lieutenants?* Borck thought. *We have within our grasp the conquest of the world, and Heisen is fretting about missing food!*

Corporal Scheimer waited at attention.

"There were no others?" barked Borck.

"No, Oberführer."

"You did not leave your desk at 1300, 1400."

"No, Oberführer."

"Thank you," Borck said to the radioman with a dismissive wave.

Orlov had said three days and it was already five. Borck decided to call Paris and have the truck ready to go. He considered having the facility's doctor re-examine the sleeping creature. He had first looked at him, before Orlov had been hurried from Paris, and surely the doctor wouldn't infect—but no, Orlov was among the world's best. They could afford to wait another day.

Maybe Orlov could make a breakthrough with the creature itself. The other scientists were hopeless. They had struck the hull repeatedly with blades of various types, but had been utterly unable to remove even a shaving. The hull had been dented by some of this hammering, but no sample had ever been separated from it. Soon the diamond drill should be there and they would try again, but Borck had no indication that it would work any better than all of the chisels, hammers, jackhammers, and drill bits that had been ruined already. The scientists would all gather, go at it until they were dripping sweat and red in the face, and then huddle together to try to understand how the drill bits could turn red-hot and fracture, while the ship remained at its normal temperature and showed only the slightest marks. It would take only minutes for the tiny scratches to disappear. Even the largest markings they had made on the hull of the craft smoothed out of existence within a couple of hours. The scientists were now jabbering that the material, while metal, behaved like an incredibly viscous liquid; that, when damaged, slowly flowed back into the gouge. Rhinehart placed a microscope against the hull and found none of the crystalline structures one normally found in metals. They were dealing with something that defied the physical laws of this planet, they said, and scratched their heads like cretins at a magic show.

Borck was tired of pacing and waiting. "Corporal, when the diamond drill arrives, ring me immediately. I will be in Confinement Area C."

The corporal saluted.

The facility had been designed with three confinement areas. Area A was outside and was nothing more than a small concentration camp for about 150 slave workers, who were to build the new rocket bombs. Area B was in the back of the second cavern, a stockade for about a dozen soldiers. Area C, however, was deep in the earth, an ultra-secure area, containing interrogation rooms for select prisoners, whose screams would never reach the sunlight.

Borck carried his own set of keys for Area C and startled a sleepy guard when he opened the first steel door. He snapped to attention. "*Heil Hitler!*" The sound echoed off the stone ceiling.

"*Heil Hitler!*" said Borck. "At ease." He looked through the wall of bars at the steel door beyond. "Has there been any movement, any sound?"

"No, sir, Oberführer."

"Nothing?" Borck noticed something in the guard's eyes.

"No."

"Out with it."

He shifted. "Well, I thought I saw some light coming from the slit." He pointed at the small trap in the door through which they would normally shove food.

"There's a light bulb in there. Perhaps it was moving."

The guard shook his head. "It was a glow, not like the bulb."

"Some kind of dream?"

The guard hesitated to admit that the endless silent waiting down here might have caused him to doze off. "I was thinking of efflorescence, perhaps. My brother-in-law was a miner; he said sometimes the walls in deep mines give off—"

"You noticed nothing else?"

"I've had the strangest feelings . . ."

"Explain," snapped Borck.

"I felt like someone was behind me, like a draft blew up my neck, or someone touched my hair."

Borck knew exactly what he meant. He had felt it when he had the creature in his gunsight. His heart pounded at the recollection.

"You've—you've been down here too long. Perhaps the ventilation changed."

"Yes, sir," said the guard.

Borck put his Luger on the guard's desk. He unlocked the barred door, locked it behind him, and walked to the door of the inner cell. He slid back the peephole and looked in. The dull yellow from the dangling ceiling light permeated the cell. An examining table sat by the usual cot. On the table rested the creature. Its glassy eyes pulsed with a faint greenish light, as if auroras were swirling within them. It was fascinating, hypnotic. Dead? It didn't seem to have moved. The arm lay limp at its side. The shifting light made its fluid tunic seem to be in motion, but that just made the limbs seem more still.

Borck froze. The mouth had moved. That lipless, tiny mouth had shifted slightly. He was sure of it! With trembling hands, he fumbled the key at the lock hole.

It was alive! He knew it was alive!

But before he could get the key into the lock, there was shriek—a high-pitched noise coming at him from all sides. He dropped the keys. As the noise faded, it took him a second to recognize that all he had really heard was the ringing of the guard's telephone. It rang again.

"Area C," said the guard.

Borck picked up his keys, hands shaking.

"Yes, sir," said the guard, hanging up. "Sir, I have been ordered to tell you the drill has arrived."

"Thank you," Borck said. He took another look through the peephole. The lips were utterly still, but the tunic had shifted colors to a pinkish maroon. What the hell was that thing?

Again he had the sensation of having his scalp caressed.

"Did you feel that?" he shouted to the guard.

"Sir?"

"The breeze! The ventilator! What you felt before!"

The guard looked bewildered. "No, Oberführer, nothing."

The creature was alive, Borck knew. It was alive! And somehow, he thought, it knows that I know it.

Almost drunk on his realization, he rushed to the spiral staircase, taking it two steps at a time.

When he reached the chamber, the scientists were all standing back from the ship, drifting around it. Most of them wore expressions of great surprise, but Erstewald, eyebrows bobbing, was talking excitedly with Rhinehart. The soldiers were as far back as they could get from it and had raised their rifles.

"What happened?" asked Borck. Rakoczy took one look at him and rushed out of the door.

Borck grabbed a quivering soldier. "What happened?" The soldier tried to speak. Borck slapped him. "Talk!"

"It hummed. It . . . There was light coming—dancing all over it."

Erstewald hurried to Borck. "It was fascinating. Only a few seconds ago, a bar of light swept over its surface. Something like the northern lights."

"It was yellowish," said Rhinehart. "A cloud like chlorine gas."

"Then, poof!" said Erstewald. "It became invisible."

"You're mad!" said Borck.

"No!" said Rhinehart.

"It only lasted a moment," said Erstewald. "A pulsation."

Borck could see from their mixed wonder and fear that what they had said was true.

"Poof!" said Erstewald with a childish delight.

Borck walked straight at the craft as everyone else gaped. "It is on. Maybe it has always been on. We can fly it if we get inside. Can you imagine what we can do with a bomber that can repair its own damage? An invisible bomber? We must open it. The creature came out, we can get in!"

Borck waved his hand frantically. Rhinehart scurried up beside him. He grabbed him by the collar. "Your drill is here?"

"Yes, Oberführer."

"Get it."

"But, Oberführer . . ."

"Get it and open the hull. You said it would cut anything, that a diamond is the hardest substance on Earth."

"On Earth, yes, but—"

"Open it!" He flicked Rhinehart back. The scientist stumbled, then began prying the slats off a large crate just inside the delivery door. "Help him!" ordered Borck. "Now!"

Soldiers rushed to obey the order.

Erstewald walked up to Borck, never taking his eyes off the craft. "We were discussing how to place the drill. Usually, the material being drilled can be secured, clamped down. How we can do it to the craft, we were debating."

"How long is this going to take?"

"Exactly, Oberführer," said Erstewald. He turned back to the craft. "In case you are interested, Oberführer, there is no danger of radiation. It is higher than normal, but no more than a watch with glowing hands. I believe that it is a liquid, incredibly enough, a liquid that holds its shape. Possibly on the molecular level it might be possible—"

"Herr Doktor, all I am interested in is getting inside—and I am losing my patience."

Erstewald tilted his head to one side, as if trying to ignore an irate beggar.

Brunnermann suddenly appeared, rolling a heavy steel cart normally used to move artillery shells. Rhinehart assembled the drill as rapidly as an infantryman forced to clean his rifle under a barrage. The frame was a large "C" with the electric motor at the top. It might have been an ordinary drill press except for the size of the motor—nearly as thick as the waist of an Olympic swimmer. The bit, as thick as a man's thumb, did not have the usual spirals, but had a savage-looking end: a sea urchin of industrial diamonds.

"This will cut anything," said Rhinehart. "It is my own design."

Brunnermann enthusiastically said, "I have seen it cut—"

"Just cut into the ship!" said Borck.

They rolled the assembly to the edge of the hull, sliding the end into the mouth of the "C." They then chained the cart to the axle of the truck and began unrolling a power cable as thick as a napkin ring.

"We will be using almost all available power from the generator," said Brunnermann. "I checked its capability. Nonetheless, the lights throughout the area will be dimmed."

"Get it open!" shouted Borck.

Rhinehart climbed on a stool and rested his hand on the pressure lever. The bit dropped to the ship's surface, and Rhinehart nodded. Both Erstewald and Brunnermann waved, and a soldier threw the heavy copper switch.

The drill roared into action, its sound rising higher and higher as its torque increased.

"Cut it!" said Borck to himself. "Cut it!"

Rhinehart pressed the lever down, and the bit whirred against the hull. There seemed to be no particles being cut loose, but Rhinehart seemed unperturbed. The bit smoked slightly and Rhinehart nodded toward Brunnermann, who squirted a white cooling mixture on the shaft.

The bit spun. Seconds passed. Then minutes. The white liquid puddled on the floor.

"Harder!" shouted Borck.

"Too hard will burn the motor," Erstewald shouted back. "It takes time!"

Cut, damn it! Borck thought, pacing. *Cut!*

The acrid smoke from the turning bit stung Rhinehart's eyes and tears poured from them. He did not let up. Borck paced like a leopard in a cage. Unable to control himself any longer, he stepped over the cable and stood in front of the drill where Rhinehart could see him.

"HARDER! Harder!"

Rhinehart shook his head and Borck pulled his pistol.

"He will burn it out!" shouted Erstewald.

Borck stepped in the growing puddle of liquid beside Brunnermann. He stared down at where the bit met the hull. *Cut! Cut!*

He thought he saw the hull give way slightly. He placed his hand on the ship, white liquid flicking against his glove. *Yes,* he thought. *Cut! Cut! Cut!*

His eyes bulged at the intensity of his thinking. Rhinehart seemed to feel a slight penetration, and also stared intensely.

All at once, the bit dropped two or three centimeters into the hull. A flutter of yellow appeared, hovering over the surface of the ship, then there was a hum sliding into a shriek.

"*Cut!*" shouted Borck. "*Cut!*"

Smoke poured from the deepening hole and then from the electric motor. Rhinehart broke the lock of his stare and let up slightly, but the bit suddenly seized in the hole, shearing off just above the hull's surface, flinging the drilling liquid in Borck's eyes.

Borck wiped the hot liquid away. "You idiot! I told you not to let up!"

"The motor was burning. We can't—"

Borck fired. Rhinehart's eyes crossed, as if looking at the bloody flower that had suddenly blossomed between his eyes. He toppled backward on the ship.

The body slowly slid off, leaving a swath of blood from the open back of his skull. It flopped down, shattering the stool.

"Are you mad?!" screamed Brunnermann. He cupped his hand over the ear which had been nearest the Ruger.

"Yes!" said Borck. "I am a madman and I want only one thing: to get inside this craft! If you fail me, you die. Is that clear?"

"Professor Rhinehart had one of the greatest minds in the Reich," said Erstewald in a near whisper.

"Well, there it is," said Borck pointing at the gore on the hull. "And what good did it do him."

The scientists looked at each other. Erstewald slumped against the cart.

Borck looked closely at the shattered bit. It was embedded in the hull as firmly as if it were part of it. It burned his fingers through his glove when he tried to wiggle it, and it did not budge. Either the bit had expanded from the heat, or the ship, trying to close the hole, had closed in around it.

A low hum suddenly swept over the ship, and Borck backed away.

"You see," he said, "it can be penetrated. Now find me a way to get inside!"

Rakoczy, however, who had been watching the entire procedure, walked away from the chamber wall, his eyes wide, pointing toward the hull.

The streak of blood and brain from Rhinehart was disappearing, like a spot of water on a hot skillet. The ship seemed to be absorbing it. In five seconds, the hull was entirely clean of flesh and blood.

25 OCTOBER 1942
EAST END OF LONDON, ENGLAND

When the cab he was in passed the Sated Swine pub late that afternoon, Logan recognized he was in the area of Musgrave Square. On impulse, he leaned forward and told the driver to turn at the next street.

"I'm going to say hello to a friend. It won't take fifteen minutes," he said.

He stepped out onto the curb and looked up. The window to Nicole DuPrix's room was open. The curtains had billowed out. He listened and heard only the thup, thup, thup of a woman beating a small carpet from the ground floor window further down. He almost got back in the car. He had no business dropping in like this. It wasn't like she was his maiden aunt. The driver turned his head, however, and Logan went inside.

He climbed the narrow stairs, listened outside her door for a moment, then gently knocked. Her voice came through the door as if she were speaking through her hands. "*Allo?* Who is there?"

"Captain Logan." He cleared his throat. "Joe Logan."

The lock rattled. Nicole opened the door just a crack and looked out. "Enh! And where have you been?"

"Military stuff—you know."

"You shouldn't come by uninvited, you know. Maybe you found me some stockings?"

"I'll go," said Logan.

She reached out and caught the starchy sleeve of his shirt. "No. I have some scotch." She was wearing only a chemise. When she turned back to speak into the room, he saw the bony vertebrae of her upper back. "Do be a darling," she said to someone. "He is my cousin from America."

"Certainly," said a very upper-crust voice. The gray-haired man lowered his head and muttered, "How d'ja do?" as he tipped his bowler and quickly slipped down the stairs.

"He is the undersecretary of something," she confided.

"And what does he get under?" asked Logan.

"*He* brought me stockings."

"I see."

She poured him a drink. "It is the price he pays for being a bore. All he does is talk. He misses his mummy."

"Maybe I should have brought something."

"You are not a bore," she said, holding up the glass.

He belted back half of it.

"Thirsty?" she asked.

"No, I'm in a hurry. I might not be back for a while."

"Oh?"

Maybe not ever, he thought.

"And so you want a little 'slap-and-tickle' before you go?"

What *did* he want? The past forty-eight hours had been like some kind of opium dream. Maybe he just wanted to find out that he had had an existence before General Anthony had told him about the World War becoming a Space War. "Don't have time," he said. "I just wanted to say 'bye."

She moved up close to him. He hadn't thought they had parted on such good terms. "It won't take long," she said.

"I like to take my time."

"Enh! That's good. I am flattered." She drifted to the window, then sat on her bed, resting her chin on her knee and holding her leg around the shin.

"So, where are you going?"

Six feet under, he thought. *A stalag.* "Someplace cold," he lied. "They issued winter whites." He paused. "I shouldn't have said that."

"Of course not."

He finished the drink. "I'll bring you some stockings next time. I promise."

"Very good. Do I get a kiss?"

He reached under her arms and picked her up off the bed. She made a small peep like a captured bird before he smothered her mouth with his. Still holding her off the floor, he pulled back and looked her in the eyes.

"Ummm," she said. "Take me with you to Norway. I'll keep you warm."

"Who said anything about Norway?" He sat her down on the bed. She reached out like she wanted to unbutton his fly, but he backed away. "No," he said, "but hold the thought."

Nicole sneered. "Go, then. Freeze it off!"

"'Bye." Logan snatched his hat off the chair and left while he was still capable of leaving.

Nicole heard his boots moving so quickly down the stairs they sounded as if they were tumbling end-over-end. She saw that he looked up at her window as he climbed into the taxi. She waited several seconds, then slipped on her robe. No one was in the corridor. She stepped down to the next flat and tapped. A man smoking a cigarette let her in.

"So, Norway," he said.

"He was lying," she said. "Americans like him, it's obvious."

"Americans like him," said the man, "might well be on their way to Norway." He gestured with the cigarette at a radio set. "Well?"

"Will it get him hurt?"

"Many people will be hurt before this is over," said the man. "Just radio it in as you are supposed to, as well as whatever you got from the undersecretary."

"Mummy, Mummy, Mummy," she sighed, picking up the earphones.

The driver pointed to the address, and Logan climbed the stairs to flat 2-B. He was still thinking about Nicole. Why did she need stockings? By any reasonable estimate, by now she should have had enough stockings to fill a Lancaster bomber. Maybe she traded them for other things. He thought of how little she weighed and the lines of weariness around her eyes. She might be dead before he was. You never knew.

He rapped on the door. He heard someone moving inside, but nothing was said.

He rapped again. "General Anthony sent me."

A stocky man opened the door. He had a revolver aimed at Logan's midsection. "What do you want?"

"You're Dr. Orlov, aren't you? The general called."

He lowered the gun. "Yes. Of course. It's just I cannot be too careful." The man's accent was quite thick.

Logan saw a brass samovar on a side table next to a photograph and candle of the Czar Nicholas. "Your mother lives here?"

"Yes, I must visit her when I can. There may be no other chance."

"I understand. Where is she?"

"She is asleep. We had vodka after dinner. Too much."

"Well, I'm sorry. We have to go."

"Yes." He slid his pistol into his pocket. "I will tell her good-bye."

Logan paced. He picked up a photograph of a man in a lab coat, and heard Orlov speaking in Russian.

Orlov paused in the doorway to say "*Dosvidanya*" tenderly. He had tears in his eyes, wiped them, and noticed Logan holding the framed photograph. "My half-brother," said Orlov. "The Bolsheviks killed him."

"Sorry," said Logan, putting it back.

"Everyone has his time," said Orlov.

"Let's hope it isn't on this mission."

Orlov put on his overcoat. "Will General Anthony be seeing us off?"

"No," said Logan. "We're each arriving separately at the airfield in case anyone got wind there might be a mission. There'll be a briefing and total seclusion after that."

"The world," said Orlov, "consists of millions of spies and my mother, who is the only honest person."

"You may be right," said Logan. "By the way, I'd leave that gun in your pocket behind if I were you."

"I feel more comfortable with it. It is true the Nazis want me, but the Bolsheviks want me, too."

"They're our allies at the moment, haven't you heard? We've got plenty of weaponry at the airfield. There's a lot more bang in it than in that popgun."

Orlov took the .38 from his pocket and put it on the table. "I suppose she will need it more than I."

"We won't be long at the airfield. Have you ever parachuted?"

"I can't say I've had the pleasure."

"You aren't the only one. We'll give you both a quick course."

"I'm sure," said Orlov, "it is invigorating."

Logan watched as Orlov checked the hallway, then, seeing it empty, hurried down the stairs.

The squad's complete, thought Logan. *All we needed was a paranoid mad scientist. Thank you, General, sir.* He felt a little guilty about that. After all, Orlov seemed very game for a mad scientist.

Very game.

27 OCTOBER 1942
NANTES, OCCUPIED FRANCE

Marcel once again slightly shifted the roof tile so that he could look out through the slit toward the tiny church two roofs over. He spent his days watching the pigeons come and go into the belfry, and also used the thin beam of light that crept in to read the books hidden under the eaves, but he found them of little interest. Karl Marx had earned a water stain up there, which had curled the pages and stuck some of them together. To pass the time, Marcel would spread out the book and try to let the beam dry any moisture which might still be left, but reading it was of no interest whatever.

He was closed in behind a false wall in the attic, in a space a little wider than he was tall. The French Nazis, who knew that the husband of the widow downstairs had been active in the party in the 1930s, searched her house just the month before Marcel was concealed there. From the routine way she had settled him in, he had the feeling she had done this many times. Levrier, before handing Marcel over to a mysterious man he called "Bleu," had told him that he was going to the safest safe house in France, but that he must never allow himself to be seen by the bicycle shop owner on that corner. That man would sell his own mother for a sou. Marcel had seen him chatting up the police and the local Nazi leader, though from a distance he looked as if he might have been simply trying to sell a bicycle.

Marcel spent a lot of time in the attic praying. He remembered that St. Joan had known she was appointed by God, but had the same problem he did. "I know what I am supposed to do," Joan had said, "but sometimes I don't know how." At least St. Joan had gone to a king who believed in God. What would the Communists make of God's messenger—if he was, indeed, God's messenger. The angel had been very strange-looking for an angel, Marcel sometimes thought in his loneliness. Could he have been instead a devil leading Marcel to ruin? But then he remembered the miracles, and kissed the glassy cast on his arm.

Levrier had said that he must be patient, but he was growing so anxious to do something, anything, that he thought about flinging the roof tile down on the bicycle shop owner as he passed.

That night, the widow brought him a lukewarm tin of milk and a hunk of very coarse bread, and, as usual, had nearly nothing to say and no answers for his questions other than, "Hush! Be glad you're alive."

After she had gone, he lay back to sleep on his side, and reached to bunch his coat under his head, banging the cast hard on a roof beam. The noise reverberated as if it were louder than the church bells, and Marcel listened as pigeons under the eaves cooed and fluttered at the noise.

He put his hand on the cast and began to pull. It would not slide at all. His arm felt fine. He wanted the thing off. Was he doomed to wear this thing forever? Nothing scratched it, nothing cracked it. What if it stayed on until his arm shriveled away? In horror, he remembered how Clemence had shrunken to a weak and helpless shell of herself. He pulled harder, felt for his bread and tried to push butter into the opening at his wrist. He was getting frantic and swung it hard toward the roof beam again.

The pigeons under the eaves fluttered and cooed.

Closing his eyes tight, he pulled against the cast with all his strength. *Come off! Please, come off!* He was squeezing his eyes so tightly that he saw light against the back of his eyelids.

His hand slipped off and he fell back on the floor.

But there was still light, and he knew it wasn't from the pressure against his eyes. He slowly opened them.

The cast had begun to glow. Curls of greenish and pink light swirled and pirouetted in the glass.

Marcel lifted it in front of him. His arm was as bright as a lantern, filling the entire attic space with light.

There was a sound then, a tiny cracking sound, something like that made in the first moment when the thin ice of a pond begins to fragment beneath your weight but doesn't quite give way.

Marcel watched a fracture line appear at the middle of his wrist; it began climbing down in a wavy line toward his elbow. As it snaked down, it sprouted other fracture lines, branching like incredibly fast grapevines into twos and fours and eights, until the entire cast was crazed with sparkling lines.

He saw it crumble just before the light disappeared.

"Boy!" said the widow, climbing the attic ladder in her nightgown. "Hush! What are you doing?"

She waddled to the false wall and clawed at the bent nail that would allow her to pull it forward. Her paraffin lantern danced weird shadows under the roof tiles, and Marcel momentarily covered his eyes from its brightness.

"Boy!" she whispered. "What are you doing? What is all that banging?"

There was something, however, about his face that gave her pause for a moment. He seemed to be in a kind of shock.

"You had a bad dream? What? What if someone had been downstairs? What if it had been heard?"

Marcel looked on the floor. The cast had fractured and re-fractured and, judging from the flickering glow in what was now fragments no larger than grains of sand, it was continuing to fracture microscopically.

"It fell off," he said.

He held up his forearm and saw that it was totally healed. The place where the bone had cracked was smooth and unblemished. The muscles flexed strongly as he clenched his fist. He turned his arm in wonderment. There had been a scar on the back of his forearm. He had gotten it after falling on a rake when he was five; his father had stitched it up with thick string. The scar had disappeared.

The old woman was still looking around for whatever had fallen off. "Aah!" she finally said. "You be quiet or I'll throw you out. I'm not going to die for you, eh?"

She hesitated, as if trying to remember something, then turned to go.

Marcel reached out and touched the material on the floor. It was now no more than a soft powder.

He crossed himself, then saw a fading glow on each shoulder and over his heart.

27 OCTOBER 1942
NEAR PLYMOUTH, ENGLAND

he men were as sullen as storm clouds riding low on the North Atlantic.

That was okay. They had more than enough experience as soldiers to know what it meant to be secluded on the base in Cornwall. And if that wasn't enough, looking at who you were being isolated with ought to tell you plenty. Their lives during the war had given them a lot to be sullen about, and Logan was sure that if they survived, he was about to stuff their brains with more painful memories. The men stood more or less at attention, watching Logan march slowly back and forth before them, hands clasped together behind his back. Orlov, head back, stood at the end beside Punchy, doing a fair imitation of a soldier.

"You didn't bring us here just to watch you march, didja?" Jonathan Tyler asked. He was chewing tobacco. "Ya march real good, Cap'n, but I ain't much for that kind of thing." He spat. The others laughed with impatient amusement. That was exactly what Logan had been waiting for, the first spark on the tinder of insubordination. Normally, several weeks training allowed you to build respect; this time, he only had until tomorrow.

He walked slowly back to Tyler, seemingly unperturbed by the outburst. Logan stopped, stood bare inches away from the hillbilly's face, noses almost touching. Tyler continued to chew, a smirk on his face, and returned the stare.

"Private, who's your commanding officer here?" Logan asked.

Tyler's sniffed like he smelled something rotten. "I guess that'd be you, if'n I remember what the oak leaves are supposed to mean. That *is* what they mean, isn't it?"

Next to him, James, tall and angly, looked down his hawk nose and said in a mock whisper, "Indeed, hayseed. You are correct."

Tyler's eyes shifted slightly at the word "hayseed," but he continued to stare down at Logan. "I reckon they promote just about anybody 'cause of the war and all."

"Tom Swift" let loose with a short giggle. McGonigle scowled. The two Welshmen raised eyebrows at each other. Carlson and Stern suppressed a laugh. Orlov held his stiff position and did not even look in their direction. Punchy, however, assumed a Mona Lisa smile and waited.

Well, thought Logan, *let those who find it amusing, find it amusing. It will be the last laugh at my expense.*

"And look what they did, Private. They put me in command of you," Logan said. "Of all of you." A contrary thought seemed to suddenly occur to him, and he asked, "You play cards?"

The change momentarily left Tyler confused, spinning mental wheels. "My momma told me that was sinning, so I done it every chance I could."

"Then you probably already know a good, solid hand beats a joker every time, right?"

"Huh?"

The wheels continued to turn, and just as he seemed to read something in Logan's eyes, Logan gut-punched him.

Tyler doubled over like he'd been thrown over a clothesline. The tobacco juice in his mouth gagged him and he rolled on the ground, hacking and drooling, trying to draw air back into his laboring lungs, but not accomplishing much more than a few, small, wracking, wheezing sounds.

"Sir!" said McGonigle, holding himself as straight as if the king were passing.

"Yes, Sergeant-Major?"

"I shall be forced to report that you struck an enlisted man, sir."

"Who was struck?" asked Logan.

Tyler crawled to his knees and looked up in pure hate.

"I didn't see it," said Pawlowski. "I must have been looking the wrong way."

"Not me," said Carlson.

"Me, neither," said Cosgrove.

"I was thinking," said Orlov, shrugging.

James cast a bemused eye on Tyler.

"How about you, Griffiths?"

John Griffiths glanced at Rhys Griffiths. "You," said Logan, pointing at Rhys.

"See what, sir?"

"Sir," said the sergeant-major.

"Yes, McGonigle?"

"I believe I was mistaken, sir." The faintest hint of a smile played over McGonigle's lips.

"Oh?" said Logan.

"I believe the private choked on his cud, sir."

Tom Swift giggled again.

Tyler had finally gotten to his feet. Tobacco stained his shirt and trousers.

"Private," said Logan, "there are reasons for the rules. This kind of accident can occur easily if you disregard them. Keep your chaw for after hours."

Tyler was pale, still holding his stomach.

"Did I hear a 'yes, sir'?"

"Yes, sir," gasped Tyler.

Logan made sure the men were familiar with the weapons they would be taking with them. If any one of them should be taken out of commission, another had to be ready to pick up his weapon and use it. Most regular military weaponry was designed to be loud and powerful—an enemy with his face in the dirt and his ears covered wasn't likely to advance on you. But this mission was different. The ideal would be that no one would know they were there until they had achieved their objective. They needed to travel light, avoid direct conflict, and, when forced into it, to fight with as little noise as possible. A troop of knife-throwers would have been perfect, but the circuses were out of town for the duration, and, hell, the Germans *did* have guns, after all.

He decided that the Brits would carry Sten .9mm carbines, and one Bren machine gun. They were more comfortable with them than the U.S.-made M3 .45 caliber—the "grease gun." The Resistance was also more likely to have the ammo. Logan gave several of the Americans a quick course in the Italian Beretta .9mm submachine gun, also on the theory that the ammo would be easier to get in Occupied France. He thought about taking a few of the captured Schmeisser submachine guns, but they would have had to have been shipped up from Bristol. Each man would carry a knife, two grenades, and a Colt .45 sidearm.

They would be throwing a lot of fire, if necessary, as long as their ammunition held out—which wouldn't be long if they got into a serious situation.

Orlov worried him. What did a scientist know about playing commando? He proved to be as lousy as Logan expected on the firing range. The Colt jumped up like Jack-in-a-box when Orlov pulled the trigger, though he did manage to keep from braining himself when it recoiled. Although the man seemed physically well-built, it was hard for Logan to imagine him in hand-to-hand combat. He'd require babysitting, and that always increased the danger.

While the men were eating a steak dinner—the "condemned man's meal," as James called it—Logan put in a call to General Anthony. He didn't beat around the bush.

"Is it still a go?"

"Affirmative," said the general. "The information has not significantly changed."

"I am worried that the package from Minsk might not have the wheels for this."

"It is the only vehicle that has a built-in map," said Anthony. "Going up those roads without the maps might mean missing important sites."

"I understand that, but it might slow down the other vehicles."

"Will it drop?"

"It doesn't seem to be bothered by the prospect as much as some."

"Let the eager beaver go, then," said the general. "The beaver has eyes to recognize what it has seen."

"I know," said Logan. "I know."

"Better with him, than not. It's too important."

"All right. Maybe he'll break an ankle later and save us the trouble."

"He knows his way around," said Anthony. "One other thing."

"What?"

"I started to say 'break a leg,' like they do in the theater. Instead I'll just wish you godspeed."

Logan nodded his thanks and rang off without answering.

"Who's going to show the virgins how to do it?"

Logan held out the ring that attached to the lift harness. Above the ring was a short chain attached to another ring around a steel cable, which stretched far down from the top of the 200-foot jump tower to its anchor in the ground. To go off the platform wasn't like jumping from an airplane exactly, but it was good enough for training purposes. Orlov and McGonigle stood to the side, exchanging nervous glances.

"Geronimo," said James in a patrician manner. He had jumped several times for the Foreign Legion.

"Head first, don't worry about the shock of the canopy opening."

"Doesn't it fail to open on occasion, sir?" asked McGonigle.

"The cord pulls it right out," said Logan.

"And if it doesn't open," said James, "there's just enough time to pray for mercy. That is, if your list of sins isn't too long. Oh, dear, I hadn't thought of that before. There wouldn't be nearly enough time for me."

"Shut up and jump," said Logan. They watched James plummet, then snap straight and slide down the long cable, tumbling to a stop in the sawdust pit at the end.

"You see?" said Logan. "Roll, like he did. Don't try to land standing up. Just roll. Like we practiced before we came up."

Orlov intently watched Tom Swift shout *"Geronimo!"* and dive off. McGonigle held his body straight as he usually did, but seemed to be trying to avoid really watching.

Punchy went off and swung particularly wide from a sudden gust of wind. He landed like a sack of potatoes.

"He didn't roll right," said Logan.

"He tangled his feet," said Orlov.

"The thing to do is just let the 'chute pull you over. Don't try to stop it."

McGonigle looked a little pale.

"Somethin' wrong, Sergeant-Major?"

"No, sir. But I believe I can see Afghanistan from here."

Logan smiled. "It's even higher in a plane, but we won't see the ground. It'll be dark."

He clipped on Cosgrove, who was shivering. "I hate this," said Cosgrove.

"You've done it before," said Logan.

"That's why I hate it."

Cosgrove jumped.

"Head first!" Logan said, "or you can be hit by the wing." Tyler was next, then the two Griffiths. Doolin, Carlson, and Stern waited on the tiny stairs, but Logan put his hand on Doolin's chest.

"Are you ready to try it?" he asked.

Orlov shrugged. McGonigle swallowed.

"You do it great and that'll be the end of it. Screw it up and you'll be climbing up again."

"I would be willing," said Orlov. "Head down, hang patiently, roll."

"In a nutshell," said Logan. "But I think the sergeant-major wants off this tower."

"Indeed I do, sir, and I suppose I will be taking the quick way down?"

" 'Fraid so."

"In for a penny, in for a pound, sir."

Logan didn't know how the "Great" McGonigle was holding himself together. He seemed to have to concentrate merely to take the two steps to the edge. Logan clicked the ring onto his harness and McGonigle stepped to the edge, closed his eyes for a moment, and shouted *"Scotland the Brave!"* as he dove. He, too, swung wildly, and landed awkwardly on his side. Logan squinted down the long cable and saw McGonigle's eyes pop open. He had done the jump with his eyes closed.

This was a man who would obey any order, thought Logan. *You're a better man than I am, Sergeant-Major.*

"I believe I am ready," said Orlov.

"Concentrate," said Logan.

"Mind over matter," said the scientist. He bent over a bit awkwardly, then jumped without shouting anything. The wind gusted again, but Orlov held tight to his parachute straps and swung into the sawdust smoothly. He flopped and rolled and lay on the ground for a moment.

"He's hurt," said Doolin.

But Orlov jumped up and unsnapped his ring, rubbing his hands together in glee. He took a bow for the others already on the ground.

"Beginner's luck," said Stern.

Maybe the son-of-a-bitch will be okay, Logan thought. *That'd be a miracle. We need more than one miracle.* He looked back over his shoulder. "Next!"

The men practiced for a while on the obstacle course, then took another turn on the firing range. Logan didn't want to make them sore, if any of them were even a bit out of shape. He knew he was still trying to win their respect, so he also took part in the training exercises. No one beat his time but Tyler; he chalked that up to the five years of youthfulness the hillbilly had on him. James and Rhys Griffiths gave him a run for his money. In marksmanship, it was almost dead-even among him, McGonigle, and John Griffiths. The others were more used to rifles than submachine guns. The Brits were best with the Sten, though Logan was far better with the pistol. The main point to all this was going some distance in earning their respect. To show that you had a competent fighter as commanding officer would count for something, he guessed. Only Madison James seemed unchanged, but he was probably unimpressed by habit, and Tyler seemed not to resent being sucker-punched and was playing the good soldier.

It was getting dark, and the men had had a full day, although it was not really as long as the nights and days would be that lay ahead of them.

After mess, a hot shower and shave, Logan entered the bunkhouse where his new platoon was bivouacked. The men started to fall in from their bunks and seats at the card table, where they played penny ante poker, but he told them to be at ease.

"You did good today," Logan said, and was surprised to realize he meant it. "You're about as good as we can be on short notice.

"Even you, Dr. Orlov," he added, drawing a laugh from everyone.

"I approach everything scientifically," he said. Laughter erupted again.

"We go at dusk tomorrow. If anyone wants to get right with God, I'll see you have time with the camp chaplain before we head out," Logan said, chewing on the end of an unlit cigar.

"God gave up on me a long time ago," said Carlson.

"Captain—" Punchy began. He didn't like where this was headed.

"No, he's right," McGonigle interrupted. Everyone turned to look at him. "If we've only a wee chance to make it, I'd rather the captain looked us in the eye and told us so."

"Perhaps we should ask ourselves, 'Is this trip really necessary?'" Carlson joked, quoting a popular stateside expression about the rationing of gasoline to aid the war effort.

"It's necessary," Logan said, striking a match. He held the flame to the end of his cigar and took several deep draws, puffing it to life. "It could be the most important mission in the war."

"Undoubtedly," said James.

"For real," said Logan quietly. He let that sink in. "This isn't just brass talking. I know you've heard that before, but this is one situation—how can I put it?—well, we can't win the war on this mission, but we can absolutely prevent us losing it. The fact that Dr. Orlov is with us should be a clue that this isn't just any sabotage mission."

"Yes," said Orlov.

"I cannot explain it until we're on our way, but you'll know then, for sure."

He scanned his men. They were a hard bunch. Most of them wouldn't be missed when they were gone, the others would only be missed by fellow soldiers. Orlov had a mother, at least; the others had been cut off from normal humanity for a long time. In that sense they were all loners and losers.

Logan's Losers, he thought sourly.

"I'm going to do this, though," he said. "I know what it means that you 'volunteered.' Anyone who wants out can get out. Just say so now."

"What happens if I do?" said Tyler.

"You get a few days of solitary confinement until the mission is done. That's just to keep you silent. I'll say you weren't what I needed, even though I think you're exactly what I need."

"Who says I want out? I was just asking." Tyler raised his long legs and stretched out. "I hear the Frenchie broads are real generous to Americans. I aim to get my share."

"Anybody else?" asked Logan.

"I've always gone for the inside straight," said Stern.

"Good, then," said Logan. "We'll start getting our equipment ready at 1400 tomorrow. Meantime, I have a little something to keep you occupied this evening." The men groaned.

"What about the poker?" said Stern. "I was winning!"

"Cover the windows," said Logan. "Full security." He signaled to Punchy to help carry in an ammo crate.

When he flipped open the latch and tossed back the lid, several bottle necks stuck out of the excelsior.

"Cap'n," said Punchy, "are you outta your mind? On the base?"

"Sir," said McGonigle, "I would regret to have to report this infraction of your American rules. But, then, perhaps I am not familiar as I thought with your regulations." He rubbed his hands together.

"This booze here was donated by General Anthony," said Logan. "It's what Churchill and Ike put away when they're hobnobbing with the king."

"A general sent this?" asked Doolin.

"Holy cow," said Tyler. "We *are* dead ducks."

There was moment of silence.

"But a thirsty duck I am," said Rhys Griffiths, and they all leapt toward the crate.

28 OCTOBER 1942
NANTES, OCCUPIED FRANCE

They came early in the morning, about the time that people would be on their way to work. That way everyone would see, would know that the widow had been hauled away to a cold cell. Those who knew of it would speak of it, and many others along with them would try to envision what the interrogation would be like and would shudder over tortures they could not even imagine. It was important that everyone knew the consequences, and it was particularly important—as the local German commander had said the evening before—that people knew it was the French police who did it. France was part of the Axis now, part of the new world being built by National Socialism.

They came to the front door, the bicycle shop owner and his wife one step behind three thugs from the French Nazi party, one of them carrying the flag of the party. Three more thugs and a constable hurried into the alley behind the house.

"Good morning, Monsieur," said the widow, opening the door before he rapped.

He clutched his hands behind him. "Madame," he said, "you are to surrender him immediately."

"Who?" she said.

"You know who."

"I do not know who, and I am not fond of riddles."

"Arrest the bitch!" said a pimply thug.

"Who are you calling 'bitch,' you worthless turd?" snapped the widow.

She clawed at him, but the police chief grabbed her arm.

"Let her out," said the thug. His friends pulled out blackjacks. "We'll teach her some respect."

The police chief raised his hand. "This will all be done properly," he said. "Madame, I repeat: You must immediately surrender the enemies of the Republic."

"Republic!" she snorted.

"If you force me, it will be more difficult for you."

She sneered at him. "If my Jean were still alive—"

The back door slammed open, and the constable was in the widow's kitchen.

Marcel heard the bang of the door and slipped aside the loose tile to look into the street. A crowd was gathering. He saw the bicycle shop owner and the flag carried by one of the thugs. He listened, and although he could make out none of the words, he knew he was captured.

No, he thought. *No. They cannot capture me until I have done whatever it is God has ordained. They did not capture St. Joan until she had made several victories against the invader. They won't find me. They won't know where to look.*

He slid the tile back into place, then checked to see that the false wall was back where it should be. Crawling back into the corner, his knee crushed his coat and the steel ball which the angel had given him rolled noisily across the floor, dropping into a hole under the eaves. He reached down and his fingertips brushed it. It rolled again in the narrow space. He strained his arm into the space between the floor boards and the ceiling below, scratching himself on rough wood and plaster. He bumped it again and pinned it against a crossbeam. He pulled it out, his hand and forearm covered with dead bugs and cobwebs, then backed on his rear into the corner, weeping with fear.

He clasped the metal ball in his hands and prayed to St. Joan, begged for her help.

"What are you pigs doing in my kitchen?" shouted the widow, rushing back from her door. "You have no right!"

The police chief followed her in. "I told you to watch the back," he said to the constable.

"No one came out," he answered.

The widow turned back to the police chief. "Monsieur, we have known each other for many years. You knew my Jean. Yes, you had political disagreements with him, but he always respected you, Monsieur, and you might show respect to his house."

"I am sorry, Madame, but I have a duty. A citizen was passing your house last night. His attention was drawn by a noise in the upper stories. He then saw light issuing from a seam in your roof tiles."

"What nonsense!" she said.

"He then saw you rushing up the stairs."

"And how would he see that?"

"Your lamp passed the window."

"Old women often have difficulty sleeping."

"Madame, you will please escort me to the attic."

"Find it yourself, you and your gangsters."

The constable grabbed her by the arm and shoved her toward the stairs.

"Let go of me!"

"Would you rather stay here with them?" asked the constable.

She glared at the grinning boys. Two of them were missing teeth. She took a deep breath and moved toward the stairs.

On the second floor, the police chief ordered the three rooms searched. The Nazis overturned furniture, and the widow cringed when she heard glass breaking.

"That wasn't necessary," said the police chief.

"We have to look thoroughly, don't we?" said the oldest thug.

"Up," said the chief.

They slid the ladder propped against the wall into the trapdoor that lead to the attic. The constable pulled his pistol and slowly climbed. He flung open the trapdoor, then tensed and waited.

"Come out!" he shouted. "This is the law!"

"In the name of the Republic," shouted the police chief, "I arrest you!"

The constable gathered his nerve and stuck his head through the opening. He quickly looked in all directions.

"Be careful," said the chief.

"Nothing," said the constable.

"Go up. Use your lantern."

The constable disappeared through the door.

"Where are the Jews, bitch?" said a thug, grabbing the widow's arm.

She jerked away. "Pig!" she said, then clutched the police chief's coat. "You see? You trouble a poor widow for nothing! Why? You know I was never political. We went to school together."

"Anything?" shouted the police chief.

"A trunk," answered a voice. "Old photographs."

The bicycle seller startled them all from the top of the stairs. "I tell you there was someone up there! I heard talking. I had my son watch the house until your man arrived."

"Go up," said the police chief. "Up!"

The old woman slowly climbed the ladder.

One of the thugs whistled, pretending to look under her skirt.

"Stop it!" said the police chief. When the widow stepped into the attic, he followed her. The Nazis scurried up afterwards.

The attic space was long and narrow; the roof beams, irregular. Light filtered in under the eaves and around the edges of some of the large clay tiles. The floorboard covered only part of the space. The police chief took the lantern from the constable and stepped carefully from beam to beam, looking in the crevices where the roof rested on the outer walls. He came back to the floorboard. There was little else to see. The trunk. A yellowing stack of newspapers from the early 1930s, so covered with dust the chief could hardly make out the Communist emblem on the masthead.

He pointed the lantern in one direction, then in the other. Back to one end of the attic, then the other.

His eyes widened. He pulled his pistol.

"Come out!" he shouted. "Out!"

"What is it?" asked the constable.

"There," said the chief. "That end is different."

"I looked down there. It's just the end."

"That," said the chief pointing behind them, "is stucco. Why is that wood?"

The constable thrust his pistol toward the wood. "I see! When this house was built they could not make small planks like that!"

"True," whispered the police chief. "But there are also tracks in the dust."

"Mine?"

"One footprint goes under the wall."

"What nonsense," said the widow, panting.

The police chief signaled the constable to move ahead. They crouched, spread out, and approached the wall.

"We know you are in there!" said the chief. "Answer me immediately, or I will fire!"

The old woman's knees weakened and she settled on the dusty floor.

The chief felt the wood and then saw the bent nail that served as a latch.

He twisted it and yanked back the false wall.

No one.

Nothing, except for old books.

"Someone has been here!" he said.

The widow was speechless for a second, then said, "No one's been up here for years."

The chief held up a book. "What is this, then? Marx and Engels!"

"That must have been my husband's. He stored things up here."

The police chief stepped back into the tiny space and sniffed. What was it he smelled? It was like urine. The pigeons under the eaves burbled and cooed.

"The birds got in," he muttered.

"Come on," said the chief.

"We'll make her talk!" said one of the thugs.

"Get out of here," said the police chief angrily. "It is that idiot Bern! I wish to hell he'd stick with his bicycles and stop imagining things!"

"We could arrest her for the books," said the constable.

"Damn the books," said the police chief. "Let's go make Bern wet his pants!" He brushed past the old woman and started down the ladder saying, "Get down! Get out of here! Go!"

The attic became incredibly silent as the noisy crowd marched away toward the bicycle shop. The widow, still trying to catch her breath after what had happened, awkwardly raised herself and staggered toward the hiding space.

When she looked in, she covered her mouth with both hands.

Marcel sat in the corner in a puddle of urine, his face streaked with sweat. His arms went limp, and a metal ball clumped to the floor.

28 OCTOBER 1942
THE FORBIDDEN ZONE

orck sat in his office, sipping cognac, smoking a Turkish cigarette, and trying to clear his mind. The drill had penetrated the hull and then seized up. Now it remained embedded, as if it were originally part of it. They had twisted it, struck it with a hammer, but were utterly unable to dislodge it. Why not? Why had the drill penetrated at that time when nothing else would?

And then Rhinehart's blood. The hull had soaked it up like a sponge, so there wasn't a trace of it.

Why?

And why had he shot Rhinehart? It was a reflex, he thought, a way to make the others know how serious he was. They were all working hard now. But they seemed to be getting nowhere. They were idiots when it came to the craft and the creature still lay dormant in the cell and where was that blasted Orlov?

He had sent a truck, but Orlov hadn't been at his laboratory. Was the Russian out drinking vodka? Had the Resistance captured him? There were a number of scientific instruments in Orlov's lab, but none of them seemed to be in the process of being crated. He had sent instructions to Paris to have Orlov immediately arrested, but the Wehrmacht was in charge of Paris and was too often careless about these things. The Wehrmacht had been told to arrest the degenerate painter Pablo Picasso. Had they? No.

His secretary rapped on the door and brought in several papers, placing them silently on Borck's desk. Borck waved him out.

Berlin wanted a progress report, immediately, particularly concerning the health of Professor Rhinehart.

Somebody had gotten the word to them. In the end, it would be handled, but there was always paperwork.

There was yet another note from the lieutenant in charge of the mess. *I should shoot him, too,* Borck thought. The lieutenant was requesting permission to send a truck into Nantes to replenish the pilfered supplies. He was, he said, very disappointed that the pilferers had not been identified. The amount clearly indicated that someone in the facility had sold the milk on the black market. Perhaps inquiries might be made in the surrounding communities?

Idiot. Put a foolish man in charge of a kitchen and he thinks he's the emperor of cheese.

Finally, there was a message, also from Berlin, advising particular watchfulness. It could have been a routine warning, or it could have been based on something gotten from an informant. There had been earlier reports of the formation of Resistance units in the area. Perhaps Berlin was reacting to those.

Well, no one would ever get into this facility, thought Borck. The perimeter was guarded constantly with dogs. A strong circle of barbed wire had been set inside that, and then, of course, there was only one door into the caves of the facility itself. The Emperor of Soup and a good machine gun could hold off an assault on the front door for months.

The Resistance, he thought. *That's what happened to the boy. If they got him, the Allies may know what we have. But even if they do, would they believe it? Suppose they have Orlov, too?*

He flung down the papers. The cognac was getting to him. What was the difference? What mattered was getting the technology. After that, the Allies could do nothing.

But how?

The damned scientists! You could never count on their loyalty. Either their egotism led them to look for ways to glorify themselves, or they sanctified themselves by babbling about "truth" and the "laws of the universe."

He could no longer count on Orlov. He'd need to get another biologist and perhaps a medical man. The creature could be dying. Somehow he knew it was not, but he couldn't be sure. There was something that was sustaining the creature, some kind of energy it drew from its surroundings, perhaps even from the ship in the hangar above. If there could be something like a death ray, why couldn't there be something like a life ray?

All he knew was that if he didn't make rapid progress, the rail line to the facility would be completed and the craft would be moved to Berlin. He would lose his chance to be Hitler's most important aide, the Oberführer who had made the Reich invincible and brought a thousand years of *pax Germanna*.

His head was splitting. He hadn't slept for days. He settled back into his chair and closed his eyes.

Relax, he told himself. Relax. Let the cognac work its fragrant magic.

The cognac, which had risen like steam into his nostrils, now swirled in his brain. He felt the caress of fingers on his scalp, but he did not open his eyes.

Soothing darkness. A vague circling cloud of light. It moved gently, its edges blurred. It was a hypnotist's watch. It was a fuzzy ball on a string.

Good night. Good night.

He bolted upright.

It was a light bulb.

It was a light bulb dangling from a cord high on a stone ceiling.

It was the light bulb in the creature's cell.

Borck fumbled for his cognac and belted it back, slopping some on his chin.

He stared straight ahead. How could this be? This wasn't a dream. He had been in the creature's cell, looking up from the cot.

He had been *inside* the creature's perceptions, seeing what the creature saw.

Somehow, their minds had been linked.

He squeezed his head between his hands.

How could this be?

He reached for a cigarette, then abruptly threw it down. He ran out of his office and down the stairs into Area C. He snatched the keys from the astonished guard and went through the first door, then threw himself on the viewing slit.

The creature lay unmoving. The light bulb, however, swung slightly.

He closed his eyes and concentrated, concentrated on trying to connect.

Tell me what you know. Tell me what you know.

He listened and heard nothing but the hum of a ventilator.

The tunic was spinning an aurora of dim light.

But suddenly he knew something which he wasn't sure had come from his own mind, or the creature's.

Yes! That was it! The drill! The craft!

He spun and rushed out the door, flinging the keys at the guard as if in a fever, hurrying up the stairs and into the chamber.

The scientists were standing in a circle, considering some problem. Erstewald held his chin in his hand and listened attentively to Brunnermann.

Borck's entrance stopped the caucus dead. They all turned and faced him like a group of schoolboys caught doing something naughty.

"Ah, Oberführer, we were just coming to speak to you," said Erstewald. "Our new examination of the microscopic structures indicates that the surface is porous. It is like a foam metal, which is why it is so light, except that it has the plasticity of a liquid. Brunnermann has suggested that if we freeze the surface, say with dry ice or liquid nitrogen—"

"Never mind that!" said Borck. "I have been inside the creature's mind!"

The scientists blinked.

He stopped in front of them and tapped his forehead with his finger. "It has been trying to make contact with me."

Erstewald looked at the others for a moment, then reached out to touch Borck's shoulder. "The work, perhaps, has been so tiring—"

Borck slapped his hand away. "Don't be ridiculous! This is a creature from outer space. In ancient times it would have been thought of as a god! It *is* a god to us. I don't know how it can enter my mind, but it can. It has come to restore the values of our society, to reverse the long degeneration of Aryan values through Judaism and Christianity."

"It told you this?" asked Erstewald.

"I did not know the Martians read Nietzsche," said Brunnermann dryly.

Borck turned on Brunnermann, who stepped back. Rakoczy stepped between them. "Oberführer," he said, "surely you understand how hard it is for us. We do believe you; at least, I do. My own mother once helped the police find a drowned girl. She did it through her dreams. The paranormal is a fact of reality."

"This is no gypsy trick, tea leaves and tarot cards," said Borck. "I tell you the creature explores my mind."

"Very well," said Rakoczy.

"There is a sensation rising from here." He touched the back of his neck.

"The brain stem."

"Then tickling forward over the scalp. It feels like a chill."

Brunnermann suddenly looked at Erstewald. "Karl," he said, "I have felt that."

"My God," said Erstewald. "So have I!"

"The other day, when Rhine—when we were drilling."

"And when the light moved over the craft!"

"Yes!" said Brunnermann.

"Could the creature have been reading our minds? Perhaps it knows everything we know!"

Borck interrupted. "But have you seen with the creature's eyes? I have. I closed my eyes and I saw the inside of its cell. Have any of you seen that? Dreamed that?"

They looked at each other and shrugged. "We cannot know because we have not seen its cell," said Rakoczy. "I have imagined it in its cell, but there may be no connection."

"Describe it," said Erstewald.

"Concrete walls? Damp?"

Borck shook his head. "No concrete. Stone. Enough of the parlor game. I think I know how to open the ship."

"With our minds!" said Rakoczy.

"Exactly. The diamond drill was useless at first. And then what were you thinking?" asked Borck.

"I don't remember," said Erstewald. "I wanted it to succeed. I tried to visualize it drilling."

"Exactly. Perhaps it was only me, but I was willing it into the hull."

"This is difficult to accept," said Brunnermann. "Are we all to concentrate on the same thing. Or is it only you, Oberführer?"

"We are going to open the craft," said Borck. "With our minds."

The scientists looked at each other.

"But what if our natural skepticism interferes?" said Brunnermann. "Ultimately, the drilling failed." He pointed at the broken bit, still stuck in the hull. It was tilted to one side.

"You bent it," said Borck.

"No," said Erstewald, "The hull is expelling it, slowly pushing it out as it heals its own wound. It is fully a centimeter further out than it was five hours ago."

"Incredible," said Borck.

"Precisely," said Erstewald.

"If the ship can heal itself so readily, why can't the creature?"

"The atmosphere? Lack of sunlight? Has it eaten anything? Who knows?" said Rakoczy. "Where is Dr. Orlov?"

"Never mind all that," said Borck. "Let us take command of this craft."

"What do we do?"

Borck ordered all the men to approach the craft and place their hands upon it. "Then you will relax and concentrate on one thing and one thing only: open."

"Perhaps you should try it alone, first," said Brunnermann. "Conflicting thoughts and all that. You are the one in most direct contact, wouldn't you say?"

Borck's hand snapped out and grabbed the engineer by the throat, squeezing until his eyes bulged. "Is this mockery? Is this the skepticism you spoke of? You will do as I say. All of you will do as I say. How can you compare any one of our minds to the minds of those who built this ship? In unison, we will open the craft and have the power of gods!"

Brunnermann tried to nod, his veins almost bursting in his forehead.

Borck flung him back. "And let me add this: if the craft fails to open, one of you shall die."

"D–die?" stammered Erstewald.

"Yes, just as Rhinehart died. You remember Rhinehart?"

"But who?" said Rakoczy. "Why?"

"I'll decide afterwards. Perhaps I'll have you draw straws. It makes no difference if we succeed; then no one will die." Borck took out his pistol and pretended to be checking the action.

"I–I must protest," said Erstewald.

"Protest noted. It will not affect whether I select you or someone else." He carefully looked at each man, then shouted for all of the soldiers in the chamber to put down their rifles and join them.

Many of them slapped their hands down on the hull to stop their shaking.

Borck reholstered his Luger with a flourish and moved toward the craft. Erstewald and Rakoczy shifted away from him, leaving him a wide space.

"Relax!" ordered Borck. "Clear your minds!"

He stretched forth his hands and brought them down slowly on the hull. "Open," he murmured. "Open!"

The ship pulsed two hums. Several of the soldiers jumped back.

"Get on there!" shouted Borck.

Licking their lips, they touched the ship again.

"Close your eyes," said Borck. "See it opening. Concentrate your will! Will it open! Open. Open."

Some of the scientists and soldiers mouthed the word. Others whispered it audibly.

The ship pulsed three times. Borck raised his head slowly and watched pink light shimmer above and within the hull's surface.

Open! I command you open. We must become friends. Open to us. Open.

Again there was a hum—loud, but not frightening. Everyone was bent forward, eyes closed, with the exception of Borck, who stared at the hull, trying to puncture it with his stare.

Open! Open!

Sweat poured down his face and into his eyes. He thought he saw something near the top of the ship. His heart pounded. He dared not even blink, but he was sure there was something irregular on the sheen.

Yes! It was the circling of dark spots, like those that had appeared on the tunic of the creature. They spun with the spiral arms of a galaxy, then, right at the center, the surface seemed to pucker, then slowly began to spread.

Open, damn you! Open!

The spinning hole rippled outward, hesitated, then whooshed and went silent.

One by one, the scientists and soldiers opened their eyes.

"Yes!" shouted Borck. "Yes!"

The men on the other side of the ship looked at each other in confusion.

"It's open!" Borck crowed, his voice echoing off the stone walls of the chamber. A cheer went up.

A perfectly round hole about a meter in diameter had formed on the slope just below the rounded peak of the ship. It looked as if it had always been there.

"Congratulations, Oberführer!" said Rakoczy. "Do you know what this means? We could will the enemy into surrendering. We could go into Churchill's mind and influence his plans."

"Or at least read them!" said Brunnermann.

Erstewald gaped at the portal. "Oberführer, you are a genius! Five minutes ago I thought you were mad—stark, raving mad!"

"Never think that again!" said Borck angrily. He laughed at the expression on Erstewald's face, then grabbed him by the shoulders and shook him like a long-lost brother.

Borck saw that one of the soldiers had climbed onto the roof of the truck to get a better view of the ship's insides.

"What do you see?" Borck asked.

"It's dark, Oberführer." He leaned over, then twisted away. "The smell is terrible!"

"Hand him a flashlight," shouted Rakoczy.

"Climb and look in," said Borck.

The light was handed up and the soldier gingerly stepped out onto the slippery craft. He fell and slid back against the truck cab, but rolled over and crawled toward the opening.

His face was pale, and he turned his head away from the opening to try to lessen the stench.

"What is in there?" asked Borck. "Do you see instruments? What?"

The soldier took a deep breath and reached the flashlight into the opening with one arm, then he lowered his head inside to look.

The opening snapped shut like a cigar clip.

The body, minus head and arm, slid down toward the gaping Brunnermann, twitching and spurting blood.

29 OCTOBER 1942
OCCUPIED FRANCE

As the plane bucked and bounced, twisting in all directions like a crazed bronco, Logan struggled to keep his stomach from exploding up his throat. He saw some of the other men vomiting on the floor, which felt like it would give way any second. The sound of the engines and their constant fight against the wind made anything other than listening to the moaning in your own head impossible.

Logan leaned closer to the microphone of the radio transmitter so General Anthony could hear him above the storm. "If you mean have we had enough training, I'd say no. We're game, though."

"Then go immediately," Anthony replied through an ocean of static. "If the weather closes in for two days, it may be too late. May God be with you."

"I hope the Big Guy's up for a mission like this."

"Amen."

Logan signed off, then headed for the cockpit. At the controls was an Eighth Air Force pilot, who turned to face him.

"Jesus!" said the pilot. "What the hell are you guys doing? I've never been asked to go up in weather like this."

"Maybe we should've used another crew?"

"My crew's the best you're getting, Cap. I was merely wondering what the big deal was."

"There's no big deal, and you keep your mouth shut," Logan said gruffly. "And that goes for your crew, too."

The pilot shrugged. "Me? I never heard of you. Just don't hold it against me if we accidentally drop you in the ocean."

With all the water battering the plane, Logan wasn't sure they weren't *already* in the ocean.

One of the crewmen slapped Logan's shoulder and leaned close to his ear. "We're in the area. The Resistance is supposed to send up a radio signal we can aim at. This is as close as we can do it." Logan gave him a thumb's-up and checked his watch. They were supposed to be down there waiting in ten minutes—if the message had gotten through about the earlier take-off.

The plane banked and turned. Logan could see the wings bucking as if they might snap off. Once the Resistance started the homing signal, they'd need to jump as soon as possible. The longer the signal beamed, the more likely it was that the Germans could home in on it themselves.

They banked again, circling again. Could the signal be dispersed by the clouds? Could it bounce and direct them to the wrong place? If they had to keep circling, the plane would surely be heard. The plane was a bomber, not equipped for aerial combat with the faster, more maneuverable ME-109s and other fighters, nor were they escorted by Allied fighters. But maybe the storm would keep the enemy fighters on the ground if they were detected. They had set it up to fly on a path approximating flights to neutral Spain because they were no longer able to fly low, but if the enemy detected the circling, they would know something was up.

Logan checked his watch again. The flight had been long, sheer torture, too much time to imagine what might go wrong. Yet, these few minutes seemed even more torturous than the rough ride.

The signal was five minutes late. They couldn't wait much longer. Logan had to decide whether to go ahead without a signal. It would be suicidal to do that, but so what? The whole mission was suicidal.

The crewman hurried back. "Prepare for jump!" he shouted into Logan's ear as he made ready to open the door.

The pilot was spiraling the plane down, taking a chance he was not off-course and over a mountain. The lower they were, the closer they might drop together.

The men, seated on the benches along both walls of the fuselage, had been rolling their heads with weariness and airsickness, but with the first blast of rain from the open door, they were instantly ready, gripping their weapons and checking their equipment. To Logan's surprise, Madison James crossed himself. James saw his look and shrugged as if to say, "Oh, well, it can't hurt."

At the airman's signal, the men stood, clicked their static lines to the rail, then staggered single-file to the open bay door. The static lines would yank out their parachutes as they fell.

"Good luck!" Logan shouted over the roar of the wind battering them through the open hatch. "GOOD LUCK!" He gave them a thumb's-up. Punchy would go first, followed by Doolin, the two Griffiths, McGonigle, James, Tyler, Cosgrove, Tom Swift, Carlson, Orlov, and Logan. The jumps had to be spaced moments apart, or the men would simply leap into one another or tangle their parachutes.

"Nervous?" Logan asked Orlov.

The scientist shook his head, just barely. "We leap, our parachutes fill with air, we float to the ground."

"We hope so," Logan shouted.

"Physics!" shouted Orlov

The light blinked over the door, indicating that the pilot thought they were over the drop zone.

Punchy looked to Logan, who nodded, and the airman gave the boxer a slap on the back. "Go!"

Punchy laughed and pushed himself away from the hatchway, tumbling away into the black, stretching out the static line. He called something back, but the slipstream from the propellers scattered his words on the wind. It didn't matter; Logan knew his friend well enough to guess what he said. He always shouted "Geronimo!"

The airman held Doolin for just a second, then slapped his shoulder. Rhys Griffiths went next, then John Griffiths.

McGonigle moved to the hatch, taking deep, calming breaths. The tower had been bad enough, but it didn't really prepare you for a jump into total darkness. He gave Logan a quick salute, then put his hands together and dived.

"Go!" shouted the airman, and James dived. "Go!" and Tyler dived. Soon, only Orlov and Logan were left, and Orlov seemed to hesitate in the open door. Logan prepared to shove him, but Orlov was suddenly gone, swallowed in the oblivion.

"Good luck!" shouted the airman, and Logan jumped off the edge.

The parachute, dyed black for this covert night jump, unfurled behind him like a plume of smoke. The parachute filled with wind, stopping Logan's plunge with a jerk. The harness tightened and squeezed the air from his lungs, but now he was feeling good. Top o' the world, Ma.

Blinking the water from his eyes, he squinted to see anything below. He could barely make out the toes of his boots.

You clamp your legs together and keep *them together,* he thought. *You could land on a roof. You could land on a steeple. You could bang down on top of a car or a German or a cow.*

Even if the moon had been out, as they'd intended, there was a chance they'd get only a few seconds to figure out if they were going to be impaled on a lightning rod.

There was nothing dull about night drops, even in a rural area.

Logan swung under his canopy, hearing nothing, seeing no sign of the other parachutes that would be drifting like dandelions on the wind.

For a moment, he felt a strange serenity, as if there were no war, no mission, no spacecraft. He was just a baby, floating in his mother's womb.

The crash came instantly. Branches clawed at him. Limbs bent and broke, as he tore through them. He stopped, bouncing, and just had time to think, *Oh, hell, I'm caught in a tree!* when he dropped again, at least ten feet, catching again and dangling.

This time he dropped no further. He could be a few feet off the ground or twenty, depending on the tree. He couldn't make out any branches below. If he dropped again, he might really take a shot. He listened carefully. The branches creaked. It was a big oak, hundreds of years old. He decided no one was in the area. He listened again, squinting in all directions. There was some vague light to his right that disappeared, but if there were anyone near they were remaining silent. He took out his flashlight with the red lens and pointed it down. A jagged boulder was just below him, but he wasn't more than ten feet above it.

Taking a chance the parachute was thoroughly tangled, he kicked his feet and began to swing, his razor-sharp bayonet ready to cut at just the right moment. Back and forth, back and forth. One, two . . . He slashed and dropped, just catching the edge of the boulder with his heels, then tumbling down a steep incline to land face-first on a hard, gravelly surface.

It was a road. What road he couldn't know yet. Now it was time to locate the others. He checked his compass and climbed the hill to go east, in the general direction of where they should have landed.

It was always a problem reuniting a unit that dropped from the air, especially at night. Each was carrying a small penny whistle which they could tweet twice in order to be recognized. The response was to be two blinks of the red-lensed flashlight.

Logan entered a pasture and barely made out the black silhouette of a treeline beyond. He fished out the penny whistle, shook the rain out of it, and blew twice. He got no response. He made his way along the edge of the pasture, close to the trees. The storm would keep most sane people indoors, making it less likely that he or his men would be spotted. On the other hand, it was going to make it very hard for them to find each other.

He backed against a tree trunk and squinted to see if anything unusual seem to be hanging in the canopy. Orlov should have landed somewhere around here, but then you could never tell, especially with a novice. A couple of good gusts and the scientist could have landed miles away.

He tweeted again and thought he heard movement in the brush. Something snapped behind him.

He pocketed the whistle and whipped the Beretta off his shoulder.

He took a deep breath. There was no sound but the rumbling of thunder. He spun, ready to fire, and a flash of lightning revealed Orlov, standing in the ferns, his bayonet raised.

"I could have shot you!" whispered Logan.

"I could have stabbed you," said Orlov. "Well, where are the others?"

"You're a bit too calm for all this," barked Logan. "Where is your whistle? Your light?"

"You didn't hear it?"

"Look," said Logan, "you're not a soldier, but—"

"I'm sorry," said Orlov. "I didn't think we were supposed to do it very loud."

"Just remember," said Logan, "I could have killed you."

"I won't forget."

Logan looked around. "What did you do with your parachute?"

"Buried it under some rocks."

"Good," said Logan.

"I landed on a hedgerow by a road."

"Unfortunately, mine is up in a tree. It will wave like a flag when the next Nazi car comes down the road. Let's move. We don't have much time. The others should be that way."

"The Resistance?"

"Them, too."

"This is quite thrilling," said Orlov.

Logan stopped in his tracks. Lightning briefly illuminated Orlov's smile.

"Thrilling? Doctor, there will be casualties from this night drop. If that's your idea of fun, I just hope you'll be able to share your enthusiasm with the guys who are hurt."

"Did you hear that?" Orlov said. "I think it was a whistle."

Logan sighed and blinked his light.

29 OCTOBER 1942
SUPREME HQ,
ALLIED EXPEDITIONARY FORCE
LONDON, ENGLAND

At the same time that Logan was creeping through the rainy French night, trying to locate the rest of his squad, General Anthony was snoring face-down on a pile of papers. He had been trying to put together the meaning of a troop movement down the boot of Italy. Surely the Germans did not intend to put more troops into Africa. If so, they would arrive too late to assist in resisting Montgomery's counteroffensive at El Alamein, but if the counteroffensive bogged down . . .

He bolted upright, instantly awake when Marston opened the door without knocking. "There's an important message. Churchill ordered that it be sent directly to you."

"I guess Winnie never sleeps, either," yawned Anthony.

"It's from the Foreign Office."

"Without going through State?"

A British courier entered the room. Judging from his suit, he was a diplomat-in-training, some boy out of Oxford whose severe myopia had kept him out of the military. His thick glasses made his head look like a grasshopper's.

Anthony took the sealed envelope from his outstretched hand. "Is there a reply?"

"No, sir, but it is incumbent upon me to remind you that this is for your eyes only."

"Thank you," said the general. He waited until the door was locked, then slit open the envelope. It was a brief official dispatch from the British ambassador in the Soviet Union to the Prime Minister:

28 OCTOBER 1942

SOLOMON INDICATES KREMLIN HAS LEARNED OF A CAP-TURED AIRCRAFT FROM SPACE STOP THEY HAVE AGENT ON INSIDE STOP INTENT TO STEAL TECHNOLOGY BEFORE WEST CAN ACQUIRE STOP

MESSAGE ENDS MESSAGE ENDS MESSAGE ENDS

The Russians? Anthony thought. The Commies were Allies for now, yes, but that, the General was sure, was only a matter of expediency. The Soviets had cause to hate the Germans more than they did the Americans. But once Hitler was out of the picture, Anthony secretly feared Uncle Joe Stalin would start getting big ideas of his own. How much bigger would those ideas be if Uncle Joe had his own Martian war machines, Anthony wondered. Stalin had once signed a deal with Hitler; maybe he would again. The Soviets were barely holding on in Stalingrad, but if they got whatever might have dropped out of space—death rays, flying saucers, whatever the hell—they wouldn't just use it on the Germans. The only thing anyone could use to keep back the Soviet hordes was superior technology. He strangely thought of the Mongol bow and how it had routed the armored knights of Europe.

"What is it?" asked Marston.

"There's a wild card in the deck," said Anthony. "I'm not sure what it means. Have we heard from Logan yet?"

"No. The plane was forced by the storm to land on Skilly. They made the drop and barely got in on the fumes."

"At least we didn't kill any Air Corps this time," said Anthony. He tapped his desk with his fingers. Solomon was a highly placed spy in the Soviet government, he knew. So highly placed that he seemed sometimes to have overheard Stalin's mutterings in his sleep, though it was hard to say how. The British wanted to keep his (her?) identity to themselves. It had also become increasingly clear that things in the British government had gotten to Moscow fairly easily. Was this another way of the Soviets simply saying, "We know what you know"?

"I'm more than a little worried," said Marston. "They haven't turned up at the Resistance rendezvous point."

"Make sure the frogs don't alert the Germans by sending too many messages our way."

"Well," said Marston, "it seems the Krauts are on alert. I was holding it because I thought you were asleep. They have trucks on the move toward the Forbidden Zone."

"It doesn't mean they're after Logan."

Marston nodded. "Not necessarily."

"But they could be," Anthony admitted. "Let's confuse them. Go to Brigadier-General Smythe. Tell him we'd like to use 'Vichy-O' to send a message. Reassure him the agent won't be compromised and all that."

"As usual," said Marston, not relishing the task. "What do we want them to think?"

"Exactly what the drop area implies—that the commandos are heading northeast and that they're after the fuel dump at St. Nicolas."

"And when they don't attack there, won't that compromise Vichy-O?"

"We'll do something to threaten it. Drop a perfunctory bomb or two. Maybe let the Germans know the raid on the dump was dropped because we knew about their reinforcing the area. It'll give them more reason to suspect the Frenchies who've signed up with them."

"The main thing is protect Logan."

"To the extent possible. Vichy-O is safe, regardless."

Marston nodded. Night after night of head games with friend and foe were taking their toll on him. He pushed himself out of the chair and left. For the first time, Anthony had noticed that Marston's temples were sprinkled with gray.

Anthony lit a cigar, then used the match on the Foreign Office dispatch. He stared at the blackened scraps of paper in the ashtray, as if they contained some mystic portent, augurs of the uncertain future, but there was only ash and smoke.

30 OCTOBER 1942
SOMEWHERE NEAR ST. NICOLAS
OCCUPIED FRANCE

D awn diffused across the entire foggy sky, as if the sun was rising from all directions at once. By steadily moving to the west, Logan had found seven of his men, besides Orlov. The first were Doolin and Carlson. Doolin had landed hard on a rocky outcropping, gashing his forehead as he smashed down on top of the radio strapped to his chest. The radio had probably saved his life at the cost of its own. Carlson had found Doolin when he fled into the rocks as the lightning grew more intense, revived him, and started on their way to the rendezvous point when they met Logan.

It was Orlov who spotted McGonigle and James in a lightning flash. They were moving along at a crisp, mutually competitive pace—probably too crisp a pace to be properly cautious. The Griffiths had hooked up with Tyler. The three of them were hiding in a wet ditch and tweeted as the group crossed another gravel road.

That left Punchy, Tom Swift, Cosgrove, and Leo Stern—with his all-important radio—missing.

Don't let them be captured, thought Logan. *Don't let them be captured*. Ever since the jump, he had been aware of a jitteriness rising up as dark and thick as the smoke from a burning tire.

Dieppe. He couldn't let the nightmares come. He couldn't allow the memory of what had happened there dull his edge. When it had all turned bad, he had suddenly found himself and eight Canadians surrounded on all sides by German soldiers. They had all thought they were dead men and one Canadian fell to his knees, pants soaked and stinking, begging and pleading for his life. This seemed to amuse the Germans, who held off firing to watch the spectacle for a few seconds. That was when the SS officer arrived, his uniform black and crisp. That strange timing had saved their lives for a little longer, only to put several of them in a living hell.

There'd be no throwing up his hands this time, even if he had to stuff a grenade up his own ass.

He waved them together after they crossed a small stone bridge that looked old enough to have been built by the Romans. Further along there was an old house with only one wall left standing. Logan waved them together behind it.

"James," he said, "watch the road to the left. Tyler, watch the right."

Logan squatted on leaves that had covered what once had been a peasant's floor and opened his map. "All right. Where are we? Look familiar, Orlov?"

Orlov squinted. "I'm not sure. Is that Mesquier?"

"That's what it says," said Logan, "but we're over in this area. I think this might be the bridge we just crossed."

"It could be that one," said McGonigle.

"If that's the case," said Logan, "the road should have—Hey, you're right. Very good. We're closer than I thought. The rendezvous should be only half a mile that way. It's an old village, abandoned fifty years ago. They say the church is about all that's left."

"We'd better move," said McGonigle. "We're four hours, thirty minutes behind schedule."

"Indeed we are," said Logan, folding his map.

"You think the others are there already."

"I hope so," said Logan. "We need them."

Carlson looked around at the other men. "Listen, Captain, isn't it about time you filled us in?"

"What do you mean?"

"Exactly what the hell are we doing? I know that I've never seen the general as worked up as I did before I 'volunteered.' I also know the general wouldn't have let me go unless it really mattered."

Logan looked around at his men. "That's fair. You need to know. Something happens to me, somebody's got to do the job. You understand? This could mean the whole war. I wanted to wait until the rendezvous point, but it's daylight already, so I'll give you the quick and dirty."

James and Tyler took a few steps back, but they did not turn.

Logan took a deep breath and then finally said, "Perhaps Dr. Orlov can explain it better."

"Yeah," said Carlson, "why is he along for this ride?"

"He knows the facility we're going into," said Logan. "He volunteered for this, and I mean voluntarily."

They all turned to him. Orlov searched for the right words. "The Germans shot down an alien spacecraft."

The soldiers looked at each other. It was Tyler who finally spoke, tossing the words over his shoulder. "Excuse me?"

"An alien spacecraft," said Orlov. "A plane capable of flying among the planets."

"Gimme a break," said Carlson.

"He's serious," said Logan.

"They're nuts!" said Doolin, mopping fresh blood from his cut.

"No, we're not. They also captured the pilot. That's about all we know at this point."

"He was a little green man, am I correct?" asked James. "I believe I know his cousin from Betsy Emerson's coming-out party."

"This is serious," said Logan. "No bullshit. If this guy, being, thingamabob, can fly from wherever he comes from to Earth, he can give the Nazis the war."

"Maybe he's just here for lunch," said Carlson.

"Whatever he's here for," said Logan sharply, "we are to make sure he never has tea with Adolf Hitler. We are to do whatever is necessary, to kill whatever is necessary, destroy whatever is necessary, to prevent it. That's the sum total."

"You guys have lost your minds," gasped Carlson.

"Think about it," said Logan.

"Anthony's been working too hard," said Carlson.

Logan just stared at him.

"Jeez," said Carlson. "From space!"

"The alien could be the factor that determines whether we live the rest of our lives in slavery," said Orlov. "If he is still alive, we can perhaps persuade his people to join us."

"And he'd better decide quick," said Logan. "The alien technology can't be allowed to go to Hitler and Hirohito."

"But, Captain," said Rhys Griffiths, "where there's one rat there's always more. If we kill this space bug, won't we irritate his folks?"

"Maybe we can just rescue his butt and let him fly away," said Logan angrily. "I don't know. I'm not for killing everything that moves. I *do* know my orders are to prevent the Axis from getting anything out of him."

The men were eyeing each other. Even McGonigle looked like he was ready to mutiny.

"Believe me," said Logan, "if there's any way to get anything out of that alien, the SS can."

"I believe the problem is," said James, "that the men are having a little difficulty with accepting that there's an alien at all."

"Maybe the Nazis are just drawing us in," said John Griffiths.

"Why would they do that?" said Logan. "What will that do for the war effort? Losing us might help the Allies."

"Maybe they want the test tube jockey," said Tyler.

"They already had him," said Logan. "He was spying for us. He slipped out of France so we could be convinced."

"So convince us," said Carlson.

All eyes turned to Orlov. "It is incredible," he said, "I know, but I saw it with my own eyes."

"Tell them about the blood," said Logan.

"It was . . . I have no words for it." He lowered his head and sank to his knees.

"He brought us a sample of the alien's blood," said Logan. "You explain it."

Orlov shrugged. "You do it better in layman's terms."

"All I know is what the general told me. It wasn't like anything on Earth. Blood is made of proteins, am I right? And carbon. This was made of proteins that hadn't been analyzed before I left, and instead of being carbon-based, it was silicon-based."

"This is all mumbo-jumbo," said Carlson.

"The point is," insisted Orlov, "it was not of this Earth. Quit if you must, but I will go ahead."

"You wouldn't stand a bloody chance on your own," said McGonigle. "It's our job to get you back there and we will."

"But not because we believe a damned word of it," said Rhys Griffiths.

"Amen, brother," said Tyler.

"I'm in just to see how nuts the general is," said Carlson.

"Count me in," said Doolin. "I hit my head. I'm delusional."

Logan stood. "So we're all in the game, right? That's good. There's only one way out and that's by way of Purgatory."

"And you'd put us there if you had to, wouldn't you?" said James.

"Just don't disobey me," said Logan.

30 OCTOBER 1942
NANTES, OCCUPIED FRANCE

I tell you," whispered the widow, "I don't know how he did it. He was gone, poof! Then he was back." She shuddered.

She was standing next to the window in a toilet stall at the back of a shoe store. The man who had followed her every time she came out was out front, pretending to look at a pair of hunting boots.

"He crawled under the floor boards," said Levrier, outside the window. A middle-aged woman from the brothel stood with him so that he could appear to be flirting with her in the alleyway. "What did he say?"

"He said God had shielded him from the police."

"*Sacre bleu!* He was under the boards. The flick was too stupid to look."

"I tell you he was not under the boards. The space is barely big enough for a mouse. I know what I know. You must get him out of my house."

"What can we do, Madame Comrade? Your house is being watched every minute of the day."

"And they will come back in when they get ready and put me in front of a firing squad." She moved away from the Turkish toilet and checked to see that her follower was still in the front of the shop. Back at the window, she insisted, "I want him gone, do you understand? I think he's mad."

"Mad?"

"He speaks of an angel who appeared to him. He says he is God's messenger. He says all this too calmly, too surely. He is mad as a hatter."

"We'll think of something," said Levrier. "We can use him now, I think. How is he?"

"He was exhausted after the search and slept for nearly a day."

"What else is there for him to do?"

"No, he was truly exhausted, but his eyes are filled with a kind of wonder. He is not afraid, I think. He truly believes he is blessed."

"Too much time in the hole. You *do* let him exercise at night? Insist on it."

The widow hesitated a moment. "Sometimes I believe he is telling the truth."

"What? An angel with big black eyes? Are you mad, too?"

"Is it so impossible?"

"Religion is just a way of oppressing the masses!"

"It certainly interferes with *my* work," smirked the prostitute.

Levrier blinked. Prostitution was oppression, but prostitutes also controlled the means of production. He shook his head to untangle his thinking.

"I tell you this," said the widow. "You will never convince me he hid himself in that space. That space is where *you* hide. It's the end of the road. Something miraculous happened, I tell you."

"If you say so," said Levrier.

"But I am too old to live in constant fear. Get him out."

"We will think of something."

He strolled down the alleyway with the prostitute and into the next street. "Angels!" he muttered.

"The Bosch are not making any serious search for the boy any more," said the prostitute.

"So you said," said Levrier.

"Though one of them said there might be a hot time to the north."

The fuel dump, thought Levrier. His last message had asked that, after they assisted a group of commandos, they attempt sabotage at St. Nicolas as soon as possible. The Bosch, however, were too well-informed for his taste. Making the Resistance act when the Nazis were ready for them was like wearing the sickle and hammer on your back.

"Come to the brothel and relax," urged the prostitute. "You are getting too worried. Rest a few hours. There isn't usually any business this time of day."

"I'm still mourning my wife," said Levrier. "But when I feel different, I promise to come to you, eh?"

"It's been sixteen months. How bourgeois!" She laughed and strutted away.

Levrier stood on the sidewalk, his arms spread helplessly. He had enough to think about without sorting *that* out!

30 OCTOBER 1942
THE FORBIDDEN ZONE

The Wehrmacht general—Von Kerner by name—was being very polite, but his message was clear. "There is some concern, Oberführer Borck, that you may have placed your duties as security officer for the facility in a secondary position."

"That is not true," said Borck without looking at him.

"You can understand, I am sure. With so much potentially at risk . . ."

Borck spun his chair and faced him, another one of those career military men from some obscure family that fought with Frederick the Great. An Old German, the kind of German who needed to be retired for the new Germany. "No one understands better than I do what this discovery means. Can they grasp that in the Reichstag? Do they even believe that, for the first time in human history, the superior race of one planet will unite with a great race from another? Can all those old generals even conceive this?"

"Now, now, Oberführer, don't be impolite. This is very difficult to believe, isn't it? But now that I have seen the craft and the, ah, being, there will be another voice on your behalf in Berlin. When the tracks are finished, the disk will be sped into the Fatherland and we shall make thousands of these craft."

It was the tracks which had begun to fret Borck more and more.

When they took the disk and the creature away from him, he would lose his chance for real power. He had to break through to the alien within three days, or the tracks would be up to the front door.

"I urge you, General Von Kerner," said Borck, "to convey to Berlin, to Speer—perhaps to the Führer himself—that this facility is like a fortress. It will be a waste of time to move the research, and it risks the possibility of something going wrong."

"I understand. Perhaps—and this is only a suggestion—if the scientists thought it better to remain here . . ."

"I will have them compose a letter."

"This is their thinking, too?"

"I will have them compose a message before you leave," Borck answered firmly.

The general raised an eyebrow and brushed something off his thigh. "I shall be most happy to convey it. We are not enemies, Oberführer Borck. My sole concern is the triumph of my nation. 'Germany over all!' Those are not merely patriotic words to me."

"Of course not," said Borck.

"In the next few days, however, you might turn your attention to some of these routine matters of the security officer. That will quiet some of those who would like to take over the research after it is relocated. If you give them an excuse, they will simply do it sooner."

"They will do it, anyway," said Borck.

The general raised an eyebrow. "Well, you have nothing to fear from *me*. I am more afraid of this than I am of the Russians."

You would be, thought Borck. *The world, perhaps the whole solar system, is in your grasp, and you are afraid to seize it because it might disrupt your comfortable existence.*

Von Kerner smiled weakly. Borck smiled back and poured him another cognac.

The general sipped before going on. "An alarming thing was said to me when I arrived."

The damned scientists. "Yes?"

"It wasn't said directly to me, I should make clear—"

The damned scientists told the two new scientists that the general brought with him.

"Do you believe that the creature has entered your mind?"

"It has."

The general thought, swirling his cognac. "And you are certain this is not overwork? Strain?"

"No," steamed Borck.

"More than one of the scientists believes you, or at least that it is possible. What closed the aircraft door on Corporal—oh, whoever?"

"Someone thought it closed."

"Excuse me? You mean someone closed it with his mind?"

"Yes. I have considered this for many hours," explained Borck. "I went to the cell and tried to clear my mind to see if the creature would explain it to me. That failed; however, I came to the conclusion that if we can think it open, someone suddenly thought it to close."

"Hmmm."

Borck couldn't tell what the general meant by that. "My own theory is that the corporal himself, upon reaching in with his light, became frightened and wished that it had not opened."

"He saw something inside?"

"Perhaps. There was a stench that issued from the craft."

"Erstewald described it as rotting flesh."

"Similar," said Borck. "A bit less sweet."

Von Kerner raised his eyebrow.

"Surely as a general you have smelled a corpse," said Borck. "There is a cloying sweetness in the odor."

"I confess," said the general, "I have only smelled the corpses of the careers of fellow officers."

Of course.

"How then shall you examine the inside? If the slightest thought can—"

"Our minds are not as disciplined as theirs. Our thoughts scatter. But consider how a chessmaster or a musician is able to remove himself from himself. He becomes the game. He becomes the violin or the piano. If we can find a comparable mind-state, we shall open communication."

"You'll *become* the craft?"

"In a way."

"It reminds me of the higgery-pokery of Buddhism. Perhaps if we bring an Asian monk or a clairvoyant . . ."

"*I* will do it," said Borck, "if I am just given enough time."

The general twisted his head to say, "That might be impossible, but I shall represent your arguments without prejudice. This is all too incredible. I will do what I can."

"The world hangs in the balance," said Borck fervently.

"But you must help me with the practical matters."

"Yes, General." Borck's eyelids half-closed. "Such as?"

"First, give a more thorough explanation of the accidental death of Dr. Rhinehart."

"Again?"

"Second, do something about this lieutenant who complained about pilferage."

"He went over my head? Damn him! I'll have him broken to private!"

"His cousin works in Himmler's office. Make a fuss about finding the milk. Send some men into the villages. See who's making cheese. Arrest someone. Shoot them."

"Milk? Someone stole some milk. Is that all this is about?"

"Well, it was three barrels, he says. The entire supply."

"Did it ever occur to him it might have just leaked out? No one got through our perimeter and into our refrigerator and out with 1000 liters of milk!"

"Just do something. It's absurd, I know."

This is so typical, thought Borck, grinding his teeth to control his temper. *With the world ripe for the taking, the bureaucrats niggle about milk!* He scribbled a note to order the mess officer in and tell him to change the locks. It would be a lecture the little bastard would never forget. "Is there anything else, General?"

"Only this," he said. "I have two secret dispatches I am to convey orally." He looked back to see if the door was closed.

Von Kerner polished off his cognac and leaned forward. "Your Dr. Orlov was only in his laboratory in Paris for a brief period, an hour at most, then he left in the company of a Parisian policeman who has not been identified. The Gestapo is of the opinion now he wasn't a real policeman and that Orlov was kidnapped. The Russians sometimes snatch back their expatriates if they can use them in some way. If they did that, then the Russians know about our craft. Fortunately, they are much too far away to do anything about it, but they might tell the Americans. If the Resistance snatched him because they view him as a collaborator, he will likely float up in the Seine soon, and we will have to assume, if they interrogated him, that the Allies will know about the craft."

"So they know, then?"

"Strangely, Oberführer, we do not believe they do. We have received confirmation from an agent in London that the Allies are planning another raid."

"On the Forbidden Zone?"

"No, I'm afraid not. Although an informer has said that something like that was in process, he seems to have been mistaken. The London agent has tipped us that the raid is intended for the fuel dump at St. Nicolas."

"The agent is reliable."

Von Kerner winked. "Got it from an undersecretary, I'm told."

"Nonetheless, we will go on special alert."

"Very good. And you may be interested in this as well. The commando leading the raid was also at Dieppe. An American. A Captain Joseph Xavier Logan."

"*Logan?*" shouted Borck. "*My* Logan? The one who escaped?"

"Apparently. Could be another, but they thought you'd be interested. I have heard it was an embarrassment for you."

Borck banged his desk. "You see this?" He pointed to a small scar on his nostril. "Logan did that!"

"Do you want to go up there and hunt him?" asked the general. "I'm sure that would be approved."

Ah, the bait, thought Borck. *Get the craft in the hands of the Wehrmacht.* "No, I won't leave my post here, but if they bring him to me, I guarantee he'd talk this time. I guarantee."

The general stood. "We must all do our duty. Now, perhaps, you could show me how to open the craft. I have brought a cameraman. That will be remarkable!"

30 OCTOBER 1942 NEAR ST. NICOLAS, OCCUPIED FRANCE

A priest frantically bicycling by might have noticed them before they ducked into the bushes by a stream, but other than him—and he didn't turn his head in their direction—only a lonely goat had seen them. Logan crept up to the top of the hill with Tyler and looked over at the abandoned village. A narrow road, little more than a path, wound through old foundations with chimneys that had mostly crumbled. The old church was the only structure left relatively undamaged by time and neglect; three of its ancient stone walls stood in place, while the fourth was reduced to a pile of rubble. The slanted roof had mostly collapsed, exposing the great beams.

Logan scanned the place carefully with his binoculars.

"Ain't nobody down there," said Tyler.

"I don't see anyone," said Logan. "Where are the Maquis?"

"Well, somebody's there. Them birds'll say so."

Logan looked to see what he meant. Several birds walked on the church walls. They cocked their heads, then flew to another spot. "Good trick," said Logan.

"Better'n sucker-punching somebody."

Logan ignored it. "You think we could get trapped in that church?"

"Pretty open all around."

"Well, it's either our guys, the Maquis, or a bunch of Hitler enthusiasts."

"Two out of three ain't bad odds," said Tyler. Logan nodded, waving the men forward.

McGonigle would swing a group of three around the hill and come up on the church from out of the sun. Meanwhile, James would pick his way in from the west among the weeds and old foundations. Logan, Orlov, and Tyler would cover from the hill.

Several minutes passed. James disappeared, then reappeared. McGonigle's men looked like olive-drab ants skittering through a trash pile. When they reached the edge of the old church cemetery, the birds fluttered up and away from the walls and they heard a *tweet, tweet.*

Punchy Pawlowski crawled out of the ruins and shook John Griffiths' hand.

Logan and his men were soon walking through a hole in what had been the altar wall. They were dwarfed by a heap of stone and beam that had once been the bell tower.

Punchy and he embraced. "Thought we'd lost you!"

"I'm ready for a few more rounds," he said.

Logan saw Tom Swift and Manny Cosgrove sitting on the floor near a stone baptismal font. "Stern?" he asked. "Where's Stern?"

He knew from their expressions he wasn't just lost.

" 'Chute dragged him through the grapes about a mile that way."

"You landed way over there?"

"Yeah," said Punchy. "Caught a tornado on the way down."

"The wire ripped his throat open," said Cosgrove, holding up Stern's dog tags. "Can you imagine? A big guy like that. Bled to death."

"Did you bury him?" asked Doolin.

Punchy looked ashamed. "We covered his face. We said a few words."

"That's all you should have done," said Logan. "What about the radio?"

"We got it," said Tom Swift.

"Doolin," said Logan, "get on that thing and say hello. Any Resistance? They were supposed to meet us here."

"Nobody," said Punchy. "Maybe we should move on."

Logan thought for a moment. "We need a few hours of rest. The walls are better cover than walking around in broad daylight. They're five hours late. Six. Something's wrong."

"How badly do we need them?" asked McGonigle.

"We know the general direction; when we get closer, Orlov can help with the lay of the land."

"I would feel better with some locals," said Orlov. "I was inside most of the time."

"We need the manpower," said Logan. He clinked the dog tags in his hand and stuck them into his jacket pocket.

Our first casualty, he thought.

The church stunk of bird droppings and mildew, beams and leaves rotting in the rain that blew in through the fallen wall and opened roof. He saw the birds in the wooden latticework overhead, cooing softly to themselves. A papery rattling of wings punctuated their conversations.

Logan posted Punchy a hundred yards to the east, John Griffiths south, James west, and Cosgrove to the north. The rest were to eat and get as much sleep as they could. In two hours they would switch with Logan, Orlov, Carlson, and Tyler. Then, if there was still no sign of the Resistance, begin moving toward the Forbidden Zone. He ordered Doolin to send out the Morse code for a successful landing: "DDD" for "down," "111" for one casualty, "MAMANOTHOME" for no contact with the Resistance. He didn't like playing sitting duck in the old village, but he wasn't certain where else would provide such good cover if they were attacked. And they needed the Resistance—if there was any such thing!

Logan glanced up from his tinned meat, sitting with his back against the crumbling plaster of the wall. The men ate from cans of C-rations without talking and washed the meal down with water;

even a small fire to boil coffee might be noticed by Wehrmacht patrols. Logan stirred the meat paste, eating it only because he knew he'd need the energy.

Suddenly, Tom Swift sat next to him.

"Somethin' on your mind?" Logan asked. The crafty demolition man had been glancing at him for some time now, like a hopeless wallflower hoping to be asked to dance. Now, of course, he seemed incapable of speech. He looked away, but casually let out the thought.

"Nobody's said it, but we've all thought it." The men within hearing stopped whatever they were doing to listen. Their eyes glittered like cold marbles.

Steelies," thought Logan. *We used to call the big ones "steelies," and what a stupid thing to remember now.*

"But, once we get in—" Swift began.

"*If* we get in," Tyler added.

"—how do we get out? Not just out of the Forbidden Zone, but out of France?" The words were coming in a rush now, as if he were vomiting them out. "You haven't mentioned that. We all know you somehow got out after being captured at Dieppe, but that was just you."

"I couldn't have done it alone," said Logan.

"I think he meant that there's a lot more than one of us," said Tyler.

"And you just needed to get across the Channel."

Logan started to say something flip and dismissive, about taking the flying saucer on a test drive, maybe stopping in Berlin long enough to kick the Führer's seig heil, but they were good men, all things considered, and deserved better than that. So he said that the Resistance, who would provide them with phony documents and civilian clothing, was supposed to move them south into Vichy France, where they would hide them until they could meet a submarine in the Bay of Biscay. "Of course, all that is a longshot."

"With no Resistance, it's a no-shot," said Tom Swift.

"We'll pilot the spaceship out," Orlov said cheerfully, as if reading Logan's earlier thoughts.

Logan looked aslant at the physicist, looking for mockery or even simple, bad taste in humor, but there was seemingly none of the former, and he suspected that Orlov never made jokes, bad or otherwise.

"That's a good one," said Rhys Griffiths dryly.

"Who knows?" said Logan. "Perhaps the doctor is right. If things like flying saucers are flying down from Mars, and spacemen are taking the waters in France, then maybe we'll just hitch a ride with them."

"Like we stick out our thumbs and could chat them up. How could we figure out how to make it fly?" Griffiths snorted.

Tom Swift silenced him with one of his high giggles. "Give me a shot, Taffy. If it's a machine, I can figure it out."

"Call me 'Taffy' again and you'll be figuring out my fist."

"Aw," said Tom Swift, "I didn't mean nothing by it. My neighborhood had all kinds: Welshies, Eye-ties, Hunkies, probably a few Martians if I'd paid attention."

"And what were the Martians like, Tom Swift?" asked Orlov.

Tom Swift giggled. "Like my uncle, Ziggy Sweissenborg! Now I finally understand what was with that guy!"

"Let's get some rest," said Logan. "We've got a hard time coming."

"But this fine hotel makes it all worthwhile," said Griffiths.

"Amen, brother," said Tyler.

Orlov found a dry corner near the steps into what had once been a confessional and was about to stretch out, when Logan snagged him by the crook of his arm and pulled him aside, away from earshot of the others. The colonel spoke in a whisper, with the whoosh of the fluttering pigeons in the roof helping to disguise his words.

"You've seen the thing, but do you really think we could learn to fly that ship? The Krauts haven't figured it out, do you think?"

"Captain Logan," Orlov began, shaking off the American's grip, "I couldn't say, but if it's possible . . ." He shrugged. "The aliens have no reason to cooperate with the Nazis, whereas they have every reason to aid us."

"Self-preservation?"

"I'm willing to bet that the will to survive is a constant throughout the universe," Orlov said. "Should we believe an advanced society would not find the whole Nazi agenda reactionary—a step backwards?"

Logan looked out a glassless window. "If self-preservation is their goal, they might well decide that cooperating was best. Believe me, when you're their prisoner, it's hard to find any reason to resist." He stood with his hands braced on either side of the sill. Overhead, somewhere nearby, a plane passed. "And what if the Nazis already decided they weren't going to learn anything from the spacemen? What if they're already dead?"

That thought had apparently never occurred to Orlov, and Logan wondered how a man who knew so much could also know so little about the people he had spied on.

30 OCTOBER 1942
LONDON, ENGLAND

cotland Yard reached General Anthony only two hours after he had gotten to his room at the Diogenes Club. It was a matter of the gravest importance.

Aren't they all? he thought, trying to think how a man was supposed to survive on an hour's sleep.

He was merciful to Colonel Marston, however, and did not call him. A man picked him up in a Bentley and directed *his* man to drive across London to the area of St. Paul's Cathedral.

The man was obviously not an ordinary policeman. Anthony thought he recognized him. "You're with the Foreign Office, aren't you?"

The man reached up and closed the window between them and the driver. "He is a trustworthy man," he remarked, "but there is only so much he is supposed to know."

"Ah," said Anthony. "MI-5. You were at one of the meetings at Downing Street last month."

"Very good," he said. "I am afraid that what I have to show you isn't very pleasant."

"In what way?"

" 'In what way?' Why, corpses are rarely a source of mirth, and this one is not in very good condition."

"Is it one of my men?" Anthony asked.

"No, it isn't, and could never have been one of your men. It is, in fact, that of an elderly lady."

"That is why you got me out of bed?"

"We must assume it is relevant to our current activities in some way. We believe the body is that of Madame Katerina Orlov."

"Orlov? The scientist's mother?"

"Indeed."

Anthony shook his head. "Orlov isn't in England."

The man smiled. "No need to be coy—I know about all that. But yesterday the lady, the doctor's mother, was found dead in her flat. She had been dead at least three days. The fiend, whoever he was, cut the throat so deeply he nearly beheaded her."

"And you think Orlov did that?"

"Very possibly."

Anthony frowned. *"Why* would Orlov murder his mother?"

"We thought you might be able to help."

"What's the theory?"

"I quote Detective-Sergeant Strether: 'Does a man *need* a reason to murder his mum?' "

Anthony shrugged. "Okay, so murder *isn't* rational. Our mad scientist *is* a touch mad, as I'm certain you also know." The man nodded. "But did he fight with her, anything like that? Do you know something we don't know about his sanity?"

"If he used a knife in the flat, I am told, he must have washed it afterward." The man from British intelligence touched the general's arm. "I have been discreet with Scotland Yard about Dr. Orlov's whereabouts, by the way."

Joe Logan picked him up at this flat. Anthony thought. *And she was already dead by then. Maybe he met Orlov on the sidewalk.* "I only saw the woman on two occasions. Couldn't her neighbors identify her?"

"I thought you needed to know. In any case, she hardly ever left her flat."

"I *did* need to know; I just don't know what to do about it. It's hard to believe this would affect our activities."

"But perhaps it would be better for *someone* to know, if you catch my drift." The agent pointed at a row of buildings "We're coming up on the apartment."

Anthony squeezed the bridge of his nose. Men from outer space, Logan and his men missing, now Orlov's mother dead—this damned mission was becoming more and more complicated with each passing hour.

He glanced down at his uniform and watched the light of passing streetlamps glimmer along the edges of the medals pinned to his chest. Unbidden, Logan's accusatory question about them suddenly rang out from the depths of his mind.

How many would have to die *this* time? the general wondered darkly.

30 OCTOBER 1942 NEAR ST. NICOLAS, OCCUPIED FRANCE

It was the scream of a man dying, seeming to come from nowhere, from dreams, from memory, and yet, here, *now*. Logan snatched the helmet off his face and blinked against the daylight. Rhys Griffiths and Orlov and Doolin had jumped to their feet, grabbing their submachine guns and crawling to the nearest openings; for Logan, it was the collapsed altar wall. If anyone were to attack them, it would be through it.

"Do you see anything?" he asked.

The grasses undulated in an early afternoon breeze. Even the pigeons were silent.

"I think it was over here," said Rhys Griffiths by what once had been the church door. The men, except for Orlov, started to move in his direction.

"Hold your positions," said Logan.

"What was that?" asked Tom Swift.

Logan waved his hand that they be silent. He stared hard across the crumbling cemetery stones. James should have been out his way. Where was he?

"Ah," said McGonigle, "there's the bugger."

"What?" demanded Logan.

"A helmet."

"Be careful. Remember our guys are still out there."

Calm as if he were discussing what he'd like for dinner, the Scotsman said, "I believe I know a Jerry pot when I see one."

"Any sign of Griffiths?"

"No."

"A movement!" said Orlov.

"Carlson," said Logan, "help Orlov cover. Murray, get over here, and keep low. Where is Tyler?"

Tom Swift seemed momentarily confused by the use of his real name, but then crept up behind a chunk of the collapsed bell tower. "Tyler went out," he said.

There was a small copse of trees and brush out the altar end. The best spot, Logan guessed, to launch an assault.

"We're in a right pickle now," said Rhys Griffiths.

"They'll be moving up for position." They would probably send men in to take out the sentries. It was supposed to be quiet, but one of them had managed to scream. He guessed it wasn't Punchy. He'd recognize Punchy's gravelly voice anytime. Punchy was still out there. Or he wished he was. Maybe it meant they had already taken him out.

"There," said Carlson.

"Griffiths!" said Orlov. The Welshman was bobbing and weaving among the low walls and foundations of the crumbled village.

Orlov sprayed a burst of fire. Carlson shoved him and jerked the submachine gun away.

"You'll hit him!"

"It was for cover," said Orlov.

"Damn!" said Carlson. "I can't see him. I think he's down. I think you hit him, you idiot!"

As he shouted, a full machine gun popped up on top of a set of stone stairs. Orlov shoved Carlson out of the way just before it opened up, shattering stone around the window. Orlov landed on top of Carlson, who clawed the rotting leaves as if he wanted to dig through the stone floor under them.

"Are they coming? Are they coming?" Logan saw no one.

"No!"

"No, sir."

"I see movement," said McGonigle.

How many were there? Just a patrol? Lugging around an MG-34? They had to have a vehicle somewhere. Why didn't anyone hear it coming?

Because they knew they were there. They'd stopped their vehicle somewhere in the distance. Maybe it had been sitting the whole time Logan's squad had straggled in.

"Any idea how many?" asked Logan.

"Enough to do the job," said McGonigle.

"And there'll be more soon," said Logan.

"We've got to break out, then," said Orlov.

"You know they're all over. At least here we've got cover."

"They'll be ready soon," said Rhys Griffiths.

A single shot cracked in the copse, and the sniper's bullet grazed Logan's helmet, right by his ear. He rolled, and Tom Swift moved to help him.

"Stay back!" said Logan, spraying a quick burst at the trees.

Tom Swift barely made it back behind his cover when a bullet ricocheted off the edge of the stone. He bent as if hit, but was only picking a fleck of stone from his eye.

"We've got to break out," said McGonigle, "before others get here."

"You're right," Logan said, "but we might just be walking into their hands. Anybody know where Tyler is?"

"Taking a crap, he said," answered Griffiths. "If he's alive."

Logan was thinking they might be better off to surrender. The odds might be fifty-fifty that they'd end up as prisoners, which were better odds than if they fought. Of course, they might be tortured for a long while and then killed. That was the nag he'd bet on.

Logan knew what torture was, and they weren't going to do that to him again.

"Okay," said Logan, "we'll break out through the cemetery. We can use the stones and tombs as cover. We just go as fast as we can and then reassemble on the other side of the stream back there." The trick was getting them all out of the main church door as quickly as possible and scattering among the graves. It would be much better to charge out through the collapsed alter wall, but that would mean right into the face of whoever was concealed in the trees beyond. "I'll be last and I'll order you out either left or right at random. That will confuse—"

"Take a gander," said Carlson. "I think the reinforcements are here."

Logan, after checking that Tom Swift was watching the treeline, scurried across the church to Carlson and Orlov's window. To the left, half hidden by a tall hedge and a bend in the road, was an open truck. A German officer stood in the rear looking at them through binoculars. He ordered someone with a gesture of his arm and stepped behind the armor protecting a double two-centimeter Flak antiaircraft gun.

"Damn!" said Logan.

"They're coming!" shouted Griffiths.

Out the front door, there were momentary glimpses of helmets among the graves. The Krauts had the same idea: use the stones and tombs as cover.

"How many?"

"Half a dozen. Maybe more."

"Watch for potato mashers. And the rest of you hold your positions. It could be a diversion."

The Germans suddenly popped up and charged, pouring bullets into the door opening. Tom Swift dove to the ground, ducking the bullets that cleared the door behind him. Griffiths made a quick spray without looking and the Germans dropped behind the stones. They were close enough to fling their "potato mashers"—slang for long-handled grenades—now. There were two *plinks* as a pair struck on each side of the old doorway.

"Grenades!" shouted Griffiths, diving away from the opening.

In rapid succession, each exploded. As the shock of the sound receded into a slight ringing, Logan heard a shout from the Germans and they began their full charge, about ten of them weaving among the tombs.

Griffiths, still stunned by the concussion, crawled back toward the door to fire, when suddenly a figure stepped out from the collapsed door of an old tomb, submachine gun blazing. Krauts dropped, unaware that Punchy was behind them. When the four who were left turned, Punchy got the two to his left, just as the two to his right opened up.

But Griffiths had also opened up and the last two went down. Punchy felt back into the old tomb, just as rifle fire *ping*ed around the opening.

"Is he hit?" yelled Logan.

"I don't know," said Griffiths. "Pawlowski! Pawlowski!"

There was no answer.

"Oh, shit!" said Carlson, looking out his window.

"The gun?" asked Logan.

"They're lowering it," said Orlov.

"Get back!" shouted Logan, but Orlov was already moving. Carlson, a step behind him, had barely made it two steps when the Flak gun fired both barrels, punching twin holes in the wall.

"Stay down!" screamed Logan. "Stay down!"

The Flak now opened up firing over 100 rounds per minute. It took only a dozen seconds to turn the wall into Swiss cheese, though it seemed like a century. When the burst of fire abated, Logan lifted his head and heard the decaying roof creaking.

He looked toward McGonigle, whose hands were still on his head. His wide, white eyes nearly popped out of his head as he looked up.

"Out!" shouted Logan. "OUT!"

They all scrambled for the nearest exits, the wall beginning to sway. Logan flopped into the grass beyond the old altar wall. McGonigle broke for the door and chased Griffiths through it. The Germans, as if stunned by the swaying church, held their fire momentarily, then opened up on the soldiers dashing for cover.

The men fired up the hill and across the foundations and into the woods at their hidden enemies. They scrambled for whatever cover they could find and then, with a growl like a dying lion, the church roof collapsed, embracing the men in a great cloud of dust.

We're finished, Logan thought, running while still invisible in the cloud.

He saw the face of the SS Oberführer who had "questioned" him after Dieppe. He smelled the strange scent of spice in his cigarette and the cognac of his breath.

"They're not getting me alive," he said. "No!"

The dust cloud was suddenly gone and he was running as hard as he could toward the trees, waiting for the bullet to tear through his heart and lungs.

But the Flak opened up. Trees began to shatter in front of him, exploding in white splinters, breaking off and dropping. A man screamed and toppled from the branches. Other soldiers ran from the brush, one even dropping his rifle.

He rolled on the ground and the Flak spun and began to rip the earth at the top of the hill that overlooked the church.

What the hell? Logan thought.

A voice shouted, "*Hande hoch! Hande hoch!*" then something else Logan couldn't make out.

"Bloody hell!" McGonigle shouted. About half a dozen Wehrmacht dogfaces had popped up with raised hands.

Logan gingerly raised himself on his arms.

The German officer stood with a pistol shoved hard against his ear, shouting for his men to drop their arms and come in.

At the other end of the pistol, his knuckles white on the grip, was His Majesty's Madison James III.

Logan got up on one knee and shoved back his helmet. Tom Swift came up behind him.

"Thank you, Master James, Esquire," said Tom Swift.

"I guess that's why the Legion has a legend," said Logan.

30 OCTOBER 1942
THE FORBIDDEN ZONE

A cameraman and his assistant backed into the hanger. As Borck strode through the door with the Wehrmacht general Von Kerner behind him, the assistant directed a white-hot light at them.

"Stop there, please, sirs," said the cameraman politely. They paused for a moment to look up at the spacecraft.

"Would you mind pointing up at it, *Herr General*?" the cameraman asked.

"As you wish," said Von Kerner, who raised his arm and began to talk nonsense for the sake of the film. "I notice it is rounded at the top to allow more airflow and to reduce friction, this is very advanced, it is obvious—"

The cameraman's assistant turned off the light and they moved to set up to film Borck's attempt to reopen the door. Rakoczy was telling them where it had opened before.

"And this blob actually flies?" asked Von Kerner.

"The coastal battery knocked it out of the sky."

"So I was told, but what could make it fly? There are no visible engines, nothing. Perhaps it was simply being dropped. It was hit as it fell. It's some sort of glider."

"I have considered that," said Borck, "but the powers of these creatures must be unimaginable to us. They may have the power of mind over matter. They may be able to fly between the stars on the sheer power of their wills."

Von Kerner cocked another condescending eyebrow. "Indeed?" he said simply.

And you, thought Borck, *are the typical smear of goose grease unworthy to be called a German.*

Something of Borck's thought must have been apparent in his face. "Certainly," the general said apologetically, "it is impossible to know. I have heard of people who are capable of moving objects with their minds."

"Well, then, perhaps there is something to it."

"I'm sure," said the general.

"And here, too," said Borck, "is a machine capable of repairing its own damage. Look here. This is the area where the shell struck."

"I have seen the photographs." But there was a tone of skepticism in the general's voice, as if he thought the ship and all the events connected with it had been concocted to deceive Berlin. Borck suddenly understood. He had been too astonished by all of it to see that there might be many who disbelieved him. General Von Kerner had clearly come not to gain control of the device and the creature, but to prove it was all a hoax.

He chuckled to himself and Von Kerner eyed him. Von Kerner, thought Borck, was about to have his mind broadened.

"Yes," he said, "it can repair its own damage."

"And, if I may be so bold, General Von Kerner," interrupted Erstewald, "we have a theory about that."

"Oh?" said the general.

"Yes. Our analysis of the oil-like substance which coats the craft has a large silicon component. There is also the presence of certain metals: aluminum, magnesium, titanium—we have not completed a thorough analysis. It isn't like a piece of stone that we can knock off a chip and analyze it."

"And exactly how would this combination of substances repair themselves?" asked Von Kerner.

"This is where a leap of imagination comes in. It came to me just as I dozed off early this morning."

"Well?" asked Borck.

"On Earth, all life is based upon the element carbon, which has an atomic number of 6. Silicon, which has an atomic number of 14, is a non-metal like carbon, and is one of the most abundant elements on Earth. It lies just below carbon on the periodic chart and share certain chemical properties."

The general raised his head and looked down at the chemist.

"In essence, what I theorize," said Erstewald, eyebrows bobbing, "is that it is possible to use silicon as the building block of a life-form instead of carbon."

"The ship is alive?" asked the general. "That's absurd."

"Sir," said Erstewald, "is a non-living thing capable of repairing itself? No. Only living things can do that!"

Borck looked at the ship in wonder. "Of course!" he said.

"What nonsense!" said the general. He rapped the rim of the ship with his knuckles. "Did it flinch? Did it move?"

"But what if it is possible to combine living and nonliving things?" asked Erstewald. "To build a machine that is still a machine in many ways, but has a structure that is vital, that lives?"

"Next you'll be telling me about robots or golems!"

"No," said Erstewald, "neither robots nor fairy tales. Better than a robot, and real—very real."

"Imagine a soldier who cannot become a casualty," said Borck. "Imagine an army of them. Invincible."

Even the general seemed caught up in a vision of thousands of them massed on a battle line.

"The blood," said Erstewald. "You'll remember the blood. The hull absorbed the blood as if it were drinking it, eh?"

"It lives on blood?" The general backed away from the craft.

"No," said Erstewald, "but perhaps somehow it absorbs the proteins into its chemistry. That is possible, is it not? Perhaps in some sense it is nourishment."

They all looked at each other as if they had each had the same thought: *The war. The carnage. It came to Earth to find blood.*

Rakoczy suddenly stepped into the huddle. "Gentlemen," he said, "I am reminded of the legend of the vampire. Is it possible that the aliens could have come before, sought blood, and inspired the legends of such creatures?"

Borck paced. He looked up at the craft. He remembered the caress of his scalp and the moment in which he had seen what the alien had seen in its cell.

Suddenly, he began to laugh. His laughter grew louder and stronger and echoed off the high stone ceiling. "Vampires?"

The other men watched him as if he were mad.

"Vampires? That is ridiculous!"

"How do you know?" asked Erstewald.

"Because I feel who they are," said Borck. He put a finger to his temple. "I know."

"Perhaps they can exercise something like possession," said the general.

"It may be true that the hull absorbs proteins. Or it may be that it simply disintegrates that which might taint its surface. But as to the creature's motivations, you know nothing." Borck pointed to his own head again. "I know," he said. "They are here to help us. They believe in the Third Reich!"

The intensity of what he had said seemed to freeze everyone. His eyes locked on the general's as if he could project into Von Kerner's mind his own faith. He felt Von Kerner coming under his sway, then the general broke the gaze and looked at Erstewald.

"Very well, then," Von Kerner said. "Open the door. Show us that they mean us no harm, or even that they mean us well."

Borck sneered, then lowered his head and closed his eyes. These fools! They were ciphers, insects, meaningless nothings that could not break his concentration. He had to be calm, to achieve the feeling he had felt when the door opened before. He took a deep breath and laid his hands on the hull.

A rippling like static electricity danced the hairs of his arms and rippled his scalp.

"My God!" said Erstewald, and the general crossed himself just as Borck turned toward him.

You are a Catholic, thought Borck. *That could be a weapon against you.* He grinned.

"There—There was a purple light dancing over you," said Von Kerner.

Erstewald struck the general's arm and pointed. Borck knew what he would see when he followed the direction of Erstewald's arm.

The porthole had opened again.

Borck raised his head, his eyes aglow like those of a lion who knows he has absolute dominion over his pride. The general shrunk back. Erstewald swallowed. The soldiers guarding the doorways shivered at Borck's stare. Who would Borck order into the craft? The craft with a guillotine port.

Borck laughed, and peered up at the opening.

He knew it would not close on him. The others might all think it would close. It had been his thought that one of the others had thought it to close before, but now he knew somehow it wasn't true. Their weak minds, their atrophied capacity to will, weren't equal to open or to close it. Perhaps when the unfortunate soldier had stuck his head in, he had been frightened and wished he wasn't there and the ship had responded, but it wasn't because of any-one else. Perhaps by being actually partly inside the craft, close to the heart of the ship, it had responded better to the soldier's thoughts.

He held his arms behind him and strode between the general and the chemist as if they did not exist. At the front of the truck, he stepped on the bumper and onto the hood, then onto the top of the cab.

He could see within the opening now. A strange, low cabin with no sharp edges, it might have been made of candle drippings or the damp walls of a calcite cavern. But the smell, something like the odor of rancid butter, rose out of the opening like a cloud.

Carefully, he stepped upon the slick surface of the hull, balanced himself, and moved toward the perfectly circular opening. He squatted next to the opening. The decapitated soldier's head lay on the floor still in its helmet, its now-green face and bulging eyes distorted by the surprise of sudden death. Next to it lay the sleeve of his uniform and part of the shoulder. It had been snipped off as cleanly as with a razor. The hand in the sleeve was nearly gone, reduced to its bones, which seemed to be melting into the floor.

He remembered Erstewald saying that they thought the material absorbed proteins. The head would have been rendered as well, except that the steel helmet had blocked direct contact between the flesh and the floor. Placing a handkerchief over his nose, he reached into the opening as Rakoczy gasped, "No, Oberführer!"

But the hole did not close. He knew it would not. He grabbed the helmet by the strap still buckled under the chin and lifted head and helmet out like the pail from a well. He held it up for a moment, then dropped it on the hull. The head rolled down as the men watching him scattered. It dropped off the edge and clanked onto the floor.

No one moved to pick it up.

Borck now took off his hat to get a better look inside. At first, the shapeless details of the interior might have been clots of cream swirling in coffee, but gradually Borck made out two indentations that looked like lidless, rounded coffins. The passengers of the craft would have lain in them, facing upward into the dome. Borck bent lower and looked up on the ceiling. A square area that might have been one huge topaz or grain of demerara sugar was directly above where the aliens would have rested their huge heads. Some kind of navigation screen? A window?

He ran his hand around the smooth edge of the opening. It was as solid and smooth as a polished chrome bumper. He glanced back at General Von Kerner and the scientists with a sneer.

"I'm going in," he said.

"Wait!" said Erstewald. "Don't!" But Borck had already swung his booted legs in.

He sat on the edge of the door for a second and slid in. The stench was still present—it seemed to come from the walls themselves—but his excitement drew him in.

There seemed to be nothing loose in the cabin. Everything was part of the walls and the walls were seamlessly united with the floors and the ceiling, which was very low. He saw nothing that resembled food or drink or the containers that might hold them. It was as if the creatures lay in the lidless coffins and hibernated through their long journey across space.

At the top of each coffin, however, he saw a twisted bluish tube. It looked like the umbilical cord of a newborn child. At its end, it branched out into a netting of similar smaller tubes. He shuffled forward and picked it up. At its un-netted end, the cord was attached to the top of the "coffin." The netting fell open as he lifted it. He spread it with his fingers, turning it. There was a flutter of light on the surface of the topaz-like square and a low humming sound. He moved his fingers and the light changed randomly. The hum shifted pitch in random ways.

He looked at it again and recognized that this was some sort of head gear. It would fit directly over the alien's head like a hair net on any *hausfrau*.

His heart pounded. "Yes!" There were no dials, no knobs, no handles. This was the only thing that could be a control for the craft. It was as he suspected.

They controlled the ship with their minds.

He hesitated, thinking of the possibilities, turned the strange netting in his hand. This was inconceivable technology, so far advanced that it could make a man no less powerful than a god. It was all so far beyond the mean state of human science in the twentieth century that it would take human beings hundreds, maybe thousands of years to reach this level.

But here it was. In Oberführer Werner Borck's hands. What was there that he could not do?

He heard the general calling out to him. "Oberführer Borck! Are you all right?"

He laughed. "I am splendid!" he shouted. "Incredible!" and he thought how their inferior minds were wondering what it was that he had found.

Slowly, hypnotically, he spread the netting. The aliens had huge heads. It wouldn't fit him at all. Nonetheless, he slowly raised it above him, like Napoleon crowning himself in the cathedral at Reims, and lowered it. Like a towel, it covered half his face and drooped to the back of his neck. He looked up at the screen, and saw the light playing on it begin to swirl and shift hue. It started out as a rainbow, then moved to black and a sky blue.

Snap!

All of the cords of the netting suddenly drew in and squeezed the top of his head like iron fingers. He fell at the shock of it, landing on the closest coffin, but not falling in because his torso was much larger than the aliens'. The pain was excruciating, so sharp he could only gasp, trying to breathe enough air to scream. He felt he was drowning, being crushed at the bottom of a black ocean of infinitely heavy liquid.

And then, suddenly, the pain dropped away from him so smoothly, so easily, that he felt he no longer needed air. He spun in a warm, sweet vortex of light, and his thoughts spun around him like beautiful specters.

This is what it feels like to be in the womb. This is what the dying must feel in their last moments. This is the becoming of pure mind, pure will, infinite and universal. I am now in the mind of the gods.

I *am a god.*

What was he seeing now?

Before him lay a plain, its soil olive-colored. A scattering of stones round and tan as peasant breads. He sailed over this surface for what seemed like dozens of kilometers. A thick ocean with sluggishly ebbing fluid appeared to his left and a boat with a circular sail slowly glided across it, though it seemed to have no pilot or passengers. Ahead of him, above the shore, a cluster of what might have been termite mounds appeared. As he came closer, they grew larger, until he recognized that they were at least a hundred meters high, with some of them rising to at least the height of a twenty-story building.

Close up, they looked more like giant candles which had guttered out after inundating their own flames with too much wax. Yet, there were openings in the sides of all of these mounds. Some of them opened and closed as the spacecraft's port did, and he had glimpses of the bulbous-headed, black-eyed, skinny-legged creatures who moved around in the tunnels. A small one pointed out at him with its spidery finger, but the others paid him no notice.

He swooped between the great structures, then landed on a balcony-like ledge before one of the largest openings. The thick liquid from the ocean was being pumped into a fountain at the center, and the creatures occasionally lowered their heads to bowls they dipped from it. As they did, their lips became tubelike and extended from their heads a good ten centimeters, and they sucked the liquid through them as if they were straws.

He passed beyond the fountain and the gathering area as their black eyes watched. He passed through a narrow tunnel which then opened into a great domed chamber. For a moment, he thought he was in the chamber to which he had brought the spacecraft, but then he saw that a tiny, unctuous white thing sat in a spoonlike chair. The other creatures rushed around attending to it, pouring bowls of liquid onto its grub-like body.

It had almost no arms, and no legs, but it had hands similar to those of the other creatures. Its head merged with its shoulders—there was no neck. Its eyes were no more than two black marbles, and a cluster of short undulating tentacles seemed to feel at the air.

What Borck felt upon looking at this entity, this strange larva-like being, was even stranger than its appearance. He felt it was wondrous, beautiful, perfect. It needed to be protected and nurtured and saved.

From what?

He remembered a hare. His hare. Soft and gentle. He had hidden it in his bedroom, caressing it and talking to it while his mother entertained the fat businessmen in the parlor below. He remembered the way the sores had sprouted on his mother's lips and face and how they had no money and she grew stranger and stranger and stranger and how one day she found his hare and wrung its neck and chopped off its head and cooked it screaming, "Stop crying! The Jews did this, not me! They have food while we starve!"

Borck was screaming, babbling. He was back in the spacecraft, the netting lying beside him. Somehow he had knocked it off in his mad thrashing.

He panted. He had wet himself, just as he had for many years as a child.

He had forgotten that. Just as he had forgotten the hare. His childhood had been a nightmare he had managed to grind out of his consciousness, piece by piece, with an enormous effort of will.

What had happened? Was he going mad as his mother had? When they took him away to the youth camp, they had saved his life, or rather, given him another. Why would the aliens throw this back at him?

And what had he seen? Was it a dream?

That grotesque creature being attended by the others, was it an infant? Somehow he knew it wasn't. It was the lord of the creatures, their leader.

No. That was wrong. It wasn't the only one. There were more, many more, in the chambers of the mounds.

How could he know that? The netting could have induced hallucinations that meant nothing, that brought out the painful memories. This could all have been a strange reaction, nothing from them and all from his own mind.

But what really stuck from all this was one incredibly powerful emotion he had felt, and he knew now why it had brought the hare up out of the hidden parts of his memory.

It was love.

He had felt nothing but absolute love from the strange creature in its chair. It was the protective, nurturing, mother-love that a good woman feels when her child nurses at her breast.

He wiped the copious sweat from his face and looked up.

The spacecraft port had closed above him.

30 OCTOBER 1942 NEAR ST. NICOLAS, OCCUPIED FRANCE

I ssus," said James.

"Issus," said Logan flatly.

"Huh?" said Punchy.

"Perhaps you'd care to explain that," said McGonigle.

James looked snide. "Perhaps the captain would."

"I'd love to," said Logan, "if I had any idea what the hell you were talking about."

"Alexander the Great," said James. "He was outnumbered, so he simply went straight at the Persian King." He nudged the German officer with his pistol. "The Battle of Issus."

Logan glared at him. James had saved their bacon, but he still wanted to punch out the son-of-a-bitch for going off on his own. "Good work," he said instead.

"*Merci, mon capitaine*," said James.

They were standing beside the truck, the German officer in the middle looking less like their prisoner than a tin soldier about to go on parade.

"Did you radio our position?" Logan asked.

"That was not necessary," said the officer.

"There is no radio," said Punchy.

"How many men?" Logan demanded.

"I don't believe I am required to answer that," said the German.

Logan pulled his bayonet and began cleaning his thumbnail. "How many?"

"*Zwanzig*," said the officer.

Punchy pointed to a German soldier rocking and holding his bloody leg. "That matches to what the sergeant over there said."

"Can we account for them all?" asked Logan.

"Eight dead, sir," said McGonigle, "and seven prisoners."

"That leaves a lot of them running around the countryside," said Logan.

"We may have missed a couple of bodies in the woods," said McGonigle.

"Five?" asked Logan, shaking his head.

They all jumped when a bush suddenly moved aside and Rhys Griffiths returned from the nearby ravine, where a half-dozen Resistance fighters had been tied up.

"Don't sneak up like that!" said Punchy.

"I wasn't bloody sneaking." The Frenchmen followed him into the open. Several of them had bleeding wrists from their ropes. A weathered man with a droopy mustache stepped forward and said something to Logan in French, shaking his hand.

"He's grateful," said James.

"I know. How did the Germans get them?" Logan asked. "*Comment les Boschs*, ah, *vous . . . ?*"

James cut in and asked for him.

"They were waiting for us," said the man in English. "We were betrayed. The pigs captured us and then waited for you."

Logan turned on the German officer. "How did you know?"

"*Ich spreche nichts—*"

"Bull!" said Logan. "How did you know?"

The officer looked at him, at James, and then the Resistance man. "I was ordered here. I follow orders."

"How did you know we would be here?"

The officer showed no fear. "I was not told."

"They were waiting for us," said the Frenchman.

"As we were ordered," said the officer.

"Why would a Flak group be ordered to do this?" demanded Logan.

"I do not question my superiors," said the officer. "Perhaps we were available."

Suddenly, the Frenchman snatched Logan's Colt from its holster. Logan spun, but it was already gone. The Frenchman leveled it at the officer. *"Cochon!"* he growled.

"Wait!" shouted the German, but the pistol fired three times. Logan reached out to grab back his gun, and McGonigle leveled the Frenchman with a stiff forearm to the chin.

The officer lay on the gravel next to the truck, his shoulder supported by Punchy. He looked at the Frenchman. His eyes widened as he saw death approaching, and he tried to raise his arms. He vomited blood and died.

"Son-of-a-bitch!" said Logan. "Why did you do that?"

The Frenchman's eyes were still rolling in his head from McGonigle's blow. Logan picked up his .45. The Frenchman sat up and sucked air. "He wouldn't have talked," he gasped.

"I don't think he knew anything," said Punchy. He gently lay the officer back. One of the other Resistance fighters stepped forward and kicked the dead officer.

Logan reached down and grabbed the still-gasping Frenchman. "Listen, you son-of-a-bitch, you don't do a goddamned thing without my permission, have you got that?"

"C'est ma patrie!" said the Frenchman coolly.

"Well, it might be your damned country, but this is *my* damned mission!" Logan said. *And what a fine mission it is turning out to be!* he thought. He shoved the Frenchman back, as if touching him had dirtied his hands. *If they knew we were coming and where, they know where we're going and why.*

McGonigle moved up beside him and spoke so that the others couldn't hear. "A shilling for your thoughts, sir."

"The price has gone up, Sergeant-Major, and they weren't worth a penny in the first place."

"If I may be so bold, sir, from what I know, Dieppe was a different thing all together."

"It was a SNAFU, like this."

" 'Situation Normal, All Fouled Up'—is that what you mean, sir? You see, sir, I know something of the Americans. You got out of Dieppe and you can get us out of this."

"Is this what a sergeant-major does—play Knute Rockne?" McGonigle blinked. "Give pep talks. Rah, rah, win one for the Gipper."

"Maybe I don't know as much about the Americans as I thought," said McGonigle, "but I do know this: we cannot extract ourselves from this mission."

Logan looked deep into McGonigle's green eyes. "I know that, too, if that's what was worrying you. How many have we got?"

"Cosgrove—"

"Was the one who cried out."

"They near gutted him, sir,"

Logan winced. "I asked how many are left."

"James, myself, Rhys Griffiths, Sergeant Pawlowski, Corporal Doolin, Carlson. He was nicked on the forearm, but it is superficial."

"Tyler's knee is shattered."

"Yes. And John Griffiths—"

"I know," said Logan. They had strangled him with a wire. "All right, then, we're about half now. If we take the Resistance men, we'll have a baker's dozen."

"They're all rather old, sir. We'll be lucky if they're veterans of the Great War."

Logan nodded. "We've got to get moving. Strip the German prisoners and tie them up in the church."

The Frenchman suddenly stood. "I am sorry, Captain. What the Bosch have done . . . I lost my head."

"You can only win this war by thinking, Mister," said Logan. "Now, are you with us or not?"

"To hell, if necessary."

"It may be necessary."

The Frenchman tugged his droopy mustache. "That is why we are here."

"What's your name?" Logan asked.

The man shook his head. "We use codenames. I am Jaune."

" 'Joan'?"

The man chuckled. "Jaune—it means 'yellow.' That way, by using codenames, even if one of us is caught, he cannot reveal what—or who—he knows."

Logan nodded—it made sense. "Get all your men up here. They've got to know the score and they've got to decide immediately. If they want to go home, they can. The Germans know we're here and I figure they know why. Our chances of succeeding are minuscule, but we've got to go ahead or it might mean the war is over and the Third Reich has won."

"It is that important?" asked Jaune.

"Yes. I can't explain until later." He suddenly thought of Orlov. "Say," said Logan to McGonigle, "where's Orlov?"

McGonigle looked around. "I don't know. Is he still in the church?"

"Damn!" said Logan. "I hope he wasn't hit. We don't know a damned thing about the place without him!"

"We'll find him," said McGonigle. "Griffiths! Carlson! Where's Orlov?" When they shrugged, he sent them back into the ruined village.

"And make it snappy!" said Logan. He looked back at Jaune, who was already explaining the situation to his men.

One man bit his lip and shrugged. Another stared at the ground. They exchanged a few words. Logan noticed their rifles: two carried German weapons, two others had World War I vintage rifles, while another had a French MAS. Not a helluva lot of good against a German tank—or a well-armed platoon, for that matter—but sometimes beggars couldn't be choosers.

"We are with you," said Jaune. "I can get more men, but it will take some time."

"We can't wait," said Logan.

He pointed vaguely toward his men. "And l'Oiseau would like to send a message to his wife."

"No message," said Logan.

"I can be back in an hour with a dozen men."

"No," snapped Logan. "You should have brought them in the first place." Logan whistled. "Listen up, and spread the word. Everybody get themselves into a German uniform, pronto. We're going to take the truck and drive like hell. Maybe we'll be able to get there before the escaped Krauts get the word out that they didn't get us."

"Uh, sir," said Doolin, "if we're caught in enemy uniforms—"

"They'll shoot us immediately," said Logan.

"Exactly," said Doolin.

"And you have some point to this comment, Corporal?" asked McGonigle.

"I suppose not," said Doolin.

"They'll shoot us anyway," said Punchy.

"So let's not get caught," said Logan.

"Do you want me to send a message to London?" asked Doolin.

Logan thought for a second. What would he say? That they were six men down and counting? "No," he finally said. "The Krauts might triangulate it. We want them to think we've been caught."

Besides, he thought, *something's leaking somewhere, and it might even be in General Anthony's office.*

Jaune stepped forward. "We have a secret radio in a farm just over there."

"Don't worry about it," said Logan. "What can London do for us? We're on our own now."

James returned from the woods. He drew his thumb across his throat. "I found one of the runaways."

"You killed him?"

"He annoyed me." He cocked an eyebrow. "I assume you are promoting me to officer."

"Why? Because you're Alexander the Great?"

"No, because my German is impeccable."

"Battlefield commission, *mein herr*?" Logan asked.

James smiled broadly. "Just call me *'Führer.'*"

Logan lit a cigarette. "You did okay today, James."

"Personally," said James, "I preferred Pawlowski's move. I wish they had seen him as he came out of the tomb behind them. It seems a shame they died without knowing how they had been outfoxed."

"You are too kind," said Punchy, waving his hand and bowing at the waist.

James bowed his head and headed toward the fallen German officer.

"Hey," said Logan, "I doubt he gives many compliments."

"Ahn, he's just playing the gent. Oh-so-modest when he's anything but."

"Still . . ." said Logan. He found himself a broad-shouldered corporal who had been killed by a shot through the eye. There was blood on his collar, but it had dried already, and the buttons of the tunic strained against his breathing. These uniforms would only hold up as disguises if nobody got a good look at them. The Germans were smaller on average than Logan's men, and the bullet holes and bloodstains on half of the uniforms might as well be Confederate battle flags.

He saw Carlson returning. "Orlov?" he asked.

Carlson shook his head. "Griffiths is up there on the other side of the church. His body could be in the high grass."

"Get yourself a uniform, or at least an overcoat and a helmet. Can you drive that thing like a bat out of hell?"

"Has it got a motor?" smirked Carlson.

Logan looked around at his men. They looked like anything but the efficient soldiers of the Third Reich. They couldn't fasten their collars, their sleeves were a good inch or two short, and on Punchy, McGonigle, and Doolin the fabric on their backs seemed ready to explode. Only the Frenchmen fit in the uniforms, but they had been on a diet ever since the Germans rolled in.

"Is Griffiths back?" he asked McGonigle.

"No, sir."

"Whistle him in, then. We've got to get out of here."

"I don't see how we're all going to fit in the truck," said Doolin.

"We'll have to," said Logan. "If we have to straddle the Flak gun."

"And the prisoners?"

"We'll leave them tied."

"They'll get loose," said Jaune. "Perhaps we could dispose of them for you?"

Logan knew what the Germans would have done to them—after a long torture session—but he still shook his head.

"It would be a pleasure," said Jaune.

"Forget about it," said Logan. "We've got to get to the Forbidden Zone."

"Pardón?"

"The Forbidden Zone."

"But that is to the south."

"What else can you tell us about it?"

Jaune spread his hands. "But the mission is the fuel dump at St. Nicolas. To the north."

"Nope."

"But we were told that you—"

"You were told *wrong*," Logan said stiffly. "The mission is the Forbidden Zone."

Jaune thought for a second. "Then I must contact Levrier. I understood him quite clearly that the fuel dump—"

"Find a way to get into the truck and find something to hold onto," Logan snapped. "It's going to be a rough ride."

"But, Captain, the Forbidden Zone is like a fortress," said Jaune. "We cannot possibly—"

"Clam up," said Logan, "and get into the truck. You want to live forever or something?"

Jaune glanced at his men, then did as he was told.

With Punchy's assistance, Tyler lurched up, using a twisted branch as a crutch. His narrow face was soaked with sweat, and his entire calf and shin were soaked in blood.

"He's got his mind set," said Punchy. "I told him we'd have to leave him."

"I can still take down a fly at a hundred yards," said Tyler. "And I don't need legs to kick your ass, if'n you don't sucker-punch me."

Logan turned to McGonigle. He was about to ask the sergeant-major what he thought. Tyler, however, was pale, could barely stand—couldn't, actually, without Punchy under his armpit. "This is going to be a rough ride," said Logan. "We haven't got any morphine . . ."

"You call this pain?" said Tyler. "My momma gave me worse whippin's."

"You shouldn't ask," said Punchy. "You know what the situation is. We could leave you with the Krauts in the church. Throw in the towel."

Logan could feel all of the men watching. "We'll put you on the floor. Maybe the Resistance can figure a way to hide you. But you endanger us and we won't have any choice."

Tyler smiled weakly. "You think I want to go with you, a son-of-a-bitch who sucker-punches? I'll guard those Heinies for you, then I'll meet you back in England and knock your head off."

"Put him in the truck," said Logan. "If we have to, we'll put our feet on him. But I'm not leaving anyone behind. Is Griffiths back yet?"

The Welshman came out of the trees, panting. "It's thick in the brush beyond the grass. I saw one of the Germans, then lost him. We could search for a week and not find Orlov's body. For that matter, I could have missed him in the grass."

"Damn," muttered Logan. "We'll be blind when we get there."

"*If* we get there," said McGonigle. He leaned close to Logan. "Tyler's still bleeding. It's slowed a bit, but—"

"I know," said Logan. "Let's roll."

30 OCTOBER 1942
NANTES, OCCUPIED FRANCE

The diversions were easy. The widow carried a large bundle out her front door and led the watcher in front to the nearest square, where she took a seat in the window of a café and slowly drank a large Pernod and water. As the sun dropped lower, she carried her bundle to the church of Saint Jacques du Forêt. They might even shove the priest aside as soon as she rounded the corner and search the bundle. They would find nothing but threadbare clothes, a pitted saucepan, and a cracked wooden crucifix.

This would all be duly recorded in a notebook and filed somewhere. Perhaps they would also record that the loyal bicycle shop owner across the street would report that he saw no one enter or leave her house while she was gone.

The diversion in the back of the house would go unrecorded. It would take a few francs for a young prostitute to entice the pimply Nazi into the potting shed, where she would entertain the boy for at least ten minutes—more than enough time for Flanne to enter the kitchen and remove Marcel.

No one could prove he had ever been there after that and the local constabulary, the Nazis, and their German masters would never even find out they had been fooled.

The satisfaction of all this gave Levrier a feeling like good cognac in the belly, and when it all succeeded as planned, it was like the best warm cognac Napoleon had ever drunk.

Levrier took Marcel to a farmhouse in the country, one that had been empty since the "Phony War," when its owner had leased it to Flanne and gone off to stare across the Maginot Line for an offense that never happened.

The boy looked pale and squinted constantly in the daylight. He had spent too much time in the dark and needed more food than the widow had been able to provide him. Flanne stole several chops from an order for the mayor, and managed to round up several parsnips, a carrot, and three potatoes. All this they set before the boy, and he dove into it as if he had never tasted such food.

Levrier watched, and poured him a glass of watered wine. "Don't choke yourself," he said.

The boy looked at him.

"Eat! Eat!" said Levrier. "You must be strong." He squeezed his fists into great hammers to demonstrate strength. "The future belongs to you. You must be prepared for the struggle, eh?"

"God—" Marcel swallowed "—will provide."

Levrier rolled his eyes and opened his palms. "What has God to do with it?" he muttered. "All this talk of God! Who hid you? Who got you out of the house when the Nazis were watching it all day and night? It wasn't God. It was me."

The boy studied him for a moment, then began to chaw on a bone.

"Listen," said Levrier, "do you know what we say in the party? We say 'religion is the opiate of the people.' Eh? Do you understand that? It means that religion keeps you from demanding what is rightfully yours. How can you build a great future for France, for the world, if you put yourself under the thumb of the priests. They are all capitalist tools!"

"We are all in God's hands," said Marcel.

Levrier rolled his eyes again. "Aah!" he said, and poured himself a large glass of wine. He took a large swallow as the boy stuffed a potato in his mouth. "Where did you hide in madame's?"

The boy chewed. "In the attic."

"But where in the attic?"

"At the end behind the false wall."

"And when the flicks came?"

"I was there."

"But they looked in there. You were not there."

"I was."

The boy was much too calm, thought Levrier. He's either mad or a simpleton. "And I suppose you are going to tell me that God made you invisible."

"I prayed to Joan of Arc. It was a miracle."

"You've convinced the widow, but she is an old woman. She is probably losing it." Levrier tapped his forehead. "She never was very bright—her husband told me. She said that glass thing on your arm turned to dust. What nonsense!"

"It wasn't nonsense," said the boy, sucking at his teeth. "It was a miracle. I was healed."

The boy sat back and belched. A fly couldn't have found sustenance on the scoured bones on his plate.

"All right, then, you're healed. You can't unheal yourself, but you can make yourself invisible. How about right now. Eh?"

"Why?"

"To prove that you can."

Marcel shook his head. "It is only when God wishes it that it comes to pass."

"Well, why not now? If you do it, I will give up women. I'll be a monk."

The boy smiled. "You wouldn't do that."

"I'll take an oath." Levrier crossed his arms. "I still see you. Where is the miracle?"

The boy sighed. "God isn't a magician. He doesn't do tricks to amuse disbelievers."

"He changed water into wine. He pulled Lazarus out of the tomb."

"Those weren't tricks," said Marcel.

Again, the boy's calmness astonished Levrier. It isn't that hard to provoke a twelve-year-old, he thought. You question the truth of what they say or believe, and they protest, even explode. But this one . . .

Levrier chuckled. "You're right—I *wouldn't* give up women. I'm an old dog, set in my ways. But how can I believe you? You pray and turn invisible? Is that why the Germans wanted you so badly? Why don't you tell me that? Never mind the invisibility nonsense."

"They wanted me because I was visited by the angel."

Levrier threw up his hands, stood, and took another hard swallow of wine. "They killed your grandparents. They probably wanted to kill you, but why? Not that they need an excuse, but—"

When he turned back to the boy, Marcel's face had twisted as he tried to hold back his emotions. He covered his face with his hands and fell forward on the table, sobbing.

"I'm sorry," said Levrier. "I didn't mean to . . ." He threw up his hands again. *Why me?* He stared down at the boy's tousled hair for a second and listened to his whimpers. He touched the back of his neck and squeezed his shoulder. "I'll be outside," he said. "Cry it all out, eh?"

He stepped out of the farmhouse and wished he had some tobacco for his pipe.

Rain drizzled in a fine mist. He turned up his collar and walked across to the shelter of the roof over the well pump. There was a wide view of the countryside here. Why was he spending so much time trying to make sense of what a farmboy said? He didn't seem to be an idiot, the boy, but with no education, perhaps he wasn't all there. So why had the Germans searched so hard for him? When that German soldier was murdered in Cholet, they had searched for the killer for only a few days, then picked out ten citizens at random and shot them. The reward for the killer was only half of what they offered for the boy. What did they think Marcel knew?

He heard Flanne's rattletrap motorcycle coughing along the road to the farm. Flanne had hooked an enclosed cart behind it. Many people joked that it looked like a gypsy wagon. It bobbed and rolled up the country lane like it was about to topple over. Flanne turned off the rumbling engine and pulled off his goggles.

"Well?" asked Levrier. "Have they contacted us?"

"Nothing," said Flanne.

"They're caught."

"No one has heard anything. If they took them prisoner, they may have sent them directly into Germany, but there is no sign of that in the rail stations."

"Perhaps Jaune walked into a trap."

"They have disappeared."

Levrier hmmmphed. "Maybe they are invisible, too."

"We have to assume the Bosch have them. Jaune knows you, doesn't he? Will he talk?"

"They all talk, eventually. Maybe, if we're lucky, they merely shot them all."

Flanne snapped his goggles into his jacket pocket.

"I didn't mean that the way it sounded."

"I know. If they've got them, it's better that they are not around to talk."

Levrier shook his head. "Damn! Nothing from London?"

"Nothing. And the fuel dump—nothing about it. There's a rumor the Bosch may be getting ready to move it."

"We'll have to see if that's true, then maybe we do some damage on the roads." Levrier clenched his fists. "A squad of paratroopers just can't vanish."

"Maybe they are in hiding. The attack may take place yet."

"What are they waiting for?" Levrier shook his head. "No, we have to assume they are taken. Let's try to contact London again tonight, a triple, switching off every five minutes."

"A triple?" asked Flanne. To do this required that three different radios attempt the same message in carefully timed relays. If the signal was located from one radio, suddenly the trackers would find the signal they were honing in on had moved. They would think they were dealing with radio signals bouncing weirdly off the stratosphere.

"And we want to know if London knows anything about our boy here. We have to find out what is going on. Our whole organization may be finished, for all I know."

Flanne reached into a jacket pocket and pulled out a folded sheet of paper. "This came, as well."

Levrier opened the paper. The coded message was written out by Flanne to resemble a listing of account numbers, with amounts next to each. "It's probably another cheerful speech about German casualties at Stalingrad." Something about it caught his eye. "It's very short though, isn't it?"

"I noticed," said Flanne.

Levrier thought about going back inside, but stepped back further under the roof and sat down. He took an empty tobacco pouch from his coat pocket, and with his fingernail opened a seam hidden under the flap. He took out a folded piece of paper with a table of numbers and letters on it. "What is the date?" he asked, then ran his finger down the side of the table and began translating. He paused, confused. He wasn't sure he was correct. He took a short pencil from his pocket and scribbled it down.

"How can this be?" he said.

Flanne twisted his head to look over his shoulder, but Levrier brought the paper in close to his chest.

"They want us to give all assistance to an operative, codename *Revolutsiya.*"

"A spy?"

"A saboteur or something." Levrier re-read the message. "We are 'to render maximum military assistance.' "

"Are we supposed to fight this entire war ourselves?" Flanne asked. "What about our Allies? They've got the weapons. We've only got what we can steal. Where is the French air force? Where is the French navy? We've just lost how many men helping the Americans?"

"Is this the same operation? How important can a fuel dump be?"

Levrier held up his translation. "World revolution is at hand, they say, as if we fight only for slogans. Russians! No style. Comrades or not, no style."

"How will this *Revolutsiya* contact you?"

"In the usual way, I suppose," Levrier commented.

And then an idea struck him.

It isn't the fuel dump, he realized. It's got to be the Forbidden Zone. All that strange activity there. Maybe the Americans are going after the fuel dump as a diversion for *Revolutsiya*'s sabotage in the Forbidden Zone. Finally, the Allies working together! He folded up the code table and stuck it in his tobacco pouch. He lit the message and watched it burn to his fingertips.

He slapped his thighs. "We are going to win this war," he said, "and afterwards build a new France."

Flanne seemed amused by his enthusiasm. "With our St. Joan in there?"

"He may be a lunatic, but he knows *something*—probably something not even he knows he knows. And my guess is that it has something to do with the Forbidden Zone."

"They are building special bombs there, that's what everyone says."

"Or maybe rockets. What I know is this: There is a great explosion in the night, the boy is chased, and at exactly the same time the Bosch begin even tighter security there. Within a few days, all of these operations are started that require our help."

"It is all related."

"Exactly!" said Levrier. "Let's get him to talk more about the angel. Then we'll try to make sense of it. We shouldn't be running around the countryside exposing our backsides to the Germans without knowing why, eh?"

Flanne nodded. They hurried through the mist to the farmhouse. Levrier opened the door and looked in. The room was empty.

"He isn't here," said Levrier. "Did you see him come out?"

Flanne spun his head, searching the farmyard. "He didn't come out."

"There's no window, no door . . ." He pulled back the curtain on the pantry. Spiderwebs. Dust. "Look around back," said Levrier. "He must be—"

He froze at the chalky expression on Flanne's face, and turned to follow his stare.

He didn't see it at first, then, gradually, a cloud began to form by the rusty stove. It was yellowish, misty, then solidified in the center into a metal ball with petals like a flower and colors swirling above it. As quick as the puff of a servant blowing out a candle, the mist dispersed and Marcel appeared. He was holding the metal ball in his cupped hands, his face serene.

Marcel opened his eyes, and Levrier's heart almost stopped.

"Now you will help God," said Marcel. "We shall raise an army and free France."

Flanne gulped and clutched the door lintel. Levrier sagged into a chair, panting. He blinked and looked at the boy, blinked and looked at him again.

"No women," he whispered. "It's a pity. I shall miss them."

30 OCTOBER 1942
SCOTLAND YARD
LONDON, ENGLAND

Stepping up to the autopsy table, Detective-Sergeant Strether said, "Brace yourself, sir. It won't be pleasant."

"Get on with it," snapped General Anthony. He had seen a lot of death in his career and did not expect this to be anything other than routine.

But it wasn't.

When the detective threw back the rubber sheet, the stench billowed up against the general's face like a wave crashing over him. Colonel Marston backed against the wall, eyes wide. The general turned away, gasping. "Good Lord!" he said.

"I'm sorry, sir," said Strether. "A bit ripe, you see. They don't float for a few days, I'm afraid."

Anthony covered his nose and mouth with a handkerchief.

The head was an anonymous white bundle, resembling a ball of rags dipped in lard. There were no nose or ears that the general could distinguish. The lips were gone and the yellowish teeth grimaced sardonically. On the side of the head, a tuft of hair had somehow remained intact. Where the eyes should have been were twin holes; inside one of them, something squirmed.

"The eels have been at 'im," said Strether.

"Christ!" said Anthony. "I didn't know anything could live in the Thames."

"Nothing you'd want to eat, sir."

Marston lowered his head, staggered to a stool, and sat.

"Please," said Strether, "I know 'e's not at 'is best."

"Well, Happy Halloween, Detective!" Anthony held his breath and looked again. He circled the end of the table and looked from the other side. He turned away. "Can't you do fingerprints or something? How am I supposed to identify *that?*"

"The fingertips are gone as well, except for a thumb, but even so, there are no records for 'im, unless you 'ave some."

"Well, it can't be Orlov," said Anthony. "I happen to know where Orlov is, and this can't be him."

Strether raised an eyebrow. "Excuse me, sir, did I 'ear you correctly? You know the whereabouts of Dr. Orlov?"

"This is a military secret, Detective, and not even what I tell you now can be repeated to anyone. Dr. Orlov is doing something for MI-5 and the O.S.S."

"Vassily Orlov is the only suspect in 'is mum's murder, sir."

"I know, but I couldn't tell you all I knew."

Strether glared at him, eyes narrowing. "You are interfering with the progress of a murder investigation, I remind you. That's a most serious matter."

Anthony matched his hard stare. "Look, Detective, it is *possible* that Orlov killed his mother. He was here in London at the time her throat was slit. But *my* impression was that he was devoted to the old woman. And I *know* that he has not been in London since within only a day of the woman's death."

"I must insist that you inform me completely about 'is whereabouts, sir," Strether said firmly.

"I can't do anything about that now."

"We'll be needing to clear this up. Can you take me to 'im?"

Anthony shook his head. "I cannot contact him in *any* way. Detective, I am thoroughly convinced that you are utterly trustworthy, but now I am going to ask you to trust *me*. I promise you that I will bring Orlov to you at the first opportunity. But I cannot do so now."

Strether rocked back on his heels. "I'll need more than your word, I'm afraid, sir. Nothing personal, you understand."

"Of course. I'll have MI-5 call you. The Prime Minister, if you like."

Strether stopped rocking. "Ahh, no need to trouble Mr. Churchill, sir."

"He's quite interested in Dr. Orlov, Detective. I promise you."

Strether nodded, obviously trying to put all this together. He couldn't help wanting to know the full story, Anthony knew. He was a policeman by instinct and by nature. "So, you assert this is not Dr. Orlov, then?"

"It cannot be, despite the evidence to the contrary."

"You mean . . . ?"

"The clothes," said Anthony. "That appears to be the suit he was wearing when last I saw him."

"There are what we believe to be French laundry marks, with what you call the *accent grave*, and the circumflex accent as well. Now it could be that this gent 'ere stole the clothes, or acquired them from the killer, I suppose. But isn't it more likely that Orlov drowned 'imself in the river out of despair over murdering 'is mum? That's fairly common in these matters."

"But that can't be Orlov," insisted Anthony.

"Well, it isn't what 'appened in this case, unless he shot 'imself and fell into the Thames."

"He's shot?"

"Through the 'eart and out the back."

Anthony shook his head. "Well, maybe he's the murderer, but he can't be Orlov. Maybe he was overcome by guilt and did himself in."

"What about a brother? Did Orlov have one, as far as you know? This gent 'ere is about the same build, am I correct?"

"Height. Weight. Yes, I'd say so, but why a brother?"

Strether reached in his pocket. "This." He held up a brass key. "It opens the flat. It was in the watch pocket of 'is trousers. It was all that was in any of the pockets."

Anthony walked toward the door. "I can't help you," he said. "I wish you luck. It seems a case for Sherlock Holmes."

He glanced back at the lump under the rubberized sheet. It was the right height and weight to be Orlov. It could have been him, but the pilot and crew were quite clear that he had been aboard and that he jumped with the rest. The initial message had indicated he had landed with Logan as well. A twin?

"We've had worse," said Stretcher, "and we got our man most often."

Marston opened the door and the general stepped out. There hadn't been a message from Logan since the initial landing, and nothing from the Resistance. He told himself that this wasn't unusual, given the circumstances, but all of this was getting too strange for him.

As if a mission to destroy an alien spacecraft wasn't strange enough!

30 OCTOBER 1942
THE FORBIDDEN ZONE

Borck examined the smooth surface where the door had been. It was utterly seamless, smooth as the outer hull, but on the inside it looked like polished stone, with opaline seams running through it.

What was the source of the light? he suddenly thought. He could see perfectly, but there was no single source. It was as if the light came from within the walls.

Above him, the viewing screen flickered, then revealed the panic outside. Erstewald and Rakoczy were arguing. General Von Kerner was pacing as the other scientists shouted and pointed at the closed spacecraft.

Borck laughed. The idiots! Maybe he should put the netting back on his head and fly the craft out over their stupid heads.

His memory of the strange creature the aliens had been serving flooded back. He remembered the reverence, the feelings of love he had experienced for what should have been a disgusting, grub-like creature. He had felt what the aliens felt. He had seen their planet, their cities, their strange viscous ocean.

But he didn't really *know* any more than he had. That's what suddenly disturbed him.

What was the ship made of?

How was it made?

What propelled it?

How did one pilot it?

The emotions and the memories—somehow those had been communicated, but it was their technology that mattered. How could he use their emotions, or the vision of some planet in some distant galaxy? He needed their science, their chemistry, their engineering in order to rule the world.

And, oh yes, he thought, *with such power I could serve the Führer—or become the Führer. Whichever makes the most sense.*

Borck closed his eyes, recapturing the necessary feeling, and the port swirled open like the iris of an eye.

"He's alive!" shouted Von Kerner, as Borck raised himself through the opening. Smirking, the Oberführer stood in it for several seconds to let them remember the soldier who had been decapitated, and to see that he was not at all afraid that the door would slam shut on him, cutting his torso in half.

He then swung his leg over the edge and stepped out.

"What happened?" said Erstewald. "The ship rumbled, the purple lightning played all around it."

"We thought it was going to take-off!" shouted Rakoczy.

"And then we were trying to think if you had air," said the general.

Borck stepped onto the truck, across the hood, then down. He enjoyed this moment, their lack of control, and his own cocky calm. "I was as comfortable as a baby in a cradle. I have been in communication with our alien friends."

No one spoke.

"I have become the first ambassador to the stars."

"Excuse me?" asked Von Kerner.

"Please step aside," said Borck. "I am going to visit our guest."

"Oberführer!" said Von Kerner.

"If you behave, *Herr General*," said Borck, "you may live to have an important position in the Reich. If not . . ." He shrugged.

"What happened in there?" asked Erstewald, grabbing his sleeve.

Borck's icy stare was sufficient to make the scientist let go and back away. "Perhaps you'd like to investigate the interior yourself?"

Erstewald swallowed.

"I thought not. We have no need of cowardice in the new world we will be creating."

Borck raised an arm and the port slammed shut above him. He laughed at the way they cringed.

"Excuse me, gentlemen," he said.

Hands clasped behind his back, he walked toward the door leading to the cells deep within the mountain. The guard opened the door for him and gave the Hitler salute; surprisingly, the Oberführer refused to acknowledge it. There was an audible gasp. Borck stopped and, without turning, glanced over his shoulder. They were all watching him, mouths gaping, silenced by astonishment at his blatant disrespect for their glorious leader.

Borck grunted derisively. They weren't worth laughing at. He strode toward the spiral staircase leading to Area C.

The guard snapped to attention as Borck approached, and offered the keys.

"Open it for me," the Oberführer said.

"Yes, sir," he said, fumbling the keys into the lock of the outer cage. The door swung open with a creak.

"The inner one," said Borck.

The guard hesitated.

"The *inner* one. You've been looking in there, haven't you? Strictly against orders."

The guard blinked. "Yes, sir. I thought—"

"You *didn't* think. Well?"

"I'm sorry."

"No, did it speak to you?"

"It?" The guard shook his head. "No! How could that—?"

Borck laughed. "Open," he said. He felt a sudden surge of energy. He didn't know exactly what it was, but he knew that he should be here, as if he had heard a distant calling when he emerged from the spacecraft.

The guard nodded. His hands shook, but the lock clacked and the steel door swung open.

The creature was still on the cot, lying on its back as before, but its tunic was glowing brightly in green and blue.

And this time the creature slowly turned its head as Borck entered.

"Feeling better, I hope?" Borck asked.

The unblinking eyes stared up at him. Then, slowly, it lowered its feet to the floor, like an eighty-year-old man afraid that the floor will shatter his bones if he planted them too firmly.

Borck felt the bristling of his hair as if, once again, the creature was using its thoughts to read his own.

"We must come to understand each other," said Borck. "Your planet and the Third Reich will unite. We will restore the rightful order to the universe and cleanse it of sickness and depravity."

He did not really think that the creature could understand his words, but he thought perhaps the gist of its content would be transferred by his thinking it as he spoke. He closed his eyes and imagined the white, grub-like creature the aliens waited on. He imagined Adolf Hitler embracing this creature with an enormous smile.

He opened his eyes, and the alien stared back at him. Its slit of a mouth moved slightly, but there was no sound. The light from its tunic glowed brighter.

"I have been in your ship," he said, "and experienced your world. But you know this, don't you? You and I have a special bond. We are like an old married couple who can know exactly what the other thinks and feels."

The alien stared.

"Your arm, is it better? It does not seem quite as limp."

It still hung lax, but the alien was able to curl it upward slightly, as if it were carrying a small bundle.

"We have much to apologize for, so allow me to do so. Your

confinement here was at the advice of Dr. Vassily Orlov, one of the best biological researchers in the Third Reich. We were afraid, you see, that you might become infected with a human bacteria. He said that such things have caused terrible loss of life in the past, as when the Hawaiians became ill with the common cold. Unfortunately, Dr. Orlov went to Paris to get his equipment and never returned. We suspect foul play. There are some Frenchmen who might have kid-napped him. There is also the possibility that one of Stalin's agents killed him.

"And I shall admit, too, that we were, of course, somewhat fear-ful of you. You have arrived at what, for many, is a frightening time. Oh, not for those of us who see the future rising from the ashes, but for many. Perhaps this is why you came? Your planet knew of the greatness being restored here? Long ago, let me surmise, you came to Earth. It was the pure days that Nietzsche writes of, in antiquity, when you were called gods. And then Judaism and Christianity infected the planet, glorifying the weak at the expense of the strong.

"Your being shot was a mistake. That came from the times we live in, and the fear, of course. You should not have been injured and you, I'm sure, are too advanced to hold this action against us."

An idea struck the Oberführer. "If you wish, we shall punish the soldier who hurt you. I shall bring him here and execute him myself."

Borck waited for some kind of response.

The alien stared.

He felt the caressing of his scalp, but got nothing from it. "You are superior. Surely you have only to wish it and you can communi-cate with me."

The alien stared.

"You can transmit images into my brain. Fill me with your knowledge. I will provide you with anything you need, anything you want. Help me build ships that can repair themselves, that can open and close without seams. Teach me to fly the ship."

The light flittered across the tunic.

"Anything you want," Borck repeated. He closed his eyes and

concentrated. As he opened them, the black dots on the alien's clothing swarmed like flies on the tunic. They swirled like a galaxy, then formed the swastika.

"Yes!" said Borck and he suddenly remembered something. That stupid mess officer. The great milk robbery. As if it made sense to commit troops to scour the provinces for milk and fresh cheeses. Borck was going to dress down the mess officer for bothering him, tell him to change the locks, and make it clear that he wanted to hear no more about it. Now, suddenly, as his mind connected with the alien's, he knew what had happened to the milk.

"When we thought you were dead, on the advice of Dr. Orlov, we put you in the cooler to preserve your body. And then he left to get his instruments and we recognized that you were sleeping, hibernating to recover from your wound. You must have gone from that area of the cooler back to the food storage area. You drank the milk."

He looked at the tiny body before him.

A huge amount of milk! How? "Protein. The ship absorbs protein. Milk has protein. You sucked the cow dry in the old farm couple's barn. It is all clear to me now. Why didn't I see it before?"

Borck blinked. "You told me, didn't you? We *are* communicating." He rushed to the cell door and shoved it open. "Guard!"

The man cowered behind the outer bars, looking past Borck at the alien.

"I want you to go to the mess officer. I want you to tell him to bring all available milk to this cell."

"All?"

"Just do it. And cheese." He turned to the alien. "Meat? Do you eat meat. Meat is almost all protein. What else?"

He didn't get the sense that the creature was still communicating with him. Perhaps they didn't eat meat; their mouths didn't seem suited for it. Or perhaps flesh harbored materials that were toxic to them.

"Tell the lieutenant to bring a good chunk of meat as well. Any kind."

"Yes, sir," said the guard uncertainly.

"Go!" said Borck. "I'll spend some time alone with my new friend." He turned back to the alien. "I feed you and then you shall feed my mind. I want to know it all. I want to know everything, my friend. I *will* know everything."

The alien stared, unblinking, and Borck felt the fingers of its thought caressing his scalp. He remembered again his pet hare. It seemed odd a superior being would not eat meat. The true *Übermensch* would do anything to survive, regardless of sentiment. He should not be affected by the weaknesses encouraged by a degenerate society.

That's what Borck's mother had done to encourage his sense of superiority—fed him his pet. But he despised her for it, and he felt weak and foolish for feeling sorry for the hare.

He could not allow the strange warmth he felt while communicating with the alien—something like an affection planted in his brain by the contact—to slow him in meeting his objective.

It was what any *other* superior being would do.

30 OCTOBER 1942
OCCUPIED FRANCE

arlson lived up to his reputation as a lunatic driver. The truck had difficulty taking hills and was too heavy to control well on gravel and dirt. Nonetheless, he took every curve as if he were trying to fling the men off their precarious perches around the anti-aircraft gun and, when the road dropped down in front of them, he threw the truck forward like he was pitching it off a cliff.

Playing the Wehrmacht officer, James prominently stood just behind the truck cab, wearing goggles and covering the bloody bullet holes in the uniform by draping a coat over his shoulder. Carlson nearly blasted a motorcycle driver off the road, but even as the German tried to keep from ending up in a ditch, he managed a weak raised-arm salute.

The truck hit a bump and the men bounced hard. Logan landed a bit to the front of his seat and hurt his hip. One of the Maquis got a bloody nose on the antiaircraft gun's barrel.

"Can't we slow down?" shouted Jaune in French.

"No!" said Logan.

Jaune pointed at Tyler, who was moaning on the floor. "Your man."

"No!" Logan repeated.

The truck rounded another curve, its rear tires catching on the lip of an irrigation ditch, then flinging mud and barreling down a long, straight road toward an intersection.

Carlson stuck his arm out the window to get James's attention.

"Which way?" James relayed.

Logan didn't hear. "WHICH WAY?"

Jaune hooked his thumb left, but another Frenchman with a round face caught the drift of what was going on and waved his hand toward the front.

Jaune shook his head. The other insistently pointed forward.

"Which is it?" shouted Logan.

"Left," shouted Jaune.

"Le Marais!" said the round-faced man. "The marsh is over there! We go east."

"Slow down," ordered Logan, and James banged the roof of the cab.

Carlson took it as a signal for an all-out stop. He hit the brakes and the truck skidded, nearly tossing James off before shimmying to a stop.

"You son-of-a-bitch, you trying to kill me?" barked James.

"Which way?" demanded Logan.

"I tell you my sister married a man in the next town," said the round-faced man. "I know these roads. The Forbidden Zone is straight ahead."

"But the zone is south," said Jaune.

"That road goes south a short distance then—" he hooked his hand "—it swings back to the west."

"Don't be ridiculous," said Jaune. "Who is in command here?"

"I am in command here," snapped Logan. He opened his map. He saw the intersection on it. "It doesn't revert to the left."

"You see?" said Jaune.

The round-faced man stepped over Tyler and crossed to the other side of the truck and pulled the map toward him. "This intersection isn't on your map. It is the next intersection. This one is called Le Marais from the bog over there. The next is Quatre Bras."

"The map says Quatre Bras," said Logan.

"But 'Quatre Bras' just means a crossroads," said Jaune. "This is the right one."

Another Frenchman had stood up. "No, I think you are wrong."

"Are we lost?" said Carlson, half-opening his door and standing on the running board.

"Any of you boys live around here?" James asked.

"My sister married a man near here, I tell you."

James shrugged.

"Do you know this area?" Logan asked Jaune.

Jaune hesitated. "Well, not really well, but I know we go south here."

"What do you say, Captain?" Carlson asked.

Logan saw that the men whose boots were closest to Tyler's leg were trying to avoid looking down. Their boots were glued to the floor by his blood. Logan ducked under, the gunner's armor plate and knelt by Tyler's head. He was very pale.

"Tyler," said Logan. "Are you still with us?" He leaned in close. "Jonathan Tyler!" he shouted.

Tyler weakly opened his eyes. He barely whispered, "Captain," then gestured toward him.

"What is it?"

"Closer."

"What is it?" Logan leaned down to hear what Tyler had to say. "Yes?" He was expecting a message for Tyler's mother or girlfriend or someone like that.

Instead, Tyler swung his fist and tried to hit him. The punch was weak, like a two-year-old child's, but Logan jerked back in reflex as it grazed him and dropped away. The German helmet Logan was wearing clanged against the armor shield.

"Gotcha," Tyler said with a smile. He closed his eyes. "We're even."

Logan straightened the helmet and listened to Tyler's chest. His heart was faintly beating.

"Is he alive?" asked Doolin.

"Yes," said Logan, but the tone of his voice said, "Not for long."

"Couldn't Carlson take it easy?" asked Doolin.

Logan shook his head. He had a decision to make. He glanced at Jaune, then at the man who said they were at the wrong intersection to turn. Jaune surveyed the horizon. The round-faced man was trying to wipe some of Tyler's blood from his boots with an oily rag and seemed afraid of getting it on his hand.

"He ought to know where his sister lives," said Logan. "Go straight."

"But, Captain—" said Jaune.

"Straight," said Logan. Fifty-fifty wasn't good odds and maybe he ought to go with Jaune's opinion. Then again, maybe it was the quick way Jaune had killed the German officer that made Logan doubt him. He had seemed to enjoy it, without thinking about what information they might have gotten from the guy.

"Sir, do you hear that?" asked McGonigle.

They all turned their faces skyward. It was low, but it was coming.

"Let's roll," said Logan.

Carlson ground the gears and the truck lurched forward.

James looked back from his porch and pointed. The fighter was coming in low, following the road.

"Shall we take him?" asked Griffiths.

"He'll think we're one of his, wave at him as he—"

"*Spitfire!*" yelled James. "*Drive! Drive!*"

The plane roared in from behind them, and its machine guns opened up. Carlson swerved, then crested a small hill and floored it. One of the Frenchman made a grab at the antiaircraft gun, but a sudden bump flung him out the back of the truck as the machine guns caught up with them and passed in a deafening roar.

When Logan lifted his head, the Spitfire had already flown ahead of them, just above the road. It then banked to the right and began climbing. Logan desperately looked for a tree, anything to hide under. Their best chance was to scatter.

"Stop!" he shouted. "Abandon the truck!"

Carlson slammed the brakes and the truck spun sideways. The

men leapt in all directions, charging into fallow fields on each side of the road. James knelt to help Tyler. McGonigle had hoisted Punchy on his shoulders and was carrying him. Two Frenchman jumped beneath the truck. Another two staggered a few feet and collapsed.

Logan crouched by a stone fence. The noise of the plane receded into the distance.

"Where is he?" asked McGonigle, panting and searching the sky. Logan and he knelt over Punchy, whose eyes were rolling as if Primo Carnera had got him again. Blood had flowered on his shoulder and his hip. The bullets had made big exit wounds.

James ran up to them. "I think it was just one pass. Maybe he was headed home. They don't usually go this far."

They listened and waited.

"He's gone," said McGonigle.

"Wait," said Logan. They listened a bit longer. Nothing. It was as James had theorized. The pilot was likely making his way back and had spotted an easy target, but he wasn't going to waste a lot of fuel and ammo on it.

"Damn," said Logan.

"Are we lucky or what?" said Carlson, running up. His ear was bleeding badly. One of the bullets had put a groove in the side of his helmet and nicked his ear.

"Well, you look lucky," said James.

"They got Tom Swift."

"But he was with you in the cab!"

"The Spitfire punched holes in it like a can of condensed milk. If I hadn't been pulling such a load I could have outrun the thing."

"Right," said James.

"Stick it, fancy ass."

McGonigle put his thick hand on Logan's arm. "Sir," he said, "it's over."

Logan grabbed Punchy's face. "No!" he said. "Pawlowski, get up! It's a five-count. Six."

Logan sat back on his heels, stunned. One lousy pass. One spray of bullets. Why had he taken Punchy? Why didn't he take people he despised—the generals, the politicians, the entrepreneurs getting rich off the powder that launched those bullets?

"They wouldn't have gone," he said.

"Excuse me, sir?" said McGonigle.

Logan shook his head. "Nothing." He wondered what Punchy's last words would have been. Everybody ought to be entitled to something, even if it was only "Damn!"

"He wasn't in any pain, sir," said McGonigle. "He isn't in any now."

Logan sat back and looked up at the sky. "You son-of-a-bitch," he said.

"Shall we bury them, sir?" said McGonigle.

Logan looked at him with pure hatred. "You know the answer to that. Don't be an ass."

"No, sir. I won't, sir. We'll cover them with some of the stones from the fence."

Logan nodded. Gently, he removed the dogtags from Punchy's neck. "They?" he asked. "Who else?"

James held out Tyler's dogtags. "And two of the Maquis," he added. "Tom Swift is still in the truck. The one who fell out broke his neck, too."

"Where's Griffiths? Did we lose him, too?"

"He dove out of the truck back that way," said McGonigle. "It was still moving."

Logan was about to say he'd probably broken his neck, too, when McGonigle cut him off.

"There he is, sir."

Griffiths was poking Jaune with the point of his bayoneted rifle, shoving him along. "Look what the cat dragged in," said Griffiths. "Didn't you say 'Jaune' means 'yellow'?"

"He was running away?!" asked the round-faced man. He turned to Jaune. "How can you be such a fool!"

"That's ridiculous," said Jaune. "I was running for cover."

"He didn't really get going until the plane left," said Griffiths. "If I hadn't been up there . . ."

"Where were you going?" demanded the round-faced man.

Two of the remaining Frenchman were muttering together. They were saying something about the way they got captured.

"One of them thought he heard something near the weapons cache, but Jaune insisted that he had already checked and no one was there," explained James.

"Verte—" the Frenchman paused, thinking of his now-dead comrade "—said he heard movement. Jaune said there was nothing there. I wanted to look, but Jaune said there was nothing."

"Then he said it was a goat," added the round-faced man.

"Why didn't you tell us this?" asked Logan.

"We didn't really think he was a traitor."

"Traitor?" said Jaune. "This is an outrage. Me? I have been in the party since 1925!"

"Yes," said the round-faced man, "and my sister lives near here."

"What does that mean?" asked James.

"Jaune tried to organize the peasants, here in 1936. He knows these roads."

"Is that true?" asked Logan.

"I was confused," Jaune replied. "There was no Forbidden Zone in those days. There were no Bosch. He is right, I know now. It is the Quatre Bras ahead. I will show you exactly how to get there."

"You know it well, eh?" The Frenchman thrust a knife at Jaune's face. "I never liked you. Levrier warned Argent to watch you, and look what happened."

"Wait," said Logan grabbing the man's arm. "Let's not do to him what he did to the Kraut. We want to know everything he knows. Who is Argent?"

"The Bosch got him. They tortured him to death. We don't think he talked, though."

"He was a helluva man, then," said Logan.

"Our friend here was a bit too eager to take out that officer," said Griffiths. "I'd chalked it up to the well-known Froggy passion."

"The officer might have said something," said James.

"Please," said Jaune, "this is ridiculous. You don't know what you're doing."

"That's exactly why we're so dangerous," said Logan. "Griffiths, truss him up and gag him. We've got to get out of the open here, then we'll chat with him."

"No!" said Jaune.

"I'll be happy to interrogate him," said James. "I learned a good bit about that in Morocco. Kind of got my doctorate, if you will."

"Let's get moving," said Logan. "It'll be dark soon."

"I never thought I'd be so disappointed to see the RAF," said McGonigle.

Logan simply covered Punchy's face with the German overcoat and gently began piling rocks on his body.

"Logan's Losers" were now down to six.

31 OCTOBER 1942
NANTES, OCCUPIED FRANCE

A boy of ten rushed into the Charcuterie Flanne just as the wife of the bicycle shop owner was criticizing the sliced ham he had just placed on the counter.

"Believe me, I understand, Madame," Flanne was saying, "but what can I do? There just isn't much ham available. I take what I can get. The Germans have commandeered so much for the war effort."

Including you, he thought. Earlier that week, he had heard a rumor that she was not only a Nazi sympathizer, but was riding a young German lieutenant much more than her husband's bicycles.

"Monsieur Flanne!" said the boy.

"You are interrupting," said the woman.

"Mademoiselle Esmeralda is threatening to kill herself!"

"That whore!" said the woman.

Flanne shrugged. "What can I do?" he said, untying his apron. "She loves me."

"It would hardly be a loss to the world," she said.

"I know," said Flanne, "but it would make my evenings lonely." He hung his apron on a peg. "Do you want the ham or not?"

"Not at that price," she said.

He picked it up.

"Thief," she said, counting out the coins.

He snatched up his money and hustled her out of his shop. He climbed the cobblestone street winding to the brothel and rapped on the side door. A peephole opened and he went in.

"*Revolutsiya* is here. That's what he said. He is in Esmeralda's room," said the pimp.

"Do the other girls know?"

"They're asleep." The pimp led him up a narrow back staircase. "The Mayor had a long party last night. You could have killed off half the collaborators in France."

"Maybe your girls will do that."

The pimp stopped. "There's no reason to say that."

"Go on, go on," said Flanne. "It's a joke."

"It's not a very funny one." The pimp glanced both ways in the hallway and unlocked the door.

A small, muscular man sat in a brocaded chair, wearing nothing but olive green undershorts. "You got the message," he said.

"Yes, I am Flanne."

They waited until the pimp closed the door behind them.

"Can we trust him, Comrade?" said the man in the chair.

"Yes, but we won't be here long," said Flanne. "You are Targa, then?"

"In Germany, I have another name; in London, another."

"Targa is a legend."

He chuckled and reached for a glass of brandy. "Every once in a while Stalin gives me a medal. He can't say what it is for, and he can't give it directly to me, but they like the propaganda. I am a shadow. The spirit of international Communism. I have infiltrated everything. I have assassinated dozens."

"Have you?" asked Flanne.

Targa grinned. "I never question the Party. Where is Levrier?"

"We will meet him. How many men will you need?"

"Two dozen."

Flanne whistled. "I don't know what Levrier will say about that."

"He will say, 'Of course.' This may be the most important action of the war. It can ensure the triumph of the people."

"It is not that we don't want to help you. It is difficult, that is all."

"These are direct orders from the Kremlin itself. They did not send me out of Germany to hear about difficulty, Comrade."

Flanne crossed his arms. "Certainly, Comrade."

As Targa pulled up his pants, Flanne noticed his underwear was stamped U.S. ARMY.

As they snuck down the back stairs, the pimp warned them that two young men of unknown sympathies had been waiting in the front parlor for one of the girls to wake up. Flanne and Targa slipped away, and an hour later rumbled up to the farmhouse where Levrier hid with Marcel.

Levrier sat outside, under the small roof that protected the well. He was smoking his last cigarette. He had done a lot of sitting and thinking since the miracle of Marcel's invisibility. It was a long dream; any moment he should wake up from it.

Flanne stepped off his motorcycle and opened the cart in back. Targa had been bounced around good, but he landed like a cat and quickly scanned his surroundings.

"Greetings, Comrade," said Levrier.

"I was told to bring you greetings from Stalin himself."

"And I was told to take everything you say as coming directly from the Kremlin."

"Good," said Targa. "Then we will have no difficulties." He flicked a glance at Flanne.

Flanne looked around, as if trying to locate the boy. A twitch in Levrier's eye told him not to ask about Marcel.

"Come inside and sit," said Levrier. "There is some bread, but that is all, I'm afraid."

"Food is not what matters now. Let us take the air."

"Flanne," said Levrier, "you stay here and keep everything quiet."

Now the message was even clearer: Levrier was going to keep the boy away from the Russian; why, wasn't clear.

Levrier and Targa strolled into a neglected orchard. Targa suddenly stopped and faced Levrier. "I need about two dozen men."

"Two dozen!"

"I am going into the Forbidden Zone."

"What? You think two dozen men could get into there? It's suicide."

"Your men are a diversion. I will get in on my own."

"It's absurd."

"My specialty is the impossible."

Levrier rolled his eyes. "Oh, well, then, why ask me?"

"Listen, Comrade, if you had the slightest idea how I came to be here, you would know I can do it."

"But of course."

"Two weeks ago I carried plans for the Atlantic Wall fortifications directly past Reichsminister Speer and out of the building. The party did not send me out of Germany for trivial reasons. There is someone, something, that must be removed from the Forbidden Zone."

"And that is?"

"You need not know, Comrade, but the war hangs in the balance. The British and the Americans have sent a party as well, but the Germans have them."

"No!" said Levrier.

"They were completely surrounded and captured, along with the Resistance fighters who were to meet them."

Levrier banged the table. "Damn!" he said. "How did the Germans find them?"

Targa shrugged. "It doesn't matter. What matters is that we succeed."

"Those men mattered to me," said Levrier. "It isn't easy building up a secret organization, Monsieur. We're supposed to be a party, not a collection of master spies. We know there are prisoners in the primary facility of the Forbidden Zone. There is a high-security prison in the old caves. If we are going in, we must get our people out as well."

Targa's cold eyes narrowed. "I understand how you feel, but friendships may have to be sacrificed for the greater cause."

Levrier barely controlled his temper. "I was not saying that they were my friends. They are our comrades! If they are the Fascists' prisoners, they are our comrades!"

"Can you get me men?" Targa asked, ignoring the comment.

Levrier stared at him coldly. "In a week, maybe, but I don't know how I can guarantee their trustworthiness."

"A week might as well be a year. I need them tonight."

Levrier's mouth dropped open. "No."

"You must."

"How can we do that? How can we plan anything?"

"You fire at them at the main entrance. Get them all excited and distracted and I will get in elsewhere."

"What do you mean 'elsewhere'?" Levrier asked hotly. "Have you scouted the place? There are dogs. There is barbed wire. And what happens after we get the Bosch all excited? They kill us? They wipe out a few villages? Are you mad?"

"Sacrifices must be made for the cause," Targa replied coolly.

"Not unless it is clear what those sacrifices are for."

"Moscow commands."

"This is *France*, Monsieur. 'To each according to his needs.' I need to know."

Targa's face went red and screwed up. He was a bulldog ready to rip out Levrier's throat.

Levrier stared directly into his eyes. "Well, Comrade?"

Targa paced. "You will find this very difficult to believe, and I will ask that you not convey this to your men."

"What? We no longer trust the People?"

"It is too difficult to believe."

"Is it too much to die for?"

"No," said Targa. "The German coastal guns struck an aircraft."

"I know that," said Levrier. "Everybody knows that. There was a light visible for miles."

"Do they know it was a spacecraft?"

Levrier wasn't sure he had heard him right. Targa explained.

"That's absurd!" said Levrier.

"No, it is not. There was a pilot, a strange creature with a big head and spindly limbs. He was wounded and is likely still alive."

Levrier suddenly understood the nature of Marcel's angel and what he had already concluded about the metal ball. It was some kind of invisibility device—not a religious or spiritual force, but a device of some kind. And a powerful one, at that.

"How do you know this 'creature,' as you call him, wasn't just a circus freak?" he asked. "Maybe this is all a German plot to draw us into the open?"

"I spoke personally with Dr. Vassily Orlov," Targa replied. "He worked in the Forbidden Zone. He was a scientist of the highest caliber and he saw not only the ship, which had—this is incredible—the ability to repair itself, but also the creature."

"And this creature? It has weapons? It is allied with the Bosch?"

"Orlov said the SS security man was certain it had saluted him with a swastika."

"So now we must fight another planet as well as the Fascists?"

Targa shook his head. "I will kidnap it, or kill it. We cannot let the Germans have its technology."

"And what of the Americans, the British? Clearly this is what their mission was about as well."

"The Soviet Union must have this technology or no one. Otherwise, either capitalism or fascism triumphs."

"I see." Levrier thought for a moment. "All right, then. There will be a disturbance at the west gate. Two A.M.?"

"What will you do?"

"A disturbance!" Levrier snapped. "You will notice it. I'll work it out, somehow."

"Thank you, Comrade." Targa vigorously grabbed Levrier by the arms. It felt insincere to Levrier.

"I'd better go," said Levrier.

"And I must, as well, Comrade."

They walked silently back to Flanne's motorcycle contraption.

"Two," said Levrier.

"I know I can trust you," said Targa.

"Excuse me while I give Flanne his orders." He quickly walked to where Flanne dozed in a chair, leaning back against the farmhouse.

Levrier leaned close. "Do you trust the Russians?"

Flanne seemed confused. "They are our comrades in the struggle for—" He read Levrier's eyes. "That Poland thing was a nasty business." He was referring to the nonaggression pact that split Poland between Stalin and Hitler and began the war in Europe. Many of the Communists had difficulty rationalizing it, but once the Germans rolled into France, it seemed pointless to fret about it.

"I did not tell him about the boy," Levrier said.

"I didn't think you would. Are we going to help him?"

"Yes. Unless I think of something different." Levrier straightened up and explained what he wanted put together for midnight. They'd make the diversion all right, but they wouldn't hang around to get caught if he could help it.

31 OCTOBER 1942
THE FORBIDDEN ZONE

Borck had felt an irritation along the back of his thighs, and his fingertips had begun to tingle. Lack of sleep? His mind had been racing so much that sleep seemed irrelevant. And how could you sleep when a being from another planet might enter your mind at any time, might reveal all his secrets to you? He paced, the irritation turning into an itch, the itch becoming unbearable.

"Where is that milk?" he shouted out of the cell.

"It is on the way, Oberführ—" The guard stopped in mid-sentence.

Borck turned to see what had surprised the guard. The alien stood, unblinking, holding its injured arm and flexing its lengthy fingers.

"What is it?" Borck snapped at the guard.

"Y-your face, sir. Your h-head."

"What do you mean?"

"It's . . . red. There are stripes."

Borck touched his forehead. It felt like a rash, except that it stretched in a straight band across his forehead. There was a tiny trace of blood on his fingertips.

"It looks like measles," said the guard, "except . . ."

Measles, thought Borck. He could infect the alien. Oh, no, not now! This is the worst possible moment for this. He quickly stepped out of the cell.

"Get me a mirror!" His voice echoed off the stone walls.

The guard, momentarily confused, quickly turned and clambered up the stairs.

Borck paced, scratching at his arms and legs. He pulled back his sleeve to find that the red rash had covered the entire back of his arm. Lice? He unbuttoned his trousers and pulled them down. The rash covered the back of his thighs. This wasn't lice. This wasn't measles. He faced the cell and tried to think. The itching was making that impossible. He had to concentrate. He had to ask the alien what this was.

Maybe it was *he* who was infected by the alien, not the reverse. Surely this was some routine ailment that the aliens could easily cure!

The guard charged down the stairs and stretched his arm to hand Borck a small shaving mirror.

The rash ran in stripes around his head, over the top, across his ears.

It was the pattern of the netting he had put on!

"The milk is here," said the guard. Two soldiers panted as they brought the big barrel down the iron spiral staircase.

Borck straightened up. Could the ship have been toxic? Did it emit radiation?

The soldiers dropped the barrel and stared at him.

"In there!" said Borck, gesturing toward the cell. "Put it in there!"

They hesitated.

"Follow orders!" he shouted. "Or I'll have you shot!"

"I'll hold the doors," said the guard.

Borck watched them uneasily carry the barrel through the barred door, then lift it through the cell door without going inside. The moment the barrel landed on the floor, they seemed frozen by the creature's gaze. One of them backed into the guard, then they panicked and fled up the stairs.

"Cowards," snorted Borck. "Fools."

He reached out and grabbed the alien's good arm. It was like grabbing a broom stick, his bloody fingers easily wrapping around to touch his thumb.

"Why am I sweating blood? What do I need to cure myself? You must cure me. No, you must tell me how. You must fill my brain with all of your knowledge."

The great, dark eyes of the creature remained as implacable as ever, though he cringed against the wall.

"You fear," said Borck. "You fear me. You are like any other earthly creature." Borck let go. His entire palm left a bloody stain on the creature's upper arm but it faded quickly, absorbed in the same way that the blood has disappeared on the hull of the spacecraft.

He reached into his holster and pulled his Luger, clicking a bullet into the chamber. He held it up, smiling.

"You know what this is. You know what it can do."

He spun and fired three shots into the cot. Enclosed by the cell, the noise was deafening. Borck's ears rang painfully, but he did not allow the alien to see it.

"You are not cooperating. If you do not obey, I will shoot. I will start with your legs."

He pointed the gun.

"Bang."

He smirked.

"Then the other."

He re-aimed.

"Bang."

He raised the pistol.

"And then your shoulder. Bang! You will have no arms. No legs. And I will continue to inflict pain on you. You understand pain, don't you? You are a living being. You feel love for your master. I can inflict so much pain that you will beg me to die, but you will love me for killing you."

He stepped back. The elusive static electricity feeling on his scalp was much stronger. It felt, not like a caress, but like strong fingers, massaging, massaging.

"So you *do* understand fear! The universal law: you want to live!" Borck laughed, giddy with power. "You will give me all your power. You will teach me all you know."

He backed to the milk barrel and banged off the metal fastener, flipping back the lid. The creature twitched from the noise, then slowly cocked its head.

"Interested?" asked Borck. "Of course you are."

The alien turned its face to the milk barrel, and then to Borck.

"Yes," said Borck. "Give me what you know and I will give you all the milk in the Reich, all the milk in America. You will live like the god you are! We shall together be gods!"

Borck edged through the narrow space between the barrel and the door frame.

"Together!" he said, clenching his fist. "But fail me and I will teach you what it is to beg to die."

He stepped toward the alien, who backed into the wall. The fluid mercury of its tunic swirled. The dots appeared again, but circled and dove without forming any recognizable shape.

"We'll start with the ship." Borck pointed to his head. "Tell me how to fly it. What moves it? How is it propelled?"

He saw the blood on his fingertips, but closed his eyes to clear his mind and receive the knowledge . . .

He was receiving his ceremonial SS dagger from Himmler. Boys were making fun of him at school because of his mother. His teacher called him an idiot, and—

He opened his eyes, pushing aside the memories, and gazed at the creature. "You are not ready. Very well. I believe we understand each other." He squeezed back through the cell door. "I will give you fifteen minutes to consider. Drink your fill, and then we shall discuss how much you shall serve me and come to love me."

The alien eased forward and as it did, its mouth puckered and began to protrude. The creature bent over the barrel, and the tube-like protrusion extended to about a meter in length, giving the alien an insect-like look. Borck shuddered at the creature, then thought, as if he had known all along, that this creature was some kind of drone. When he had flown across their planet, he had seen drones or worker ants waiting on the queen of their hive. Their masters did not venture into the vastness of space, only their slaves.

What had the scientists said? That they believed the ship was a silicon-based combination of the organic and inorganic. Perhaps the creature was an automaton, a robot. The ultimate robot—not merely a collection of gears and wires, but with a brain, with a will to survive, capable of fear, able to respond to differing situations.

What's more, he sensed, it was always connected to the home planet, at least in the ship. Could all the brains of all the creatures constitute one great brain? As all the Aryan peoples shared one collective consciousness given to them by their race, so it was with the aliens.

He closed the door without locking it, then strode out to the guard's desk. The guard moved away as Borck approached, grinning. There was no greater elixir than inspiring fear. It was adrenaline, cocaine, and an aphrodisiac rolled into one.

The guard was quivering so much, he appeared ready to collapse, and nearly did so when Borck snapped up the shaving mirror on the edge of the desk.

The rash on his forehead had spread some. Tiny beads of blood, a mere mist, covered the areas, as if sprayed on.

"Do I bother you?" he said to the guard. "This is a mere inconvenience, some reaction to the miraculous substances of the spacecraft. You will soon be one of the lucky ones, you sniveling excuse for a man, living in the greatest empire that has ever existed. I will soon rule the world with your Führer, and then, soon, maybe other worlds!"

He collapsed into the desk chair, panting. He was exhausted, but he was not yet ready to rest. He would let the creature drink, then he would get his answers.

31 OCTOBER 1942
LONDON, ENGLAND

Colonel Marston rushed into General Anthony's office. It was empty. He charged down the back stairs just in time to see his car pulling away from the curb. He shouted. The sun had just set and the streets were nearly empty. It'd play hell to catch a cab, he had thought, when he realized that Anthony's car had stopped half a block away. He ran toward it as it slowly backed up.

He snapped open the door.

"And I thought I was making a clean getaway," said the general.

"Sir, we've heard from them!"

"Logan?"

"Yes, sir."

"Get in!"

Anthony ordered his new driver to circle St. James Park, then closed the divider. Marston shoved a paper at him. The message was:

SIX BROTHERS MET MOTHER AND HER BROTHERS. ARGUED WITH NEIGHBORS. EIGHT IN ALL AND ONE OLD MAID. GOING TO DANCE IN THE DARK TONIGHT.

WISH US LUCK.

"There was a traitor," growled Anthony.

"Hell!" said Marston. "Can they do anything with eight men?"

"Probably not." Anthony lit a cigarette. His hands were shaking badly. "It was too much to ask. Logan is a helluva soldier, but—"

"The odds were very long."

"Impossible."

"Some of them are still alive. Maybe they'll get out."

"Only if they're out of there by dawn."

"You could call it off."

Anthony looked out the window. An air warden smoked his pipe in the middle of a pile of sand bags. "It was always a backup. We can't let them take the spacecraft to Berlin."

"We could re-direct the bombers to concentrate on the rail line."

"We can't take the chance. We're going to hit them hard. It's a dangerous mission over a lot of enemy territory, but I don't know what else we can do."

Marston said nothing.

"No," said Anthony, "we can't wait to see what Logan gets done. We're throwing three waves of bombers at the port at Vannes and letting the Germans know about it through Vichy-O and others. They will be waiting for a raid which is basically a diversion and those bombers will take heavy casualties. Just pray that it allows for a thorough cleaning of the Forbidden Zone. It's a good way to let Berlin think that their spy network is still intact, but it will cost us."

"It's a son-of-a-bitch of a thing to do," said Marston.

And I'm the son-of-a-bitch who does it, thought Anthony.

Marston suddenly recognized what he had said and faced the general.

Anthony took a drag on his cigarette and gave Marston a pass. The colonel said nothing compared to what Anthony often said to himself.

"The damned Russians are a wild card in this, too," the general continued. "One of their best is going in, codename: Targa."

"Stalin's superspy," said Marston.

Anthony nodded. "But we haven't located him. They seem to

know our moves even before we do, and we don't have the slightest idea what he is up to."

"And the 'Old Maid'?" asked Marston.

The general shrugged. "Who knows? It isn't like you can run a want ad for reliable Resistance fighters."

"It could have been Orlov. A guy who'd kill his own mother! You can bet he whacked the guy in the river, too. "

"Maybe she figured out he's a Nazi spy. Maybe she cooked his borscht wrong and it's got nothing to do with all this." The general shook his head. "This business of ours!"

"It's a credit to Logan he isn't in the hands of the Germans again. You've got to put him up for a medal."

"Don't jinx him. He's got one coming for Dieppe. That's jinx enough." The general shook his head. "I should have sent someone else. The SS gave him a bad time after Dieppe. Even though he escaped, it was too soon to send him back in."

"You needed somebody as resourceful as that."

Anthony sighed. "I just hope I haven't sent him to get blown to pieces by our own damned bombers." He rolled down the window and flicked out his cigarette, which exploded in a plume of sparks against the side of the car. "He'd better be out of there by dawn. . . ."

31 OCTOBER-1 NOVEMBER 1942
THE FORBIDDEN ZONE
1600-0200 HOURS

The first roadblock they'd encountered was at the Quatre Bras intersection. With James standing high in front of the antiaircraft gun, the soldiers manning the machine gun nest on the corner even stood up and returned his Hitler salute.

Carlson didn't slow too much. They wanted the soldiers to see their uniforms, but they didn't want to give them *too* good a look. A sergeant, however, seemed to be a little more interested than the others, maybe in the holes made by the Spitfire.

"*Zuttritt Verboten?*" shouted James, pointing down the road to the left.

"*Ja wohl!*" returned the sergeant.

James slapped the roof above Carlson, who immediately accelerated, throwing dust in the machine gunners' faces.

The second roadblock consisted of a heavy pike, a booth, and a half-track just beyond. There was no choice but to stop. James immediately jumped down as if stretching his legs and began jabbering in peremptory German. Logan, resting his machine gun across his knees, slid it hard into Jaune's midsection. The Frenchman's breathing whistled through his nose.

"Keep your head down," said Logan. He wanted the helmet to shield view of the gag.

"Stand ready, men," whispered McGonigle.

Griffiths moved to arm the big Flak gun, but Logan waved him down. One of the guards drifted toward the truck, maybe to check it out, maybe to chat, or cadge a smoke. James, however, raised his voice, distracting him.

"They want written orders," said McGonigle.

"But they're not getting ready to resist us," said Doolin.

"Be quiet," said Logan, who was watching for any sign they were suspected. He was also trying to see in the lowering dusk if there were any telephone wires running to the booth. They might have a radio, but they were certain to check with higher command if they had a telephone.

James snapped his heels, saluted, and was marching back. The pike was rising. Carlson slipped the truck into gear. When they were safely past, Logan tugged James's sleeve.

"The main gate is a quarter of a kilometer away," James explained. "They said we were supposed to have orders to approach it. I told them we weren't supposed to go all the way there, but to set-up as another defensive post."

"Then tell Carlson to pull over." Logan suddenly saw an opening in the trees leading up a hill. "No, tell him to back up there, all the way to the top."

"We'll be sitting ducks," said Doolin.

"No," said Logan. "We'll be another gun emplacement for the Forbidden Zone."

"Perfect!" said James.

"Very good, sir," said McGonigle. "It'll be dark soon."

They were soon perched on top of the hill, the Flak gun raised, and at least one of them always searching the sky with binoculars to give the appearance they stood ready to defend the facility—instead of preparing to destroy it.

"Did they suspect us?" asked Logan.

"They're bored out of their minds," said James. "If anything, they were simply looking for someone to talk to—to break up the monotony."

"Great," said Logan. "I'm more than happy to oblige them—later."

"But what do we do now?" said Rhys Griffiths.

"We reconnoiter," said Logan. "Then we play it by ear."

"Maybe we can bluff our way in," said James.

"Don't think your life's all *that* charmed, rich boy," said Carlson.

Logan took the round-faced Frenchman and Rhys Griffiths with him and left James to play officer if anyone showed up. It was dark by the time they got back.

"Gather up," said Logan. "Griffiths, keep an eye on the road."

"So, what's the game?" asked Carlson.

"A lot of barbed wire, a lot of dogs. Search lights for when there's an alarm. There's a level area between the outer fence and the next one—you can count on it being mined. Did I miss anything?" Logan turned to Griffiths, who raised a hand above his head, then extended his thumb and forefinger to signify a gun. Logan nodded. "Oh, yes. There are towers equipped with MG-42s, one every hundred and fifty yards."

"Piece of cake," said James.

"Can of corn," said Doolin.

"It's a cinch we're not sneaking in." Logan pointed out. He gestured toward the east. "Over there, the bed for the rail line has been laid. It goes right up to the wire."

"They wouldn't mine the rail bed," said McGonigle.

"No," said Logan, "but they've set their latrines there, just inside the inner wire, along with a kennel to the left. When the rail gets close, they'll move all this, but even if we could get through the wire without being noticed, or past the kennel without the dogs acting up, there's always somebody around the crapper."

"I would say they really don't want us in there," said James.

Griffiths nodded. "There's no welcome mat, that's for sure."

"Sir," asked McGonigle, "how far is our objective from the wire?"

Logan gestured toward their round-faced guide. "The Maquis isn't sure, but he thinks it's at the base of the big outcropping in the middle, on the other side. About half a kilometer."

The Frenchman nodded.

"Don't tell me," said Carlson. "His sister was married there."

Logan grinned. "He explored the caves when he was a kid."

The Frenchman said something which James translated. "He says it's possible he remembers it wrong. The caves were closed up when a big wine dealer bought them. It was a long time ago."

"Damn it," said Logan, "if that crazy man Orlov hadn't been killed—"

"Chickened out," said Doolin.

"*Whatever* happened to him," said Logan. "He'd been in there only a few weeks ago, so he knew the lay of the land. Without him, we've got to get in as quietly as possible, until we get the layout. Until we find out what they've got that will blow the place sky-high."

"I see," said James. "So, my role as the loyal and efficient Wehrmacht officer has been such a success it is being held over."

"That's the general outline," said Logan.

"I am the toast of the continent."

"So, we'll wait until everybody's good and sleepy, then we'll bluff our way through the gates. I wish there was another way, but I don't see it."

The men were silent.

This was it, Logan realized. The end of the road. A barbed wire gate that needed a sign: ABANDON HOPE, YE WHO ENTER HERE.

"We're going in there, we're destroying the spacecraft and anything else we can manage," he continued. "We're killing the alien if we have to do it with our fingernails. The United States is *not* going to lose this war because of little green men from Mars."

"Nor the British Empire," said McGonigle.

"*Et pas la France,*" said James.

"*Vive la France libre!*" said the round-faced Frenchman.

"Which reminds me," said Logan. "Bring that sorry son-of-a-bitch Jaune over here. We've got some talkin' to do."

McGonigle and Carlson moved swiftly, dragging their resident troublemaker from the rear of the truck, then sitting him up just under the edge of the bed. James stuck a red-lensed flashlight in his face. Jaune's eyes were wide and filled with tears.

Logan played on his fear by showing him his keen bayonet, then cut loose the gag. Jaune spat out the rag which had been stuffed in his mouth and coughed loudly.

James jammed a pistol beside his head. "Death will cure that," he said.

"Exactly," said Logan. "Now, tell me everything you know about the Forbidden Zone."

"Please, Monsieur, I know nothing."

"Tell me about the inside."

"I have never been inside, but I know they have prisoners in there."

"How many?"

Jaune shrugged.

"You're *not* proving very useful." Logan glanced at James, who took the cue and nudged Jaune's head with the gun.

"I—I know the SS security man is a Colonel Werner Borck," Jaune said quickly.

Logan's heart stopped. "Borck?"

"Yes." Jaune paused. "I also know the security is quite strong. Stronger than even secret sites in Germany."

"And *how* do you know this?"

Jaune choked up, unable to speak.

"You'd better talk!" James warned.

"B-Borck told me. When I reported that there would be a raid on the fuel dump. He bragged that no raid on the Forbidden Zone would ever be successful, especially now."

"Why now?" Logan asked.

"Because he had redone the security."

"Did he say why?"

" 'To protect the future,' he said."

"And then he sent the squad to trap us?"

Jaune nodded. "He said they had confirmation of your raid on the fuel. He told me to volunteer to lead the group supporting you."

"And you led your friends into a trap." Logan grabbed him by the throat. "They'd have killed you all—all your friends, and you, too."

"Borck said I would be spared," Jaune countered. "He said I was too useful to kill."

"And you believed him." Logan turned to James. "Gag him again. The Maquis can decide what to do with him."

Jaune tried to call out, but his cry was cut off by the rag being stuffed back in his mouth. His muffled whine was probably the last noise he'd ever make.

Logan didn't care. All that was racing through his mind was the name Werner Borck. And the horrors he had witnessed—and experienced . . .

He remembered the long needles. The pliers. The surgical clamps. The smell of the hair and flesh of his forearm burning. The pain, he could not remember; it was too powerful to remember. The mind couldn't retain a memory like that.

And, yet, for all that, Borck had barely begun. Logan knew that because of what he was forced to witness. The big Canadian—what was his name?—had died particularly hard. Logan had thwarted Borck's plans for even more creative tortures by pretending to pass out. Borck ordered the doctor to listen to Logan's heart, to make sure he wasn't dead yet. Tied in a chair, Logan had kicked the man back into Borck, then spun the chair, clipping Borck in the cheek and knocking him senseless long enough for Logan to get a scalpel off the table and get his arm free. Borck rolled around, trying to get his consciousness restored. The only thing that saved his life was the thunder of boots in the corridor. Logan dove through the window into the courtyard; the rest was a blur. He ran until his lungs felt like burnt liver. And sometime after that, there were the faces of a myopic nun, and the gravelly-voiced fisherman who eventually sailed him into the English Channel.

He owed Borck for Dieppe. He owed him plenty, but he couldn't let that screw up the mission. He had to remind himself of that. He had to make sure he never forgot it.

The mission. Borck, if there was any chance, but the mission first.

They rested and listened to the random sounds that rose up from the Forbidden Zone. A car passed on the road below around midnight, and an hour later they heard men walking, probably to relieve the soldiers at the guard post.

The crescent moon suddenly disappeared, ending the dim light their eyes had grown accustomed to. The vague separation of the tree shadows and the stone outcropping against the sky blended into uniform darkness.

"Did you hear that?" whispered Doolin.

"Silence!" whispered McGonigle.

Something was moving in the underbrush below them. Then it stopped.

"Do you think they have discovered us?" whispered McGonigle.

"It was a deer," said Carlson.

"At night?" said Doolin. "A dog, maybe. A badger. Not a deer."

"Quiet," said Logan.

Another noise. More like a *clink*. Only this was behind them.

"Oh, hell," said Logan.

"Brace yourselves, men," said McGonigle.

Logan edged along the side of the truck to where James had been. "James!" he whispered. "James!"

He jumped when a hand reached out of the dark and slapped his shin.

"Jesus!" said Logan. "What are you doing?"

"I think there are at least two," said James on the backside of the hill.

"Speak German," said Logan. "Casually. Talk about women. It doesn't matter."

James patted him on the shin again, then rolled out from under the truck. *"Meine Mutter hat etwas gesagt der Rotkohl die Nacht-maren heilt. Ja! Du lachst! Warum ... ?"*

James kept up his steady patter while Logan whispered "Get ready to roll! The Heinies are out there. Get ready!" as he felt his way from man to man.

They readied their weapons, muffling the clicks with coughs and spitting noises, then aiming out into the darkness.

"They're moving, sir," whispered McGonigle.

"Let's open up on them," said Doolin.

"Wait," said Logan. They couldn't see a thing. What were they going to shoot at? "Carlson," he said, "get ready to start the truck if necessary."

"I'm not Carlson," said Rhys Griffiths.

"He's already in," said McGonigle.

"Make sure the Frenchies know what—"

Logan never finished the sentence. Suddenly, the word *"Maintenant!"* rang out from the trees, and muzzle flashes threw deadly fire at them. Bullets *ping*ed off the armor plating, and Logan's men returned a spray of fire into the dark.

"Let's go!" he shouted, and Carlson began grinding the ignition, pumping the accelerator. The truck window shattered as bullets poured through it, but Carlson had laid flat on the seat and the engine cranked, roaring to life.

Griffiths quickly vaulted into the back and, keeping low, began to arm the Flak gun. McGonigle flung a German "potato masher" grenade into the woods. It went off with a flash that revealed several men knocked flat by the concussion.

The siren went off in the Forbidden Zone, and the search lights raked the hill, silhouetting the men attacking them from that side. They dove for cover.

Logan yelled, "In the truck! In the truck!"

One of the Frenchmen grabbed Logan's arm, frantically trying to say something. A bullet ripped through his neck and he fell, clinging to Logan's trousers. Logan laid another spray into the woods and peeled the man off.

"Go!" he shouted to Carlson. "Go!"

The truck rolled downward because of the slope, as Carlson tried to catch the gear. The rear tire bumped over the downed Frenchman. Logan barely caught the swinging door at the back.

A grenade went off where the truck had just been, and Logan felt McGonigle's massive hand reach out and grab him by the collar. His heels dragged on the uneven road, then McGonigle shouted for strength and hefted him up as another spray from the enemy *ping*ed against the door.

They could see Jaune, still gagged and tied, running toward the enemy. A burst of fire ripped off his legs and shattered his torso.

Griffiths spun the Flak gun and began to pump fire into the trees. Trunks exploded.

Logan scrambled over his men and shouted to Griffiths: "FIRE HIGH! FIRE HIGH! THEY'RE FRENCH!"

The truck had barreled down the hill to the main road and climbed up onto it with a thump. Fire was still coming down on them from the Resistance, who did not know who Logan's men were.

Logan reached out of the back and pointed Carlson in the direction of the main gate, and the facility beyond it. Carlson floored it and Griffiths chopped the top off several trees, as Doolin bounced out of the back.

Someone stood up beside the road and a grenade bounced off the Flak gun's shield. It exploded behind them as the gate came into view.

German soldiers scurried in to position. The MG-42s opened up, aiming at the flashes of light on the distant hillside. A tree was on fire.

"CRASH THE GATE!" Logan shouted. James raised up from the floor just slightly to fire. His head exploded, spattering Logan with blood and brain matter.

Logan wiped the sticky blood from his face. It burned in his eyes like acid. By the time he had blinked it clear, he could see the round-faced Resistance man cowering in a ball on the floor. Logan grabbed James by the tunic and hefted him half onto the roof of the cab.

The Germans would see him, even though they were avoiding the truck with their searchlights and trying to see the attackers instead. One of the searchlights was hit and exploded in a shower of sparks.

"BRACE YOURSELVES!" shouted McGonigle, as the gate grew closer, but miraculously the outer gate swung back just before the truck reached it. It banged off the right wheel well, knocking a fleeing guard into the barbed wire and ripping out its hinges.

A dozen yards beyond, men scrambled to open the inner gate and the truck should have missed it, except the guard let go of it. It swung back to catch the truck and shatter at its lower end. Griffiths continued to fire at the highest part of the hill. The Germans rushed past them to get ready for a counterattack.

Logan's Losers were now down to five men: Rhys Griffiths, Carlson, Logan, the "Great" McGonigle, and a Frenchman who was shivering, immobilized by terror.

But they were inside, and all the Germans were too busy to notice.

1 NOVEMBER 1942
ALL SAINTS DAY
THE FORBIDDEN ZONE
0147 HOURS

Idiots!" Targa muttered to himself. The maquis had started their diversion too early. For only seconds, he had been lying still a mere five or six meters from the wire. A moment sooner and he would have been standing beside the railway bed as obvious as a naked man in the snow. The lights came on and swept the area he was in, but the brush he had covered himself with was just enough to make him unnoticeable on the gravelly slope.

They would switch on the wire now and he'd never get past it.

He looked toward where he had cut the wire. It was wide open between there and the second fence. The lights were turning toward the action on the hill, and there was less attention being paid to his direction as a shot exploded one of the searchlights near the gate. He was certain he could take down at least one guard in the nearest tower, but if they had armored the inside, one was all he would get.

He crawled on his belly to the top of the slope and peered over its level surface. A tree was on fire in the hills. A grenade exploded. Maybe Levrier's men weren't entirely idiots. He had told them that a noisy attack on the pike booth would probably work best, and draw men away from the enclave with the least number of casualties for Levrier's comrades. It would have been necessary to turn off the fence wiring in order to send out soldiers.

And then Targa heard the roar of a truck. It was barreling down toward the gate, spitting fire from an antiaircraft gun mounted on its bed, chewing up the hill behind it. An officer was dead on top of it, maybe the driver, too. The Germans rushed to open the gate, but the truck never slowed. The first gate bounced off the truck and fell off its hinges. The second had a big chunk blasted out of it as the truck finally skidded to a stop.

Targa looked up at the guards, transfixed by the action, and bolted for where he had cut the wire. The lights were all turned toward the firefight. He dove flat and wriggled under the wire like a snake. Up on his feet, he ran hard for the second fence. The gravel seemed almost like glue. Each step seemed to take hours. He decided to veer toward the tower, taking a chance that the mines weren't too close to the railroad bed. With each step he expected gunfire or an exploding grenade to finish him, but somehow he made it to the wire, panting, trying with sweat-blinded eyes to control the metal shears, listening for any sign above that they had spotted him.

A soldier was running behind the latrine to the dog kennel, but was too preoccupied to notice Targa behind the big leg of the tower. The dogs were snarling and barking at the battle, and the soldier had a bad time trying to control them.

Targa continued to clip the tangle of wires one after another, sometimes clipping the same wire twice in his haste, sometimes cutting his hands. He glanced toward the kennel, and one of the dogs strained at its leash, pulling the soldier toward the fence. The soldier smacked it and forced it to go in the direction of the gate. There, soldiers were setting up a machine gun, and taking positions to defend against any force trying to come through the broken gates.

Finally, Targa thought he could make it through. He was about to dive under when he saw something running through the mine field between the fences. It was the dog. It had broken away and was charging straight for him. He looked up. The guards hadn't seen him. He lifted his PPsH submachine gun, ready to take down the dog and the guards above him, if necessary.

The dog's luck ran out, however. It set off a mine, and then two more exploded as the pieces fell. Targa tumbled onto his back and squirmed under the wire.

He was almost through when his trousers caught. He tugged. The sharp spike cut into his thigh. He fumbled frantically for his wire cutters, and was about to clip himself loose, when a helmet appeared over the rail high above him.

He did not hesitate, firing into the man's shadowy face, then ripping up the floor of the tower from beneath.

He cut the wire and ran for the latrine. He got into the shadow of it and looked up. The spotlight in the tower was smoking, and flames burned on the railing. There was no sign anyone was alive in there. The machine gun in the next tower blasted the field beyond the rail bed, as if the shooting had come from there.

Targa smiled. He had asked for a diversion, but this was chaos. It would only take a few minutes, however, for the Germans to pull themselves together. He didn't have much time, but, then, he was Targa, wasn't he?

Targa *never* needed much time.

1 NOVEMBER 1942
ALL SAINTS DAY
THE FORBIDDEN ZONE
0230-0300 HOURS

evrier had planned to go into the fields east of Quatre Bras, moving past the marshes and circling back over the hill to the last roadblock Targa had recommended. His men, however, had stumbled into a new gun emplacement near the top of the hill. The Germans had placed a mobile antiaircraft gun at the top. The soldiers who manned it were sleeping or exchanging meaningless conversation. It looked like a better spot for the diversion. He told Bleu to wait ten minutes while he got into position to observe the reaction from the Forbidden Zone, then to attack the gun. If they could take the gun, so much the better. They could fire down toward anyone who came up the road. But there had been more men there than they thought, and the fight was ferocious.

Levrier had left Bleu in charge and continued with his own personal mission, joining Marcel where he had left him—behind an embankment that held back the marsh water. "Well, boy, you say you can save France."

"I—I must."

Levrier clutched his shoulders. "Marcel, you must not think that brave men, brave girls like Saint Joan, never felt fear. Touch my face."

The boy did not move.

"Touch my face." He placed Marcel's hand on his forehead. "You feel all that sweat? I am not much of a warrior. Circumstance has forced me to be one. There's not a drop of liquid left in me, I promise you."

"You were chosen," said Marcel. "As I was. I know that Saint Joan felt fear. I can master it with God's help."

Levrier sneered. "All that religious stuff..." He shook his head. "Well, let's not talk about it now. All I know is that the Bosch have imprisoned your angel. If you can use your miracle, now is the time. It is even easier than I had imagined. The gates are open." He looked up toward the burning tree.

The boy licked his lips. Levrier took him by the shoulders. "There is something else I must tell you, because you may stumble into it yourself."

"Yes?"

"The Bosch have prisoners in the caves. They are men and women who are not just ordinary prisoners. They are the ones Ober-führer Borck has taken a special interest in. People who can reveal secrets about the Resistance, for example. He may have tortured them until they are half-dead. Or they may already be dead. Do you understand me?"

Marcel glanced toward the fortress. "If they capture me, I will not talk."

"That isn't what I mean. I mean it is more important the fortress be destroyed than that the prisoners live. The prisoners understand that. Some of them may be out of their minds with the torture, but they knew the risks. If there is a choice between releasing them and failing the mission or letting them die to accomplish the mission, you *must* finish the mission. Do you understand?"

The boy lowered his head. This was far too much to put on the shoulders of a thirteen-year-old. Levrier looked up toward the burning tree. "Are you certain I cannot use the ball? I will gladly do this for you."

"If you have faith, Monsieur Levrier, it will work for you."

"Call me 'Comrade,' " he barked. "I am not your 'Monsieur!' " He sighed and shrugged. "I don't pretend to understand it, but I hate to sent a boy to do a man's work."

"I am only the instrument of God."

"Yes, yes, yes," said Levrier impatiently. He took a deep breath. "There is one other thing else I haven't told you. But I—"

How was he to say this? He had determined to keep this to himself, but somehow he couldn't. How could they win the war without discipline? What was he doing keeping secrets from Targa, yet revealing things to Marcel that might keep him from accomplishing the mission?

"What is it, Monsieur?"

"The Bosch took your grandparents here."

"Grandpere! Papeau! They are alive?!"

Levrier grabbed Marcel's shoulders and shushed him. "No. Impossible. Even strong young men die from the agony Borck can inflict. As soon as he discovered your grandparents had no information for him, the best we can hope for is that he quickly ended their suffering."

Marcel's eyes were filled with tears. "But if they are alive?"

"That is why I told you. If you can take a look around, do so. If you can maybe unlock the cells and give our people a chance, do so. But don't get caught, and don't fail the mission. Otherwise, your grandparents will have died for nothing."

Levrier was silent, again questioning his fitness to command. How much easier it must be to be one of the Nazi Supermen—or Targa, for that matter—who holds the individual human life to be of no consequence. He watched the boy staring at the frenzy in the enclave. It took several seconds, but the boy composed himself, straightened his back, and raised his face to the sky.

"The Lord asks too much, sometimes."

"The Lord!" said Levrier. His voice grew more gentle. "So you are not going?"

"I must."

"I will not think any the less of you . . ."

"We must defeat them. I thought my grandparents were killed by the shots I heard while I ran away. And I want them to be alive. But one of the last things I remember Grandpere saying was that he would rather the Allies drop bombs on him than allow the Germans to win."

Levrier's head swirled with conflicting feelings. How was a boy so young to understand the preciousness of life? You needed to be older for that. How could he, Levrier, a man who thought he was a champion of the oppressed, send this boy on such a suicide mission? Targa hadn't asked for it. He sure didn't want to do it any more. Only the boy was ready.

He took a deep breath.

"But can you get this material into the enclave?" He lifted a heavy backpack. The boy put it on. For all his scrawniness, the hard work on the farm had made him quite strong. "And you remember how to set the timer?"

"Yes, Monsieur."

"I told you—Never mind. In about five minutes, Bleu will begin to withdraw. The Bosch will pursue, of course, but the fighting will have stopped and you'll be able to walk straight in. Just watch for trucks and—"

"I know what to do."

Something bothered Levrier. It had irritated him like a mosquito bite since he had seen the boy disappear, then reappear right in front of him. Something about invisibility. When he was adjusting the straps, he again remembered a movie he had once seen in Nantes. It was an American movie with Claude Rains. He had thought of it many times since he and Flanne had seen the "miracle." But, of course, he hadn't really considered the movie seriously—and then it clicked in his mind.

The invisible man in that movie had to remove his clothes. His empty suit had danced around, terrifying the English villagers. Marcel's clothes had disappeared when Marcel disappeared. He hadn't given it any thought. He assumed the backpack would be as invisible as Marcel and his clothes. But why? It wasn't about Marcel alone. It was the contact with the metal ball. Marcel's *clothes* couldn't have faith. Somehow, Marcel's mind set off the invisibility, but it wasn't limited to him.

"Boy," he said, "didn't you tell me that both you and the angel were invisible when the soldiers searched for you?"

Marcel nodded. "Yes. The angel took my arm and wouldn't let go. They looked directly at us."

"If you held my hand, would I be invisible, like that?"

"Only if you had faith, Monsieur."

Levrier rolled his eyes. "Test me," he said. "Test my faith. Eh?" He peeled off the backpack and put it on himself. He then took the boy's hand and began tying their wrists together with his handkerchief. "I am going with you."

"But you do not have the faith, Monsieur."

"Don't tell me what to believe! How do you know what I believe? I can believe in God if I want, can't I? Even if he doesn't exist!" He flicked his cigarette over the earthworks and into the marsh. "All right, then, make us vanish. The angel waits!"

Marcel suddenly embraced him. The guns rattled in the darkness, and a searchlight exploded with a loud sizzle.

"Come on, let's go," said Levrier. "Who do you think I am—your father? It's a fine world when a man like me puts children in the war. Even if it is to save France! Even if it is for God!"

Marcel squeezed his thick hand.

Logan slid into the seat beside Carlson and signaled him to move the truck forward. Soldiers were running on both sides of them toward the broken gates. "We'll make like we know what we're doing. Casual. Go down and around, like the Maquis said."

Carlson nodded. It had always been easier for him to floor it than to creep along. "Why don't we ditch this thing?" he asked.

"I like having the Flak gun," said Logan. "Do you realize we've lost more men to our allies than to the Krauts? Damn!"

"Maybe this means we're going to win the war."

Logan searched the passing soldiers. The dim light made it impossible to see clearly, and none of these enlisted men had the right uniform he was searching for. He was looking for Borck. He couldn't help himself. *Deliver me Borck and I can die happy.*

When an officer did appear out of the gloom, he wasn't SS. He watched the passing truck and seemed ready to speak, but turned away.

James was still doing his job. His shattered head turned the Flak truck into a funeral procession.

They were past stacked barrels, surrounded by a thick wall of sandbags. Logan could smell the diesel fuel, but even if they blew, they were safely outside the mountain itself.

McGonigle suddenly jumped over the side of the truck and ran to the cab. He jumped on the running board next to Logan and leaned in. "Sir," he said, "I believe I saw Dr. Orlov."

"What?"

"The weasel's dead," said Carlson.

"No, I caught a glimpse of him back there. Those barracks."

"You've got to be seeing things."

"I don't believe so, sir."

Logan shook his head. "The little bastard slipped away. He came back to his Heinie friends. No wonder we've had so many surprises!"

"Two traitors in our squad," muttered McGonigle.

It was probably the science, Logan thought. Those scientists didn't care about politics unless it got them a bigger set of test tubes.

"If I see him again . . ." said McGonigle.

Logan pointed. "That's the rail bed," he said. "Turn and follow it. That should take us straight to the spacecraft."

1 NOVEMBER 1942
ALL SAINTS DAY
THE FORBIDDEN ZONE
0300 HOURS

Borck had watched with horrid fascination as the alien sucked up a third of the barrel of milk with its proboscis. It then faced the Oberführer and waited.

"What is it? It's not sour, is it? We have had some problems with supplies. The Eastern Front. When Russia is put out of its misery, which will be soon, the war is essentially over." Borck laughed. "No, never mind Stalingrad. It is over when you teach me. Fifty of those ships of yours and—"

The alien's head began to pulse, as if it were a heart beating. The color of its skin shifted from its normal chalky greenish tint to blue, then purple, then red.

Borck stood.

The alien cupped its skeletal hands and spewed a clear syrupy liquid into them. It then raised the sticky liquid to its injured shoulder. The dripping fingers seemed to disappear into the tunic like it was thrusting its hand into a silvery liquid. The creature repeated the process four times, then returned to the barrel and bent its head into it.

Borck eased toward the droplets which had fallen on the floor, and stuck out his finger to touch the liquid. But there was no liquid; the drops had solidified and become like lead crystal cabochons, ready to be mounted on a ring. The blood on his fingertips smeared on the clear surfaces.

He pulled back his sleeve and saw that the mist of blood coming through his pores had covered his entire skin. He felt his face and it now seemed to be coated with blood, though he thought he might be feeling what was already on his palms.

He felt hot, so hot. It was a fever, and he was sweating his blood. Arsenic poisoning, he remembered, could do this. It had happened to a king of France, he thought. Why didn't he feel weak, though? On the contrary, he felt powerful, better than he had for weeks. Was it merely the dizzy euphoria that can come with blood loss? He had seen a prisoner laughing once as he watched the blood pump out of the incision Borck had made in his leg. He had wanted him to suffer, to know he was slowly dying. Instead, the man had laughed. It was an embarrassing failure Borck never repeated.

I need help, thought Borck. He thought of the high-powered minds he had brought to the Forbidden Zone, those great scientists Erstewald and Brunnermann and Rakoczy and that idiot Rhinehart. What good were they?

When he raised his head, the alien had stepped away from the barrel.

"Tell me how to cure this," he demanded. "I gave you the milk you wanted. Is it arsenic? Has one of my own men been poisoning me. Is General Von Kerner behind it?"

Again, the alien's head pulsed and changed color. When the activity settled down, the creature moved toward him.

"What are you doing?" said Borck. He backed away. "Wait. Communicate with me. Tell me."

The alien moved closer to him. He hit the cot with the back of his knees and crumpled to a sitting position. He could smell the strange odor of the creature, who now moved the proboscis closer to his face.

He turned away. It was going to stick it down his throat!

"No!" His voice echoed off the stone chamber.

He dropped flat, trying to squirm away, reaching, fumbling for his holster, then losing the gun off the back of the cot.

The alien reached out and tried to hold down Borck's head. The clear liquid had begun to ooze from the proboscis, dropping in long swirls around Borck's ear.

But then the alarms went off.

The alien straightened up, confused by the drilling sound of the electric bells.

Borck spun away and felt for his Luger, pointing it at the alien. What clear liquid it had oozed on him was already hard, and he could not claw it away.

Boots clattered on the iron stairs. "Oberführer! Oberführer! We are under attack! They are firing from the north!" Three soldiers had come to get him.

"Are there enemies inside the perimeter?"

"We are holding—our position, Oberführer. We are holding."

The sergeant's eyes had widened as Borck stepped over the threshold of the cell. Borck might have been dipped in gore. Even his uniform had changed color as the blood soaked through.

Borck listened. Deep in the stone bowels of the hill, no sound came through. "Air?"

The sergeant didn't answer.

"ARE WE BEING BOMBED, SERGEANT?"

"Gr—ground only. All defenses are going according to your orders. Sir."

"It's the Allies," said Borck. "They want the ship. They want the creature. Orlov disappeared because he is a traitor. Or the Resistance got it out of him."

He opened the cell door completely. The soldiers could now see the alien. Two of them blanched. The sergeant had been with Borck when it was apprehended.

"He is our ally," said Borck. "He will bring the stars to our aid, but we must not let him be taken."

"Sir," said the sergeant, "should I send for Herr Doktor Scheinmann? Your face—"

"Never mind that! It is a mild infection which our friend will cure."

The soldiers looked at each other; their superior officer's condition didn't appear to be very minor to *them*. Was it catching? When Borck moved forward, they backed up. If it hadn't been for his Ruger, which they knew he would use without thinking, they might have run.

"You are the Imperial Guard," said Borck. "You will escort us to the ship. The creature and I will fly it to Berlin. Tell General Von Kerner to notify the Reichstag immediately."

"General Von Kerner has gone to the fighting."

"After we take off, then!"

Borck turned to the alien. "Come, my friend. You will meet he whom all Aryans worship. You will see that we feel the same toward him that you feel toward your masters."

The alien's proboscis retreated into its head and became the tiny slit of its mouth.

"Come! We shall fly! I know we can do it together."

Borck felt the caress of the alien's thoughts.

The swastika again formed on its tunic.

1 NOVEMBER 1942
ALL SAINTS DAY
THE FORBIDDEN ZONE
0300-0400 HOURS

Logan's first glimpse of the hanger doors came from the flash of an explosion behind them. They were about thirty feet high and made of steel plates riveted together.

"How the hell do we get in there?" said Carlson. "It's a cinch I can't drive through it!"

"We'll get them to open up," said Logan.

"And might I ask how, sir?" asked McGonigle.

"We'll knock on the door and ask to borrow a cup of sugar. How the hell would I know?"

"Well, you *are* the captain," said Carlson.

"Too bad for you," said Logan. "How's your German, McGonigle?"

"Worse than my Erse, sir, and I only know five words of that."

"Griffiths?"

"Welsh, I'm afraid."

"Don't look at me," said Carlson.

"Crap! There wasn't much reason to like James, but he'd be useful now. Tell Griffiths to make like he's watching the sky for an attack on the hanger." Logan pointed through the broken window. "Pull up directly in the middle, but keep the motor running."

"You got it," said Carlson.

"And load up on ammo and grenades."

Logan slipped out of the cab. The fighting seemed to be subsiding, though they no longer had a view of it. The noises echoed off the outcroppings and sounded like they were coming from every direction.

"Just look earnest," said Logan to Griffiths, and stuffed his pockets with grenades from a locker in the back. "But lay into them if they get any ideas."

"What shall we do, sir?" asked McGonigle.

"Try to look Krautish. We'll borrow that sugar I was talking about." He paused. "Maybe James can help us out again." Most of the back of James's skull was missing. Logan took a deep breath and reached into the exit wound, greasing his fingers and wiping the grisly mess on his throat.

"Help me walk," said Logan, and McGonigle wrapped his massive arm around Logan's torso and staggered with him toward the access door.

McGonigle banged hard on the door with his fist. "What will I say?"

"Leave it to me."

Logan covered his throat with his hand.

McGonigle banged on the door with the butt of his submachine gun. The booming echo faded into the hanger.

A dot of light opened in the door as someone slid aside a metal flap. Logan clutched at his throat making wet choking noises. The peephole closed.

McGonigle banged again. Then again. The peephole opened again and with tight lips Logan sprayed it with spit. The hole closed again as the guard jumped back.

"*Bruder!*" said McGonigle. "*Bruder!*" He banged again and the soldier said something through the peephole. Logan shrugged and McGonigle continued to bang until they heard a latch thrown.

The guard was babbling angrily about the *Lazarett*, which Logan remembered was a hospital. As the guard was about to close the door, Logan rolled his eyes and fell forward against it. The exasperated guard bent in a reflex to catch him. Instantly, McGonigle grabbed his collar and yanked him forward. The guard fell on Logan, and McGonigle kicked him in the face. The guard waved his hand helplessly and McGonigle drove a fist into his nose, flattening it.

Another guard yelled, and McGonigle dove through the open door, swinging up his Bren and blazing heavy fire across the open chamber. Logan squirmed to get loose, but the fallen guard had trapped his leg against the high threshold. He tugged, but couldn't get loose.

Across the wide concrete floor, he saw a door open.

"Left!" he shouted, and McGonigle sprayed it.

Logan then saw men moving to his right. A lot of them. He fired at them, but they took cover behind the big truck in the middle of the hanger. Bullets *ping*ed off the steel hanger door and a bullet—or its fragment—clipped McGonigle's shoulder.

Logan pulled a grenade from his pocket and turned on the fuse. He flicked it hard across the floor. It skittered end over end and came to a rest directly under the bed of the truck. Logan ducked.

The concussion felt like a wind of fire. When he raised his head, the truck had lurched to its side as one back wheel had blown off. Its cargo—what looked like a huge aluminum disk—had slid to that side, and a soldier shrieked. It had crushed both of his legs.

Logan finally jerked his way free and McGonigle hurried to the left to get behind a protrusion in the stone wall. The door at the end had closed. It was a steel door similar to what they had just gotten through. Keeping his Beretta submachine gun aimed at it, Logan tried to close the door to the outside, but the guard's body was in the way. He scurried to join McGonigle.

"Sir," said McGonigle, "I don't believe we'll get through that door in the same way."

Logan strained to look around the twisted truck. The second door also seemed to be closed.

"Look at that damned thing," said Logan.

"Are we to suppose that thing flies?"

"If this is a sucker play of some kind, I'll haunt that son-of-a-bitch Anthony until hell freezes over." He signaled with his hand that McGonigle should take the left door, while he'd take the right. Five soldiers were dead behind the truck, while the one whose legs were crushed was unconscious. Logan kicked his rifle away from him and took the grenade from his belt.

Somebody would eventually open the door, and he would have a gift for them.

As he stood flat against the side of the door, he looked over the hanger chamber. The place was lit by only a couple of lights hanging from the ceiling. There were three desks against one wall, with telephones on them. A strange apparatus that looked like a giant drill press sat against another wall, where a series of lab tables steamed. The laboratory glass and reagent bottles had been shattered in the fight and chemicals mixed, sending off foul odors. There might be something to do with those—acid, explosives—but there was no time to look them over now.

Behind those doors the Nazis could be telephoning for help. Logan decided he'd have to bring Carlson and Griffiths inside and close the access door. He squinted up to see how the whole door was moved and saw a heavy pulley system. The motor appeared to be inside, however, and he hoped it couldn't be opened from the outside.

He whistled and by gestures indicated that McGonigle should watch his door as well. Then he ran around the truck and shoved the still unconscious guard out the door. He heard shouting and some gunfire, but most of the fighting seemed to have died down.

"Carlson! Griffiths!" he called out. He stepped out and heard the truck still running. But Carlson was nowhere to be seen, and Griffiths was slumped against the Flak gun.

Something was wrong. As he turned to go back in, a knife came up and pricked his Adam's apple.

"Inside," said Dr. Orlov.

"What is this?" demanded Logan.

"Inside. I don't want to cut his throat. I really don't." Orlov checked to see if any of the Germans running toward the gate had noticed. "Actually, I don't care," he added. "I'll kill him, too," he said, twisting his chin toward Griffiths. "It will cure his headache."

Logan saw the terror in Carlson's eyes. Carlson was barely holding himself together. Orlov moved forward. His submachine gun became visible in the weak light coming through the door. Logan backed inside. Orlov slid Carlson sideways and tilted his head to indicate Logan should close the door.

McGonigle looked back in surprise. "Sir?"

"Behave," said Orlov, "I suggest you drop your weapons or I may, on a whim, cut your boy's throat."

"You damned Nazi," said Logan. "Tell me, was Jaune innocent? Was it you who betrayed us?"

Orlov laughed. "You are a fool! Me, a Nazi? I could take a bath in all the medals Stalin's given me."

"So you're a deep cover spy. Aren't we supposed to be Allies?"

"Drop the weapons," Orlov repeated. Carlson raised himself on tiptoe. A thin line of blood appeared on his neck.

"Whoa!" said Logan. "You want to disarm us? What are you going to do with those Krauts on the other side of those doors? Have you got a scientific answer for that?"

Orlov laughed again. "You just don't get it, Captain. I know nothing about science. My real name doesn't matter—I am known as 'Targa.' Your Dr. Orlov has been dead since the night you came to get him. You mistook me for him."

Logan tried to absorb this. The man was in Orlov's apartment with Orlov's mother. Was the mother a traitor to her own son? Logan hadn't seen the mother, however. And then Anthony had not seen Orlov after Logan had picked him up.

"You took to parachute jumping rather fast," said Logan, remembering. "You seemed a little too calm in the abandoned church."

"I didn't want to look too proficient, but it is my nature." Targa. "It was such a convenience, your dropping me right where I wanted to go."

"You son-of-a-bitch!"

"She was a *kulak,* actually. And so, how shall we remove the creature from space?"

"I'm here to neutralize it."

"Only as a last resort," said Targa. "The Soviet Union will make great use of him." He gazed at the disk. "And that? That is the craft? It is as Orlov said, no engine, no rivets—"

The German soldier whose legs had been crushed by the spacecraft suddenly waved his arms and raised his torso—a sadly pathetic final attempt to fight off death.

Targa instinctively whipped his knife around against the threat. Carlson wasted no time in taking advantage of the distraction. He dropped, spinning, and drove his fist hard into Targa's belly.

The Russian waddled back, momentarily stunned by the blow, and tried to raise his submachine gun, but Carlson had gripped the barrel with one hand, raised himself on one knee, and smashed his fist into Targa's face. The gun erupted, and bullets punched craters in the concrete floor, but Carlson hung on, twisting the gun away from him with both hands. Targa whipped down the knife to hack at Carlson.

Logan was already on him, however. He gripped Targa's elbow and slammed the forearm backward. Logan was stunned by the steel in that arm—a weaker man's arm would have been broken, but Targa still held the knife and the submachine gun.

Struggling against them, Targa gritted his crooked teeth with new determination and smiled. "Dead man," he said as the knife began slowly to move forward. "Dead man!"

It was the "Great" McGonigle who broke the tie. He banged the nose of his Bren against Targa's ear.

"Stand back," said McGonigle. "Now. And hands up!"

Targa's eyes shifted toward the barrel. Logan could see that Targa was, even now, assessing the odds of him taking all three of them. He shrugged and slowly released his submachine gun. He was still holding the knife, however.

"Drop it, Targa," Logan said, still holding the elbow and pressing against the thick forearm, "or the Sergeant-Major fires!"

Everything that happened next was almost instantaneous. There was a *clank* at one of the doors. Targa spun, driving the knife into McGonigle's upper arm as Carlson fired at the door. Logan dove, firing at the door to his left. McGonigle, falling backward in agony, slammed Targa in the face with his mighty fist, then cut loose on the second door.

And then grenades came through the door. Two? Three? There were two bright flashes, a *crash* like diving into water, and then the floating silence of being beneath the surface. Logan went deaf.

Several soldiers madly charged out the door. Carlson brought down the first and the second, while McGonigle drove those from the other door back inside. Logan ran to the truck to use it and the space disk for cover. He got there just as the "Great" McGonigle ripped the knife from his shoulder and dropped writhing on the cement.

The door opened again, and Logan threw a grenade at it. It hit the door and fell outside. The explosion knocked the door open, however, and he ran toward it, firing. The soldiers were desperately trying to shove it closed, but an unconscious soldier blocked it. Logan threw another grenade through the door and in the confinement of the tunnel it shredded everyone in there, including several men in white coats he took to be Borck's scientists. Slipping on pieces of flesh and internal organs, he ran to the end of the corridor. A sign indicated AREA B. He ran and discovered a line of about a dozen cells.

The prisoners looked out at him, their eyes blank, as if they didn't believe Logan was real. One of them raised his hand and wordlessly pointed. Logan knew what had created those vacant eyes: pain, absolute pain. There was a point at which your mind would run away from itself to escape, at which it would try to forget everything it had ever learned. You would want to be anyone other than yourself, and if you tried hard enough, you would cease to exist. You'd become a book with blank pages.

"Borck, you son-of-a-bitch," he muttered through clenched jaws. He moved from cell to cell, looking for the alien. More blank faces. A man who appeared dead. A woman whose face was swollen and purpled into a grotesque parody of an eggplant.

"Are there more prisoners?" shouted Logan. *"Plus de les prison-niers?"* They stared. He moved back to where he had come in. There was a rack, but the hook was empty. "I'll find the keys," he said. *"Les clefs.* Is there another way out? *Une autre porte?"*

One prisoner, a tiny ghost of a man with swollen eyelids, had managed to stand and cling to the bars. He pointed back from where Logan had come.

Logan had gone up a dead end.

Maybe he'd missed something. He ran back, checking every alcove. There was a guard room with a rack of rifles, a modest supply of ammunition, no keys, and a pitcher of drinking water. He was soon back to the long corridor into which he had charged.

No one could get him in there without taking many casualties. All he had to do was fill the tunnel with bullets. On the other hand, there was absolutely no way out—except in a coffin. And then there were flamethrowers as well.

He took several deep breaths and ran through the carnage he'd caused. He was astonished to reach the door alive and even more astonished to find the hanger in total darkness, except for an undulating purple light dancing over the flying disk's hull.

Sweeping his gun from side to side, he stepped over the threshold, rolled, and came up standing. He was all that was left of Logan's Losers, he thought. Why him?

The lights came on, and he saw Targa, McGonigle, Carlson, and Griffiths in chairs. Soldiers had pistols pointed at their heads. Other soldiers popped up from behind the truck and along the side walls behind him.

"If you fight," said a familiar voice, "your friends will die as well. Surrender and I will show mercy. To *them,* Joe Logan. *Just* them."

Logan turned, and found himself staring at the cause of every sleepless night he'd had since Dieppe. The same darkly-garbed bogeyman who had haunted his every waking thought.

"Borck," he whispered.

1 NOVEMBER 1942
ALL SAINTS DAY
THE FORBIDDEN ZONE
0400-0700 HOURS

Logan instinctively stepped back, trying to fight the fear that rose within his gut.

This man—if you could call him that—wasn't anything like the Borck who had tortured him. Every inch of this grotesque version of the SS Oberführer who had once delighted in his pain glistened with blood: his face, his ears, his hands. His uniform was darkened by the blood soaking through at the knees and thighs and elbows. When he spoke, his mouth was a gory hole. At first, Logan thought Borck had been drenched with the blood of someone caught in an explosion, but the blood on the SS officer's uniform had soaked through from the inside.

"Well," said Logan, "is this the new standard for military decorum, you son-of-a-bitch? You look like hell."

Borck smiled. Even his teeth were coated with grue. "Not hell. You'll find out what hell is soon enough." He turned to his soldiers. "Gentlemen, meet Captain Joseph Xavier Logan. He and I have some . . . unfinished business. Some 'catching-up to do,' as his fellow Americans would say." He pointed at Logan's rifle. "Be a good boy and put down the gun, Captain Logan."

Logan laughed sharply. "And what if I don't? What if I kill you?"

Borck slowly shook his head in mock sadness. "That would be a *very* unkind gesture to your friends, Joseph, because my men would have to kill them in turn. You wouldn't want *more* blood on your hands, would you? Not after what happened at Dieppe." A shark-like smile spread across his face, and Logan had to fight the urge to fire, anyway. "However, if you surrender quietly, after they have been held for a month or two in a Stalag, we will send them home, just as we found them, if not in better condition. Resist me, and they will beg me to kill them before I am through." The smile widened. "You *know* I can do that, Joseph."

McGonigle mumbled something. Logan could now see that he was not just wounded by Targa's knife, but had been hit by shrapnel, as had Targa and Carlson, who was missing part of an ear. Targa was slumped forward against his bonds. Targa's face bore the type of bruises that could only have been made by rifle butts. One eye was bloody and probably useless forever. Only Griffiths, whom Logan had assumed was dead, was relatively uninjured. He blinked as if he were having trouble focusing, and there was a nasty bruise on the side of his face.

McGonigle took a deep breath. "Did you hear me, sir? I said, 'Tell the bastard to bugger himself!' "

Borck laughed. "He is trying to provoke me, but he cannot. The Reich has now entered into an alliance with a race that will win us the war. It will only be a short matter of time before our spacecraft are sweeping across the globe, destroying all those foolish enough to oppose us. And then those swine Churchill and Roosevelt will be dragged before the Führer in Berlin, where they will have no choice but to beg him to spare their lives."

"That's a helluva imagination you got there, Borck," Logan said dryly. He pointed at the Oberführer's dampened uniform. "You sure you're not just woozy from blood loss?"

Borck sneered. "Imbecile." He turned on his heel, went behind the truck, and led the alien into Logan's view.

"Holy ..." Logan muttered. He stared at the lozenge-shaped black eyes, the stick-like arms and legs, the strange padded tips at the end of each of the six fingers. This creature was real, then. It *wasn't* a figment of the late Dr. Orlov's imagination, then.

"God in Heaven!" said McGonigle.

Targa raised his head and blinked. Griffith's eyes rolled like the cherries on a slot machine.

The hair was rising on Logan's neck and scalp. This was it—the alien he was supposed to terminate. It looked so fragile, but if it could make the disk fly . . .

He braced himself to attack. *This is it,* he thought. *The end. The terrible moment that has no reversal.*

Oddly, then, he suddenly thought of that day he had come home from the first grade and Father Hamilton had been waiting on the stoop . . . to tell Joe that his father had died. And no matter how much Logan had prayed, he couldn't bring the man back. It wasn't fair, he thought then. His father had promised to take him to Yankee Stadium the following Saturday. They were going to get Babe Ruth's autograph on a ball Logan had bought just for that purpose.

Logan shook his head. What had made him think of *that*, in *this* hellhole, of all places?

He glanced at the creature standing beside Borck. Black dots suddenly appeared on the alien's silvery tunic. The tunic itself flowed like water, or so it appeared, but dots spun in the fluid, circled and formed a shape.

Borck stared. "What is that? Chinese? Japanese?"

Logan shook his head. He was seeing things.

"It must be one of his symbols," said Borck.

Logan met the creature's eyes again and stared. He felt naked, as if the creature was somehow in his head. He knew that the creature knew Logan was supposed to kill him, but he also sensed the alien wouldn't resist.

He also knew, he didn't know why, that the alien was no one's ally. Not his, not Borck's. He aimed his submachine gun straight at Borck.

Logan growled. "I might be about to die, you son-of-a-bitch, but I'll see you in hell with me!"

Borck quickly stepped behind McGonigle. "By all means, Joseph, fire away!" He placed his gore-soaked hands on the Sergeant-Major's shoulders. "I'm sure there's room for *three* of us in Hades." His glance flickered across the other captives. "Perhaps there's room for *all* of us . . ."

Logan hesitated in pulling the trigger. His confrontation with General Anthony crept into his thoughts: *"How many men had to die so you could wear scrambled eggs, General?"* How many men had died under Logan's command, though—not just on this mission, but at Dieppe? How many names could he recall from the "honor roll" he always carried around in the back of his mind?

He shuddered. He wouldn't—couldn't—add more names to that list.

"Shoot the bugger!" said the Sergeant-Major.

And then silently, almost gliding across the hanger floor, the alien suddenly moved between Logan and Borck.

"Get out of my way!" shouted Logan.

"Don't shoot!" said Borck, and Logan realized that Borck was panicked that he might take out the alien.

Logan stared into the alien's eyes and felt a shiver, as if there were a draft blowing over his face and head. "I'll—I'll shoot him so full of holes," he said to Borck, "you'll be able to read the paper through him."

"Back away!" said Borck to the alien.

The creature looked back at him, then moved closer to Logan, who was feeling . . . he didn't know what. He just knew the creature shouldn't be killed. What was it trying to tell him? But he also knew he would kill it if he had to. What's more, he knew the alien knew.

But it didn't seem to care, either. The alien turned and began to move toward its ship.

"Hold it!" said Logan. "Hold it!"

But the creature kept moving. Logan followed it, shuffling crab-like to keep the barrel close to it. "Hey! Hey!"

He could see Borck holding his Luger hard against McGonigle's temple.

"Tell your men to drop their weapons or your man is hamburger! One, two—"

The alien abruptly turned its head toward the steel door leading to the Area B cells. All at once, everyone on both sides, except Logan, stared at it in astonishment.

"My God!" said Griffiths.

Logan didn't dare look back, but detected some movement in his peripheral vision.

"Jesus!" said Carlson.

His curiosity got the better of Logan. He glanced away from the alien.

The prisoners were staggering out, subhuman beings lurching forward.

"Back!" said Borck. "Back in your cells!"

One prisoner let out a squeak when he heard Borck and fainted. The others scurried, dragging their wounded legs, holding their bony arms, feeling along the wall. The alien moved toward the collapsed man and stood over him for several seconds. The man was old and pale and seemed to have died. The alien turned back toward Borck, then knelt and stretched its grotesque fingers over the man's chest.

"What is he doing?" asked Logan.

"No! You must not save him!" Borck yelled at the alien. "That man is a traitor! The enemy of all that we stand for!"

The alien abruptly looked back, but Borck had raised his head.

"Silence," said Borck. "SILENCE!"

There was a rumbling. A humming. Someone was pounding on the access door.

"Bombers," said Logan, peering upward. "It's a surprise party!"

The soldiers all looked at the stone above then, when the first dust began to drift down, anxiously glanced at Borck.

"Oberführer, shouldn't we go—?" one started to say.

"Oberführer," suggested a sergeant, "we should get away from the doors."

"The bombs can't reach us," said Borck, but the next blast rattled the steel hanger doors like cheap galvanized roofing. Tiny flakes of stone rained down on them.

"Hold your stations," said Borck, trying to be heard as the steel hanger door boomed with the concussions against it. Flakes again pattered on the concrete floor. The first soldier broke and ran, then a stream of soldiers rushed through the access door to the deeper caves, tripping over the threshold.

"*Halt!*" screamed Borck. "*Halt!* Nothing can penetrate this!" He brandished his Luger. "I'll shoot!"

When Borck moved his gun away from McGonigle's temple to fire on his own soldiers, Logan charged forward. The alien, for the moment, was forgotten.

Revenge was all Joe Logan had in mind. Revenge, and retribution.

He leapt forward, his shoulder catching Borck in the midsection, nearly bending him in half. They crashed to the floor and slid across the rough concrete, leaving a smear of Borck's blood.

But the Oberführer wasn't finished yet. He crashed the butt of his pistol against Logan's shoulder, just missing his head, but Logan rolled with the blow and kept the gun barrel turned away. With his free fist, he smashed Borck's face, once, twice, again, relishing the sound of bone striking flesh, loving his own overpowering hate.

Borck momentarily weakened, and somehow Logan managed to twist his Luger away. It was slick with the Oberführer's blood, however, and it slipped out of his hand, skittering across the concrete, which rolled like an earthquake as three bombs in succession exploded nearby.

The spacecraft lurched and slid completely off the truck, nearly dropping on Logan and Borck and they rolled among Griffiths, McGonigle, Carlson, and Targa, who were struggling to get out of their bonds. Logan and Borck clawed and punched, kicking mindlessly, frantically, consumed by only one desire—to kill, to hurt, to destroy.

Then Logan took a blow that emptied the air in his lungs. He rolled on his back and stared up at Borck's bloody, grinning mouth. Borck was holding a dagger. It was the ceremonial dagger that all SS officers received at their initiation. Logan realized that Borck had stabbed him in the side with it and was raising it to drive the sharpened blade into his heart.

"I'd prefer to do this *my* way, in the interrogation room," said Borck, his blood dripping like sweat. "But—"

Logan weakly flailed out with his legs, and suddenly the downrushing blade was knocked aside by some invisible force, sent flying high.

Borck looked around in astonishment. The prisoners who had stayed to watch the fight now watched the dagger's strange arc until it struck the floor. They then began to close in on their former torturer, their hands extended like gnarled claws.

Borck stood. "Get back, you vermin!" Some of them cringed, but others continued to close in. "You'll be sorry, you swine!" he continued, then looked over at Logan. "What—?"

An old man and an old woman had materialized from a fuzzy cloud of yellow light. Logan momentarily thought he was hallucinating, but the rumble of the ground hurt his wound.

"You!" said Borck. "You're ghosts! I shot you." He blinked. "No, I forgot about you." He laughed madly. "I can't keep track any more! So many pigs!"

The woman leaned on the old man. There was a wide bandage and a makeshift wooden splint on her leg to keep her festering knee joint straight. She lurched forward with a piece of wood in her hand, a heavy chair leg, stopping only a few feet from Borck, who would not back away, his eyes filled with defiant disdain.

She lurched forward. "Let me show you how I kill a pig," she said in French, then swung the club hard at Borck's head. It struck him a glancing blow. He spun and fell against some of the prisoners. She swung again, audibly cracking the forearm he raised to protect himself.

It was as if Borck suddenly awoke, as his defiance was shattered along with his arm.

"Help me!" he called out. He crawled toward the alien, who lifted its head as if it were trying to hear something. Ignoring its bloodied host, the alien turned toward its ship. Light shivered over the craft's surface, and the portal opened.

"Yes!" said Borck. "Perfect! We can attack the bombers! We'll rule the universe! GET THEM AWAY FROM ME!"

The old couple stood back as the prisoners fell upon Borck like a pack of hyenas, beating and clawing and even biting him. He disappeared under them and when they were finished, about the only thing recognizable of him was his skinned head as it rolled under the truck.

Logan struggled to raise himself. He twitched at someone grabbing his arm.

"Rest," said a Frenchman. "I am Levrier, with the Resistance. We'll get you out of here."

Logan looked around in confusion. There was another rain of stone flakes.

The alien now stood on the hull of its ship, having no difficulty on its slippery surface.

"We were almost too late," said Levrier. "But we were trying to find the boy's grandparents. The bastard tortured them with electric shocks."

Logan closed his eyes, remembering the aftermath of Dieppe.

"They are tough and crafty old peasants. They pretended to faint many times. Still, the bastard found out they knew nothing. Why he didn't kill them, I don't know."

Logan saw a farm boy, about twelve, hugging the old man and the old woman. They were all weeping. Carlson and McGonigle were helping each other walk. Griffiths staggered behind them. Targa was still slumped in his chair.

"Dead?" asked Logan.

"They cracked his thick head," said Levrier. "Stalin will give him a state funeral, eh?"

The boy ran toward the spacecraft and fell on his knees as if praying. He was offering up a metal ball. Logan couldn't make out what the boy was jabbering, but the alien, who had already stepped into his portal, stared at him, then slowly climbed back down. It took the ball from the boy and thrust it into its chest, or under its mercurial tunic.

The alien stopped in front of Targa for a moment, barely glanced at Carlson, then leaned toward McGonigle, who grunted and tried to crawl back from it. The alien seemed satisfied, then approached Logan, who was now grinding his teeth at the pain from the stabbing. The alien leaned over him and studied him. The boy was saying something, but Logan was dizzy and beginning to shiver. He thought he saw the alien's tiny mouth forming into a long tube, something like the paper tubes they used on Coney Island to hold cotton candy. He squirmed, trying to get away, but the boy spoke in a soothing voice and Levrier held him down. Sickened by the struggle, Logan closed his eyes, weakening. The pain softened and gradually evaporated. At first, he held on to the pain. To live meant to feel pain.

Suddenly, then, he knew that he wasn't dying. He felt for the stab wound, and it was covered with a strange, warm lump of what felt like glass. Some kind of plug, he realized. He was still weak from loss of blood, but when he recovered a bit, he sat up and saw the alien oozing its strange liquid over the old woman's festering knee. The knee was soon encased in a cast of glass. It glowed with a strange light inside it. His own "plug" was doing the same.

Logan blinked. The alien stood and quickly moved back to its spacecraft, standing atop it, and facing the great steel hanger doors.

Griffiths knelt beside Logan. "What did he do to you?"

Logan touched the strange blob stuck over his wounds. "It's like glass," he said, "and it won't come off. But the pain is gone!"

"I'll take him out," said Griffiths. He reached for Logan's submachine gun.

"No! Open the hangar doors for him," said Logan. He now felt strong enough to stand.

"But it's—"

"It's not against us," said Logan. "It was an accident. They don't understand us. They're just cataloging the planets. They're making a record of life."

"How can you know that, Captain?" Griffiths' eyes widened in fear. "Maybe he's taken over your soul!"

Logan laughed—as much as his wound would allow. "Jesus, Griffiths! There's nothing to take." He placed a reassuring hand on the man's shoulder. "You have to believe me. Haven't you seen enough today?"

"And Targa knocked me hard on the head. Captain, if more of them come! Can we take that chance?"

"Yes," said Logan. "It's hundreds of years old. I can't explain it, but it's like a machine of some kind. It's the only way they can travel across the distance."

"You're saying it's a . . . a *robot?*"

Logan shrugged. "Don't ask me how I know. Somehow, it gets in your head."

"Well, forgive me, Captain, but you've lost a lot of blood, so I'm not exactly sure you know what you're talking about." Griffiths began to rise, and he threw back the bolt on the gun. "The one thing I *am* sure about is that we *still* have a mission to complete."

Logan gripped his arm. "But *it* patched me up, didn't it? If it really was on the Krauts' side, why didn't it try to kill me? I couldn't have stopped it if it had tried."

Griffiths hesitated. He glanced from Logan to the alien, then back again.

"Open the hangar doors," Logan said quietly. "His ship has healed. *He's* healed. Let him go."

Griffiths looked at McGonigle for advice. The Sergeant-Major was sweating and looked weak. "Obey your commanding officer," he mumbled.

Griffiths looked at Logan, at the boy embracing the old woman, and then at the alien. "Ah, what the hell do *I* know?" he said.

The Welshman threw the lever and the hanger doors widened. Outside, the ground had been blown up, churned, mixed with pieces of human and dog flesh and bone and shrapnel and splinters of the latrine and barbed wire and the towers. Everything in the Forbidden Zone had been utterly devastated. It was a vision of smoke and fire and emptiness. Nothing was recognizable except the far, far fields, losing their pink as the sun rose.

The bombers were turning high above those fields and were coming in for another run, but Borck had been right. The heart of the facility was as yet unharmed.

The alien looked out at the destruction with utter indifference, then back at Logan, then at the boy. It quickly turned and climbed through the portal, which hissed shut and dissolved into the glistening hull.

The B-17 engines screamed and the bombs began to fall. Wind and dust began to blow in from the concussions. Everyone crawled or scurried or was dragged to the back of the hangar.

Carlson and Logan knelt over McGonigle, who was sweating and breathing heavily, covering his face and head against the battering of the concussions. The wounds he had were not life-threatening, but he was too woozy to run for cover and too big to drag. The bombing run lasted a long ten minutes and ended like the grand finale of a fireworks display with a sustained loud staccato of dozens of bombs. Still, the hangar had held again. The fortress could be reactivated by the Nazis later.

In the strange silence, an aurora of light played over the hull of the ship. It rose without the slightest noise, leveled itself, then whooshed out into the dawn sky, seeming to suck the air with it, instantly becoming a tiny speck, then vanishing.

McGonigle awkwardly raised himself to his feet, took one look, said, "Bloody hell!" and sat back down.

"I was supposed to kill it," said Logan to himself.

"Not to question your decision . . ." said McGonigle.

"You saw the symbol that appeared on his whatever—that chest thing. It was an interwoven 'N' and 'Y.' I was thinking about dying. I was thinking about my father. He was going to take me to get Babe Ruth's autograph. Who knows? Maybe they've catalogued the Yankees on their planet. Maybe the Babe. I mean, why not the best?"

" 'Yankees'? Ball? Is this the American game?" Levrier had approached and overheard the exchange. "Marcel thinks the creature is an angel. Perhaps he knows your father." He pointed. "Up there. You can bet there is no capitalism where he comes from!"

"How did you guys get in here? What were you doing?"

"Later," said Levrier. "We've got explosives and we'd better hurry."

"What about the Germans in there?" Logan pointed at the door to the deeper caves.

"If they strip, we'll let them go," said Levrier. "They will give a lot of laughs when they get to the villages. My people could use a few laughs."

"Sounds good to me," said Logan.

"We'll get you and your men to the coast," said Levrier, "and then to England. The old couple, too."

"What about the boy?" Marcel had joined them.

"He insists he must stay. His God has work for him, he says. For France. We can certainly put him to good use. We will greet you with champagne when you Americans come back."

"You see?" said Marcel to Levrier. "You have done God's work. You were willing to die with me. God knows you are a good man."

"God! Good!" Levrier shook his head. "If I was willing to die with you, it was because—Well, it wasn't to get to some imaginary place in the sky!" Marcel smiled.

Logan pointed to the door that led to Area B, the one he had gotten caught in. "Put the explosives in the tunnel there. It's narrow, and the rock will fracture better."

Marcel serenely stared out where the ship had vanished. They followed his gaze. Nothing would ever be quite the same, knowing that these things were out there somewhere.

One day in a few weeks, Logan would be knocking on Nicole's door. He be asking her to give up "the life," and she (given permission by General Anthony) would explain how she was actually "Vichy-O," a spy coerced into the service of the Nazis, but feeding them significant pieces of baloney among the steaks that gave her legitimacy.

He would never stop having nightmares about "Punchy Pawlowski" and the other members of "Logan's Losers" who had died, but at least she would be there in the bed with him, stroking his brow until he fell back asleep.

No, he couldn't know all that was in his future that morning, but he had some sense that all of his life had taken a turn toward the good.

"Let's put these Krauts on the road," he said to Levrier. "I think I'm going to feel really good when I see this damn place crashing down!"

And he did.